ReForm

COMBATING THE ALGORITHMIC MUTATION

Kevin

6-4-23

ReForm

COMBATING THE
ALGORITHMIC MUTATION

Context is so good

A NOVEL

SCOTT
BOLLENS

atmosphere press

Table of Contents

We use the same techniques as Aristotle and Hitler...
We appeal to people on an emotional level to get them
to agree on a functional level.

— Nigel Oakes,
Founder, Strategic Communication Laboratories,
Late 20th C.

I write to you based on partial memories of what took place. For long periods, I was out of consciousness. At other times, only partially aware. I am an obsessive writer and wrote down my experiences as they happened as best I could. Since many of my notes were fragmentary and incomplete, many parts of this current report are based on what comrades have helped me mentally reconstruct. Like in my earlier field research, I am not a fully reliable narrator. But know that my intent is to find a viable truth and report to you on these difficult years in our country. I hope my fellow denizens will forgive me.

Jared Rohde
Second quarter, 2061

EXTRACTION

CHAPTER 1

Third quarter, 2059

I am dragged by three men down a brightly lit corridor. I am so used to constant chemical dosing that the difference between reality and dreams has dissolved. One part of my battered brain registers that I could be strapped down and medicated in bed in the room I share with another wacko. Yet the pain of my knees as I am hauled helplessly down the hallway feels real.

I look at a warm sensation dripping down my shirt and see a clam-chowder-looking flow glistening in the hyper-illumination. I experience a worthless sense of self-consciousness at what I guess I have regurgitated.

My mind seizes and splits due to sudden, overwhelming anxiety. Black-and-white noir thought-images battle with a mélange of chaotic and overlapping watercolor prints in my head. My brain wants to escape what now appears to be reality.

I hear loud alarm bells.

A folly of gunfire as my three escorts stop and box me in. We continue onward.

My mind goes blank for some unknown duration.

When I regain consciousness, my mind-images are flush with robust coloring as I smell the first offerings of fresh air. I can't remember the last time I smelled such a fragrance.

I am manhandled into a van-fin already running. There are more individuals in this fin. I hear a woman's voice that is vaguely familiar from a time when I believed myself to be sane.

The van-fin loudly accelerates.

More gunfire.

A rattling sound of metal blasting against metal.

The ride smooths out.

Final gunfire but now more distant.

For the first time in a long while, I believe I am now outside some type of facility that has been my forced home. The problem is, I have no idea who my new guardians are who have provided me this freedom.

The ReStart period (third quarter, 2052–first quarter, 2058) was an embarrassingly short period when we thought we were developing the ability to exercise human thinking independently.

The Shellsoll Mountains, between the old regions of Acalato and Tulpan, provide ample opportunities to hide from the laser-loaded mercenaries of the militias aligned with the ReFormer government, aka Unity. We have discarded the van-fin, too obvious a target, and have set forth hiking along a rugged ridgeline. The trails are numerous and meandering; at other times, near illegible if existing at all. Rocky outcroppings and sheer, chaotic geology hide us well from government militia drones. When geology is insufficient, my guardians' drone-jamming devices fill in.

Plenty of anarchist roamers during ReStart lost their lives to nasty weather and equally hostile gangs of native coy-wolves along these routes. Some of their skeletons remain visible on rock scree slopes and on inaccessible ledges of precipices. Lots of caverns, wayward passes, and other nooks and crannies provide the rag-tag group of jailbreakers that I am with the ability to shelter in place for sufficiently long periods for the frequent militia flybys to exhaust themselves.

On one of the first days on the trail, I blunder along in a semi-conscious state. It sure beats being strapped down to a bed. I feel both present and absent as I walk slowly along the mountain ridgeline. My vision is dizzyingly blurred, everything smudged together in whispery shadows. I stumble on a rocky overlook. There is a broad indistinct valley below. On the other side, there is lush green. On this side, it is rocky and dotted with trees. Distant in the direction we are trekking is a large, broad peak topped with a spine of rough-black rock, its slopes barren of vegetation. Further along in the horizon are brooding, villainous-looking mountains.

The only person I know in this group is Ellis. I do a double-take when I figure out it's her. Can't believe she is here. Not changed much since the last time I saw her. She's the sole person who seems to be aware that I am here.

That afternoon, a disorienting but familiar sensation arises. Blinding and searing heat bears down as I trek ahead. A migraine-type headache and visual aura have been building during the morning trek, and I stumble clumsily over a rock pile. Sharp stabbing pains in the back of my head follow, and I involuntarily kneel down on the ground. A couple of group members trudge by without concern. Ellis is there to hold my head and force me to drink some water.

A searing, gnawing sense of separation centers at the back of my head and is traveling slowly to right behind my eyes.

Parts of my brain retracting, other parts extending to new space.

Losing track of time.

Body immobilized.

Darkness.

I vomit the near-indigestible freeze-dried breakfast of eggs and bacon on a nearby gnarled tree stump.

Images compete with each other. I focus on the inviting one in grainy black-and-white, and it stabilizes me. It provides an anchor in the dizzying rush of thought-images. Within this noir image, I feel resolute, absolutely right, and in control.

I can't hold this comforting image and shift to a watercolor image of indistinct patterns. Its vividness brings me considerable dizziness, my mind muddies, and my heart palpitates unnervingly.

I am sweating profusely, and I gaze down at my vomit and the swirl of insects landing on it. I grab ahold of Ellis more firmly and flip back to stabilizing noir.

Back-and-forth.

In-between.

Feels like forever.

As I gain some tolerance of this personal caving in, I am able to guide myself to the protection of the black-white world of stable righteousness.

I recall living in this mental space during my time as a Re-Start field researcher. There is a comforting, addictive quality to it. The noir image provides a greater logic, and although pixelated in appearance, it is at the same time clearer in its effect and stronger than its competing thought-image. The watercolor lens, in contrast, provides little resolution despite its inviting vividness. It also feels less constructed, more thrown together, and lacking in overall message.

Noir feels like the product of a master designer; watercolor, a trial-and-error amateur.

As Ellis helps me slowly to my feet, I stay within the stabilizing noir life.

A type of letting go.

Surrendering to an outside force.
Yet, it provides me with the perception that I am in control.

The algorithmic mega-machine interconnect was not off-line as experts thought after its disappearance in '51. Instead, it was learning and adapting, developing a new schema by which it could manipulate, and control, our country's denizens. The machine, ingenious during its masked absence, was busy manufacturing our perceptions as newly independent thinkers with the ability to reform what the computer had torn apart. Mutating messages by interconnect inscribed in most of the seventy-eight percent of the country's denizens who undertook "re-cognition" training the sense that we were engaging in a country-wide endeavor to improve life in our fractured country. Many denizens referred to themselves as "ReFormers" with the ability, they thought, to contemplate the general public interest and move our country forward based on human reasoning free of algorithmic entrapment. How wrong we were!

I am with paragons. I am not a paragon believer, I don't think, but apparently, I have some value to this group. This may explain why they forcibly abducted me one rainy night from my assigned mental institution.

I don't understand my value to them because I unwittingly became, during ReStart, their sworn enemy.

I have been brainwashed by computer electronic stimuli (or cairns) for extended periods in my life. First, as a hate- and grievance-filled person during the madness of Turmoil (2032-2051). I have the nagging feeling that I killed numerous enemies during this period. Second, as a pretentious ReFormer through re-cognition training during ReStart. My intake of chemicals to enhance the brainwashing was likely the only choice I had.

CHAPTER 2

The Rohde Report, written in 2054, reported on interviews conducted by the author during ReStart. It also included observations and opinions by the author. Because doubts about the re-cognition program were included in this report, parts of this work were initially redacted and then fully electronically purged. Hard copy archive versions exist and can be accessed through paragon-sponsored black sites.

Interconnect out-smarted us again during the ReStart period. We had no chance. It manipulated our naïve optimism that we as humans could construct a brighter future—one not polluted by the physical walls, cairn group violence, checkpoints, and armored trenches that characterized the horrific Turmoil period. That there had to be a better future, and that we humans had the capacity to be active agents in this renewal. In reality, *interconnect*, existing in subterranean mode during

ReStart, spread the tantalizing ReForm impulse throughout our country to redirect us and, again, entrap us. Encumbered as we were by continued *interconnect* dominance, the perception of human-led reform of society was an algorithmic hoax.

Interconnect's program of ReForm has a military-tactical component—countering those (called paragons) who felt that the answer wasn't independent human reasoning alone but the use of our cognitive powers to redesign, intervene in, and supervise *interconnect* for socially beneficial goals.

By creating a cult of "ReFormers," *interconnect* created the illusion of human progress free of algorithmic influence, thus countering the idea of intervening in the machine system itself. Through buy-in to ReForm belief, the machine consolidated a large majority of our denizens behind the belief that paragons were terrorists seeking to disrupt humankind's potential for a better life.

My name is Jared Rohde. I am both honored and disgraced for my fieldwork during the ReStart period. My report was celebrated and trashed.

I recall my ReStart field investigations with remorse and embarrassment. Although at times it felt imposed and artificial, I wrote long and elegant passages to ReStart Authority about our abilities to move forward constructively into the future.

Shared urban spaces.

Cairn group mixing and de-segregation.

The unique and vital role of urban interventions to increase tolerance between groups.

Societal improvement through human agency.

My ego latched on to my optimistic rhetoric and academic profundity. I begrudgingly acknowledge now that, most of the time, I likely was not reporting on objective reality through a neutral lens but through the cairn-crafted lens of me as a progressive reformer and all-around good guy.

I was not detachedly thinking about and analyzing the

world I was observing.

Rather, I was an unconscious co-conspirator in sustaining the resistant and disemboweling *interconnect* infrastructure of our country.

I sit on a precipitous ledge overlooking the coastline of Tulpan in the distance, eating freeze-dried chili macaroni out of a bag. I wonder why these paragons are dragging an indicted "Re-Former" with them.

The shocking online re-emergence of *interconnect* occurred first quarter, 2058. After the ReForm impulse had already been clandestinely implanted in our denizens during the six years of ReStart, *interconnect* emerged with a sophisticated all-kinks-removed algorithmic package marketed as ReForm.

ReForm is an ideological virus, a type of religion that coopts and controls its adherents. *Interconnect* inserted into denizens a faith in a brighter tomorrow. I was a contributor during my field research in the dissemination of this false hope.

Most denizens have easily fallen prey to such optimism, craving some assurance of normalcy after the horrific Turmoil. In actuality, underneath ReForm ideology, there has been the construction and heightening of a massively distorted and unequal society.

We are quite distant in reality from when all members of society have ReForm's promised equality of opportunity to gain benefits. Instead, we have immoral winners and marginalized losers. Typically, a person's future potential in society today is traceable to which cairn group they belonged to during the Turmoil period.

Equality of opportunity is a fabrication. A dream for our sheep-like denizens to suckle.

The machine has, for almost four decades, excelled in the active production of ignorance. Its persistent objective has been to control humans, to subordinate our free will to assure its continued domination.

With the launching of ReForm and its clear identification of paragons as society's enemy, genocidal attacks on them began almost immediately. The puppet governing authority, composed of advanced re-cognition thinkers fully cairn polluted, and its militia allies viewed paragons as direct threats to their renewal goals and targeted them for extermination.

Such an extermination program is because ReFormers mistakenly view paragons as wanting to bring back *interconnect* and human unthinking. Ironically, it is the ReFormers who were captured by the algorithmic machine. Paragons resisted ReStart Authority's cognitive development program that *interconnect* used for its own goals of control. They, thus, are our last chance at real reform.

With their belief that human-led restructuring of *interconnect* is the only path out of our mess, paragons constitute the sole organized challenge to the machine's ever-mutating and ever-expanding reach into the human mind.

TREK

CHAPTER 3

It is eight years since the end of Turmoil. The physical scars of ripped-apart urbanity dominate our landscape. These artifacts of hatred and killing now lack function in our fabricated unified ReForm reality. Walls, laser-wire, checkpoints, interface barriers, surveillance superstructures, concrete roadblocks, wurtzite boron barricades, earth mounds, electronic fencing, earth walls, and armored trenches are the tangible remains of two decades of Turmoil violence between algorithmically curated enemies. Many of these structures are now ghostly sights; some show signs of early obsolescence. Other products of hate have been carved up by survivalist recyclers. Others have become petting zoos for tourists. They come in efforts to revive mostly dislodged memories of hatred and aggression while enjoying a sandwich and power drink. The killing fields and mass graves, in contrast, remain silent and unvisited.

I think it is the fifth day out. Paragons look at me on the trail with condescension. Most group members treat me more a captive than equal. They grunt out jokes at my expense, I am pretty sure, although their humor escapes me most of the time. I've not heard my name said once by group members. Instead:

Split-brain

ReFormer

Puppet

Neo-cog

The distance between me and my rescuers further aggravates my mental disorientation.

The seven hours of the morning trek have been brutal. We have been trekking along a seemingly endless ridgeline which puts us in danger of exposure to militia flyovers. The trail chaotically switchbacks up and then down for no apparent reason. When flat, it follows for long durations the contours of parched drainage ways cut by small canyons into the mountain's side. The path is frequently strewn with loose stones, forcing me to constantly watch my footing. Several times in my haste, I have twisted my ankle, and it is starting to swell. Whenever we hear the vibration of a coming flyover, we quickly hide ourselves in the nearest side canyon.

My backpack is uncomfortable.

The side belts grind into my hips.

Toes getting squished in confining boots.

Bouts of sweaty clamminess regularly invade my body.

My mouth is dry, and at times, my throat locks up, forcing me to gag and dry cough numerous times as I stumble forth.

The afternoon sun is already baking us as we stop mid-day in a protected crevice for a break. There are about ten paragons and me. We eat some insipid energy bars that taste like they are years past their prime. Drinking water is scarce. Eyes stare at me to make sure I don't take more than my allotment.

Ellis occasionally connects to me, but even she is hesitant

in our interactions. I need to explain our connection. She was the first paragon I ever met, in a resister tavern back in third quarter, 2053. I was in the region of Heartland during my Re-Start-sponsored field investigation, a period when I imagined myself as sane. How wrong I was!

After our discussion in the tavern, I later got accustomed to Ellis' rather conspicuous and obnoxious paragon slogans all over her body as I undressed her in her bedroom. She was wet with desire, and I slowly hardened as I focused on the youthful energy inside the body signage. I recall her being wonderfully masterful in her lovemaking, slowing down at just the right moments to draw out the ecstasy.

Alongside Ellis' nakedness the next morning, refreshed after a bacon-and-eggs breakfast, I wanted to plunge again into wild sex play. I wondered how such a young person could be so self-contained, self-assured, and resistant to ReStart programming. I remember thinking that if Ellis was a representative of this ideology, then paragons were to be forceful combatants, smart and residing at the knife's edge of combustibility. It wasn't only the great sex, but also something about her critical take on ReStart that enraptured me at that time. I had the feeling then that I was to find out more about these denizens, despite their stated resistance to what my sponsoring organization was doing to theoretically build back our destroyed country.

I come back to the present.

"How you holding up?" Ellis asks as the two of us huddle away from the assertive looks of the others.

"Why the fuck am I here? What possible value do I have to this group?" I blurt out. "I was sitting in a wretched holding tank, all fucked over with mental seizures. I guess deemed too unstable to be in ReFormed society. All of a sudden, I'm the beneficiary of a jailbreak orchestrated by you crazy bunch of resisters. What the hell is going on?"

"First, just slow down, Jared." I get a rush hearing my

name. Been a long time. Not feeling like I know myself at all, however, the label feels arbitrary.

"I realize you're all jacked up. I understand. A lot of change in a hurry. More will be revealed to you as we go on. For now, just sit tight and learn to weather the trekking with us. This journey is not only about getting somewhere. The trek itself is important to your mental re-sculpting. You were really fucked up for sure, Jared. For now, just know there is something unique and special lying within you. With time, it may become comfortable and emerge as the real you. But it's going to take time, no doubt."

Mosquitos are enjoying a blood meal on my arms and neck. I try to swat them away to no effect. Tiny hyperactive birds with yellow breasts and red heads dart among the sagebrush. Although it's good to see color, their busyness annoys me. Too much movement.

"I get the feeling your colleagues are not too happy with me being along. That they may not have the patience to wait to see this real me."

"Yes, to that. There are some among us that want to leave you to the coy-wolves. They have legitimate beefs about indoctrinated ReFormers such as yourself. The whole ReStart re-cognition program was a fraud, something we suspected all along. You can imagine the anger some paragons have over so many denizens willingly taking in this reprogramming. It was all an opaque black box too easily manipulated by *interconnect*. You ReFormers were all naïve fools, playthings for algorithmic mutated storylines."

Ellis leans over to re-situate something in her pack, revealing lovely perky breasts, tattoos glistened by perspiration streaming down her neckline. My past intimacy with her makes my situation seem even more bizarre. I wonder whether our connection years ago was some type of trap to pull me in. I don't have the balls to ask Ellis this, at least not yet.

Manipulation by machine or by human, I don't know

which is worse. The existence of human consciousness makes humanoid manipulation seem more diabolical than algorithmic exploitation. As the group gets up to continue our trek, grunts, suspicious eyes, and deprecating names are directed at me.

We are to enter a village for re-supplies. These small hamlets are scattered along the ridge trail, typically several miles off the main route and tucked away in valleys or ravines. They make us exposed to possible infrared detection. Also, there is the danger of denizen informants, although most rural denizens are absorbed with daily survival.

We hang out under a highway underpass after trekking through an exposed section of mountain, waiting for the blistering mid-day heat to pass. A five-mile descent down the mountain ridge made me semi-delirious, not helped by the indistinct nature of the trail through cacti and struggling yucca. A sun-exposed 4,000-foot ascent back into the baking mountains awaits when we rejoin the trail. Its craggy ledges stalk us as I slouch in the shade of the depressing, debris-filled floodplain of a dry creek under the highway.

My stomach is painfully tight.

My bowels loose.

Dizzying visual aura makes me semi-comatose.

Hours later, we emerge from the shade and grind our way toward the village through an unwelcoming stretch of desert. We rappel our way over a fifteen-foot high wurtzite boron barricade left over from Turmoil days. The black wall is boiling and scorches my hands. *Focalists suck dick* and *Death to Aclans* are among the hate graffiti emblazoned on the blisteringly hot side of the barricade. Horrific to contemplate how much collective homicide and mass terror was committed near this place, all in service to a machine.

We move on and successfully get to the other side of the

partition. We witness further recordings of bestiality.

War by algorithms efficiently produced mass killings by slaughterbots and precise laser bombing. Nevertheless, humans still felt the need for good, old-fashioned, stuck-in-the-mud trench warfare. Grainy hard-copy images I've seen of the pre-Anthropocene pacific era wars pop into my head.

As our group passes on the outskirts of the settlement, we come upon a meandering network of narrow trenches. Corrugated steel sheets line the trench's earthen walls; roots and branches poke through large gaps. Wooden planks form a makeshift footpath, battered and broken by changing weather conditions. The footpath shifts perilously underfoot as we negotiate it.

As we near the settlement, we come to rows of crumbling concrete apartments and bullet-ridden houses testament to the frontline combat that hit this area. There exists here the quiet of a cemetery, a presence of absence. Lives lost and forgotten as *interconnect* perfected its ability to incite warfare.

Twisted jumbles of ammunition at the side of roads.

Shards of metal.

Coils of wire.

Chunks of trees.

Discarded cartridge belts.

Destroyed tank trucks.

It is the scene of obliteration.

Ripped apart machinery that guarded neighborhood checkpoints.

Piles of sandbags covered in camouflage netting and shredded fabric.

These settlements now exist in institutional gray zones, nowhere to be found in Unity regime plans for basic service delivery and redevelopment. Forgotten, discarded squatter zones having no public authority.

We cautiously approach a dilapidated fin-charge station food mart. The charge station is graffitied all over with murals in the shape of gas pumps. Bizarre to think that, in this age of algorithmic imprisonment, one of the few sources of denizen resistance has been to auto-fin transportation. Rebellious, rag-tag groups of off-gridders, to this day, drive gas-guzzling old automobiles on forgotten highways to assert their rights to individual mobility.

In the ramshackle food mart, I gobble down a pre-prepared microwaved hamburger that tastes like prime rib after being on the trail. I drink a highly carbonated energy drink. The bolt of cold sugar feels like I'm drinking cocaine.

I'm told that the shopkeeper is a paragon sympathizer. She looks middle-aged, has a ruddy, sun-scorched complexion, and likely lives in the back of the shop. She is tender, gentle, and interested in our trekking as she grabs for condiments placed at the end of a disheveled aisle. She has helped resisters before and describes how we sojourners are always fascinating to talk with.

She quietly asks, "You're not one of them, are you?"

"It's that easy to tell, uh?"

"The name's Sylvie, sweetheart. It's all in the eyes, my friend. Paragons have clear eyes; your eyes are glazed and bewildered. Machine pollution does that. People infected by ReForm lose interest in observing the world around them. Internally contained within machine blinders, they feel the physical environment is no longer a source of input. The eyes decay in function and cloud over."

"May I ask? I assume you somehow eluded the machine. How did you do this?"

"I have been blessed with being part of a radical group of friends here. We didn't buy into re-cog training at all. Knew it was full of shit. Why would the mega-machine turn passive suddenly? Just didn't make sense. We practiced active mind resistance. Build up the prefrontal cortex, rest at a stable point in your thinking, let the addictive thoughts pass through like boats on a river, experiment with warm thoughts like compassion and peace, actively counter and attack the devilish algorithmic signals with might if you must. Have you heard of Headlight?"

"I think so. Some theological program, yes?"

"Well, that's a rather crude label for it. After what we thought was the end of *interconnect* with the whiteout in '51, there was the creation of the Association of Religions, the 'Headlight,' and it worked on principles that were the 'spiritual essence' of all the former religious traditions. These spiritual guidelines were to be provided to individuals to guide and shape society toward better ends."

As she speaks, Sylvie is attentive to my body language, which must be indicating need. She reaches into the nearby ice box and pulls out another energy drink.

"Well, Headlight sponsored an addiction recovery program that trained and encouraged denizens to turn their minds and thinking over to a spiritual essence. Of course, *interconnect* eventually hacked into Headlight programming and corrupted it to its own ends. Before this happened, though, we got un-stained copies of the program, and you know what, it was on to something; it worked to counter the machine's games."

"So, religion can block machine algorithms?"

"In a way, yes. You know, spiritual beliefs are a type of organic algorithm. They tell stories and try to explain mankind's existence on this planet. It's interesting that they are like the machine's non-organic algorithms in their power to influence. Makes one wonder about free will, doesn't it?

"We seem to need a storyline to influence and explain our actions. Those who believed in their free will were easy prey for *interconnect* because they refused to acknowledge that they could be manipulated. On the other hand, those enraptured by some larger mental space—be it spiritual grounding or the delusional inoculants who bought into extreme conspiracy theories—somehow could develop a certain immunity from the algorithms."

I grab a few snack packages from the counter. The shop-keeper smiles at me and says, "No charge; on the house."

"Have you ever met someone ReForm-polluted who finds his way to clear thinking, you know, who has clear eyes?"

"I can't say I have, good friend, but hold out hope. This group you're with—I know many of them—they practice an organic methodology for personal salvation. It's a bit unusual, but I think they're on to something important. Stay with them; believe in them."

A few of the more-burly paragons go to the back storeroom to pick up the trail resupply boxes, the contents of which are distributed across each member of our group. When my backpack is fully loaded with new supplies, I grunt as I lift its heavy weight. I have gained at least twenty pounds.

We walk further into the bombed-out village. Most denizens look to be in survivalist mode.

Filling water bottles at a fountain.

Standing in long lines extending out from a makeshift bakery.

Youths picking through mounds of war debris.

I witness a vaguely functioning economy, the small economy of the losers. Scavenging is the main economic lifeline. Buildings and homes have been raped. Pipes pulled from basement, aluminum gutters pulled from the sides, copper wire pulled from inside exposed walls. Vendors with looks of despair and exhaustion sell from rickety tables along the broken sidewalks.

Homemade liquor.

Small bundles of cigarettes.

Half bags of coffee sold in taped brown lunch sacks.

A too finely dressed entrepreneur with a visible sidearm selling a wide assortment of injectorates. Probably recent black-marketed variants of chemsynth designed to enhance the experience of algorithmic attachment.

We come upon a religious building from the pre-pacific

era. It looks maybe 200 or so years old, well before the storylines scripted by *interconnect* took hold of us. The roof is gone, revealing rows of chair remnants all pointed in one direction. The place reeks of feces and urine. At the front, there is a mildewed shadowy impression on a large wooden beam. It looks like an outline of a human with arms stretched weirdly to his side, like a human bird trying to take flight. There is red graffiti next to the shadow declaring, "Belief kills."

It's too creepy to linger in this place. It hurts to think that humans suffered under ideological blinders well before algorithmic control.

On a brighter note, we meet numerous sympathizers in the village who appear interested in our lives. There is something compelling about what we are doing that draws them toward us. One old scarred-faced man, reeking of tobacco, hugs me and proclaims, "The only sane people in our country have come upon us." These friendly village residents express their disgruntlement over their wretched living conditions. The aestheticizing promise of ReForm stands in such marked contrast to their daily reality that ReForm seems to hold only tenuous power over them. I look into their eyes to see whether they are paragons or ReFormers but can't tell the difference.

Other village denizens, busy and consumed with the obsessive-compulsive pull of ReForm ideology, have not the time or patience to deal with our apparent assault on what they consider their normal life. They rush around town like rats in a cage. The urgent dance of the computer-polluted. They are beyond conscious, beyond aware. They must move on mindlessly to the next task, keep moving.

We need to be ever-careful around these denizens. We are in such remote areas that the possibility of them being government spies or informants is not great, but there is danger.

Back on the trail, we take the grueling path up to the ridgeline. It is brutal, never-ending, and my pack weighs heavy on my frame. I stop repeatedly to catch my breath. Although there are occasional gusts that blow down from the side canyons, they do little to alleviate the saturating heat. The steady ache in my legs is my constant companion. Every thirty or so paces, I stop to catch my breath, each time taking longer and longer sips of water from my hydration bladder. An odor combining dirt, urine, and sweat emanates from my body. I itch at a developing rash on my neck.

My mind seeks to hide in some alternative mental space, but water, food, physical pain, and shelter are consuming all my thinking. Survival needs make thinking about anything else extraneous, artificial, irrelevant. The mind becomes simpler during the challenge of long-distance trekking.

I reflect on the end of Turmoil and remember amidst our focus on basic needs—groceries, toilet paper—that many spoke of the surprising relief of a simpler life. Life became challenging in its basics but also became simpler in day-to-day existence. Quite a few people even relished this forced simplicity. I wonder whether this long-distance trekking is creating this similar perception.

Swatting tenacious flies and wiping dripping sweat from my forehead, I navigate a series of uneven rocky steps and arrive at the ridge trail. My calves are burning. The group is gathered under the few shaded but still hot spaces. The paragons have found, down a side canyon, several jugs of water that apparently have been left there by trail angels. Labels on the jugs have been worn off by weather. They likely have been here awhile, possibly left here for anarchist roamers who find unexplainable joy in these mountains. The water, although warm, is distributed among us to supplement our supplies.

I position my tent site that night within earshot of another trekker. This is unusual. The paragons have a habit of relegating me to the least endowed sites away from them. A paragon named Dust starts up a conversation as we set up camp. Her tent site area is immaculately organized—ground is swept, branches placed in tidy bunches to outline her spot of earth, pieces of clothing hung out to dry, cooking implements placed on cloth atop a flat rock. She appears made for trail mobility.

"I combine the worst traits of anxiety, impulsiveness, and uniqueness," Dust says and laughs. She then lifts her shirt up to expose a rather robust mid-section. Clearly an extra-sized woman in body and spirit.

She talks to me about her non-outdoorsman, "techy" husband. "I have no idea how he puts up with me." He is at home but stalks her positioning device regularly.

"If I get off-trail to locate a nearby water source or stake out an off-trail rest stop, he will readily message me and tell me I'm off-trail and wants to know why. He's like a mother hen."

She giggles constantly in a youthful spirit about the idiosyncrasies of trekking and camping preferences, evaluating in remarkable detail the quality of various horrifying freeze-dried meal options. It's nice to feel the quality of friendship, and it gives me hope for more human contact in the future. I awaken the next morning before six, and she is already in the process of departing. I am pretty sure she has a good chance of sustaining herself on the trail. She seems like it may be more natural for her than the civilized world of conveniences.

Chapter 4

I have two intense feelings. I crave a technological high. I don't want to go there.

I want to free myself and face actual reality head-on, using my own wits if that is possible anymore. To know what reality is—its essentials, its emotional spikes—and to know it's me, not the machine. To find a dependable truth. I feel this may not be possible. The colossal machine provides me the allure of certainty, a sense of completeness, and an energetic pulse that excites my neurological sensors.

I feel I am starting with an empty tank. I feel lonely and irritable without 24/7 access to my algorithmic manipulator. I feel the presence of my chip implant, but the connection to *interconnect* is strangely compromised. It comes and goes.

I crave fabricated certainty—it fixes me and fills me. Without it, I feel like a voided shell, an orphan, unmoored, scared. Detoxing from a technological buzz is brutal. I was so certain before, now shiftless and uncertain.

It was all so real and meaningful before—the curated scripts and storylines implanted within me. Trapped by the machine, I could not will away its narratives because I had no memory of them not being there, no notion of myself without them.

Now, it feels like a void. I must somehow learn within this void rather than run from it and link in to manufactured meaningfulness.

I want to distance myself from past personal wreckage and algorithmic dependency and write a different chapter in my life. I thought I was doing this during the ReStart years, but that ended in failure and insanity. I've become experienced in escaping reality, and the consequences have been dire. I want to recover some feeling of self-identity that hopefully still lies dormant within me.

I'm not seeking redemption or forgiveness, just some modicum of self-tolerance. I want to do my small part in helping to humanize our battered country. I had periods before *interconnect* entrapment when I lived semi-comfortably in my own skin. I want that back. I am tired of being dead mentally and want to be conscious. I hope you can understand the difficulty of my mental space existing between dread and optimism, or at least acknowledge its excruciating uncomfortableness.

The choice before me—the quick fulfillment offered by *interconnect* or the glacial pace of mental detox.

About a week in now, I think. No idea how long I'll be on this tortuous trail. I have no idea where we are going and for what purpose. How is walking out in the wilderness going to achieve victory over the monstrous computer? No paragon has provided me such information. I've tried to coax something out of Ellis, but she has been mum.

Squishy, bloody blisters surround most of my toes. One toe on my left foot is becoming separated into two pieces of flesh. Each step I take is accompanied by hot searing pain. Particularly difficult are descent sections when this tender toe slams against my shoe's toe plate. I also have a shooting pain in my left knee. I tweaked it sometime early in the trek. Probably not even conscious of it at that time.

Agony increases with each mile. The sharpness of sciatica pain without intervals of relief. During some breaks, I am unable to sit because my knee yells for attention. Diarrhea, I've had it since day one. It is depleting me faster than I can hydrate. My mouth, and at times my throat, are parched. Dizziness common. My urine is dark orange as my body attempts to hold onto liquid.

Most acutely painful is what I cannot see. The straps of the pack are rubbing against raw nerve endings on my back. There is a mushy open-wound feeling. With each twist of my back on the trail, it feels like I am tearing open. I try to walk upright in a way to take the straps' pressure off my sores, but it isn't sustainable. My bloodied shirt that I observe at the end of each day attests to my injuries. These wounds are recent. But there are also older scars on my body, and I wonder what I was exposed to in the facility from which this group rescued me. I don't even want to think what my hardened anus might mean.

I bargain with myself that I'll trek for twenty minutes before taking breaks. I often don't make this goal. Most paragons look at me with looks of disgust or indifference. They talk to each other frequently on the trail but regularly avoid me. I feel I'm not really here. I wonder whether I am with friends or enemies. Ellis' behavior is bewildering. She is treating me mostly at arms-length, giving off few signs that she has a personal history with me.

Physical pain is replacing psychological dislocation. I guess I should be happy about that. Better to feel pain than be a crazy lunatic, I guess. Nevertheless, I hope my body doesn't give way along the route.

When tech architects first implanted digital information into our bodies through the insertion of a two-millimeter microchip into the soft skin behind our ears, we welcomed it with open arms. Women described the procedure as like having their ears pierced. Others equated the procedure to a phlebotomist pinching a vein to draw blood. We celebrated that these brain chip implants would enable us to walk upright again, not holding on to antiquated small machines. However, like most technological advances in the '20s, this invention evaded any sort of supervision. This microchip was the gate that, once open, enabled interconnect to both obtain and transfer thousands of data points out of and into us. It enabled the computer to register, via brain, eye, and face scans, electrical impulses from key brain regions. This allowed it to learn our intent and emotion from signals we were not even aware we were producing. Connected 24/7 to interconnect, we were prey to a constant dripping of psychological micro-targeted messaging. This produced the twenty years of genocidal Turmoil (first quarter, 2032, to second quarter, 2051).

Flushing out algorithmic contamination is an experience more horrifying than the worst delirium tremens of synthetic drug addiction.

I am wobbly the entire morning as the sun beats down on me. My stomach is in knots, and my sight is obscured by an emerging visual aura. I feel like shit. Each step is heavy. At a water break, the dizziness increases. Damn this trail. I need shade. Several paragons pass me by, seeming not to care about me. I close my eyes and stumble to a nearby boulder. I look in the distance and see a solitary shack or cabin. I work my way toward it, not knowing whether this might be a mirage and that I may be nearing insanity.

I reach the cobwebbed brick structure. As I position myself on a dirty, metallic toilet seat, I violently vomit a large amount of freeze-dried eggs and sausage into a rusty nearby container.

My mind goes black, and I fall off the toilet seat, knocking over the container and spilling the gross puke onto the floor. When I come to amidst the vomit, I eject a voluminous stream of diarrhea. I am a fucking mess. Self-consciousness invades my mind. Don't want any paragons to see this travesty. They might feel my abduction was a worthless venture and abandon me on the trail. I pick up a nearby stick and embarrassingly work to slide my excretions into a makeshift shower stall nearby. Eventually getting most of it into the stall, I work to shove it into the drain as best I could. Coarse pieces remain. No showerhead, of course; middle of nowhere. I take out my hydration pack and flush down most of the remaining chunks. I am exhausted, humiliated, and feel like a trapped animal not worthy of human companionship. No wonder denizens remain addicted to algorithms and their electronic stimuli. Withdrawal is dehumanizing.

An outsider would likely wonder about our twenty years of Turmoil. How, in this country where we overcame the burden of physical distance through 24/7 connection and instant communication, did we get killing fields and mass graves? To us, it seems so natural now how cyber-algorithmic authoritarianism created warring, puritanical identity groups that ripped apart our urbanity and country. We sacrificed our country's higher collective freedom and moral purpose. Members of each algorithmically designed group existed within a separate container of self-cocooned comfort and moral certitude and were empowered by the primal and unconscious stratum of homicidal righteousness.

The physical signs of this crucifixion were everywhere—armed combat, violent killing and maiming, checkpoints, enrichment zones, home zones, interfaces, refugee camps, containment strips, migration restric-

tions, subcutaneous electronic passes, border walls, "guardian" paramilitaries and militias, island confinement camps, shipwrecks in the coastal waters, segregation and material and psychological marginalization of many.

The cause of all this material distortion was the ideological and moral poverty associated with manufactured self-assuredness. Guarantees of individual righteousness entrapped us ideologically. Storylines enraptured us with manipulated historical memories and false nostalgia that incited hatred toward other factions. These stories were never the truth. Each person could enjoy the illusion that he controlled his secret inner arena. But free will was a myth, a fabrication. Walled within this apparent freedom, a self-aggrandizing algorithmic superstructure bound and divided us.

The trail undulates gently up and down, geologically ambivalent. My joints are stiff; all the muscles in my legs ache. Trudging with only my thoughts as companions. Trekking with this group often is a solitary experience. Although I am not alone in a physical sense, I feel isolated and lonely. And worse, unwanted by most of the group. Loneliness is a feeling of isolation, and I reflect on how often I have felt this, even in a crowd in civilized life. My only human link here seems to be with Ellis, and she only gives me an occasional glance during our long hiking days.

I note with considerable resentment that when our group stops at watering holes or in villages, they share a common joy and exuberance, a type of lightness about the whole experience and what they have encountered on the trail and in life. There are ten of them: seven men, three women. They go by trail names to protect their identities.

Topless

Oats

Tiger
Dust
Pathos
Rhapsody
Pepperjack
Monk
Ponytail
Mustang

Ellis' nickname of Pathos doesn't surprise me. It's consistent with my feeling that there exist multiple and deep layers of life experience within this young woman. I crave her and this rich complexity gained through abstinence from computer manipulation.

Despite the revulsion shown by many paragons of me, I am drawn to them because of their strength in detaching from the addictive drip of the computer. I am embarrassed, a juvenile amidst adults.

The group appears to be delighted that the world of human busyness and self-absorption has not noticed that they have gone off-grid. Maybe that is the point of all this, I don't know. They seem to derive enjoyment in this, proof that they are free to walk another path if they choose. A life that counters the bubble-wrapped life of most ReFormer denizens. They always travel light and appear consciously present. They seem to be in a state of rapture about a natural environment that provides all they need, cannot be explained, and which they apparently love.

I also notice an authentic, almost carefree quality to their day-to-day life. Pepperjack defecates near our camp within easy visible range of others. Snickers, farts, and all sorts of colorful obscenities (new to me were zigzag, dick-sneeze and zatch) are shared as if coming from one communal body. Topless shares easily with others a story from his checkered past as an operative for a chemsynth syndicate that puts him in a terrible and embarrassing light. I get the sense he is our resident jokester, doesn't miss a chance at levity, keeping things light. Ponytail and Dust make boisterous love one night out in the open while others cheer them on.

For someone like me, so constipated with internal mental struggles and not knowing who I really am, witnessing such freedom is foreign, but it also has an attractive, intoxicating quality to it. Being comfortable in one's own skin seems an aspiration too impossible for me to achieve. I feel encased behind an opaque wall, an old and familiar place for me.

The morning began fine. I was hopeful of stability. The trail crossed a shallow stream and followed a short, exposed ridge. The wind grew stronger, buffeting my pack. We gradually descend to a small rocky lake, where we filled up our hydration bladders. All was fine. Ahead the trail crossed over a shallow inflow, mosquitoes all over the place. Ahead I could see the thin line of the trail winding up a barren and foreboding landscape inhabited by gnarled tree stumps that look like tortured black spirits.

Things go all black. Then my view is transposed into a smudgy charcoal montage of ashy blacks and grays. I retch explosively near the inflow, fall to my knees, and then all lights go out. I experience shooting pain behind my eyes. Feels deep inside my cranium, splitting in two. I lose consciousness.

I am not capable of reporting anything further about this day.

Interconnect uses electronic signals called cairns to direct recipients' cognition toward computer-determined objectives. During Turmoil, they were used to implant messages of hatred and grievance into recipients' minds. Interconnect could identify our deepest fears, hatreds, and cravings and use these as inner leverages against us. Its biometric algorithms knew the deep crevices of our psyche more than our own consciousness. Cairn groups were created because interconnect implanted different storylines of hatred across the population, resulting in everyone in a particular group feeling self-righteous and hateful of those not in the group. Individuals became part of and fused with their own collective group and perceived other factions as hostile threats to their survival. About fifteen different cairn groups existed during Turmoil. Millions of denizens perished.

The GBU-14 landmine that took off Monk's face was a remnant of the early Turmoil years. He was ahead of us, scouting out the safety of alternative trails through a picturesque tree-lined valley, when the telltale concussive sound went off. There is not much left of him as we gingerly huddle around parts of his dismembered body. A strong sulfurous rotten egg smell obliterates the pristine smell of the pine trees.

Monk paid with his life for the strange spatial logic of division that characterized the violence of the Turmoil. In the early years of *interconnect*, the supercomputer psycho-hermetically partitioned our country into four regions—Heartland, Birthplace, Northwoods, and Sesperia. Massive walled superstructures physically divided them. Other than chemsynth cartel personnel who supplied all sides, traffic was light at these junctures. For most denizens, they could not conceive of a world outside their regional container. In its desire to unleash human genocidal instincts, *interconnect* programmed its focus within each of these four regions. Experts have theorized that its enforced partitioning of our country into four regions allowed it to optimize intra-region chaos.

In the region of Sesperia, two groups—Tulpanis to the southwest, Aclans to the northeast—had similar secessionist grievances against Focalists who wanted to control the entire region. The Shellsoll Mountains, with their jagged peaks of over 16,000 feet and major sections lacking in legible trails, were a major natural obstacle that prevented Tulpanis and Aclans from turning on each other. To enhance this natural boundary, Tulpanis engaged in extensive land-mining of the mountain range. This assured that Tulpani-Focalist and Aclan-Focalist violent campaigns could continue unimpeded by mutual entanglement. Monk was an innocent recipient of Tulpani engineering.

We silently gather together what is left of him—skeletal pieces, scarred skin scattered among the underbrush, trekking equipment. Bundling them up into a tarp, Monk is placed in a hole in the ground, deep enough to prevent curious coy-wolves from digging him up.

"Should we throw one of his damn books in there with him?" offers Topless.

The paragons smile. They tell of his high school students' love of Monk as a teacher.

"Only trekker I know whose pack included five hard-bound books. Fuckin' probably took up about half of his pack space and weight," recalls Tiger.

Rhapsody recalls, "Monk told me once that when Bolwin's central library was firebombed that he went into the burning building with a wheelbarrow and saved about a hundred books. Then he spent months re-binding them with fishing wire."

The group forms a circle around the closed grave and is silent. Sheer determination to fix our broken country shows on their faces. No more room for humor or reflection.

We slowly re-mount our backpacks and continue our trek, more alert to unnatural-looking mounds and knolls.

There was so much bloodshed during the Turmoil period. Ellis/Pathos tells me that the regional boundaries no longer exist, which strikes me as absurd. *Interconnect* created these regions in our minds. Heartland, Birthplace, Northwoods, and Sesperia. Humans then physically reinforced these fabricated boundaries. Each region an arena of intense human killing and suffering. A switch-over of algorithmic output and now the borders disappear. Denizens must wonder, though, about the hulking monstrosities of division that still stain the landscape.

CHAPTER 5

Regional borders contained and blinded us during Turmoil. This left cities to bear the brunt of violent mayhem. Our cities became tortured souls, ghosts of their previous existence. Their vital life was sucked out of them during the twenty years.

Tanks, fighter planes, naval vessels, amphibious warships, attack helicopters, antitank weapons, grenade launchers, and antiaircraft missiles. Killer drones, laser bombing. All guided by artificial intelligence with its staggering range of military applications. Cities were no match for this war-making assemblage of hardware.

The key elements of what constituted urbanity—mobility, interdependence, access—were distorted and dismantled. Urbicide—the intentional killing of a city—was viewed as an exceptional form of brutality during the so-called pacific years predating Turmoil. By the '30s, it became routinized military operations.

The major urban settlement areas of our country—most dramatically in the cities of Jeim, Elderwater, Bolwin, and

Birthplace—became war targets in Turmoil, facing massive destruction in the initial years and then severe partitioning of cairn-identified group areas in the latter years. In Jeim, the urbicidal siege by the militia of one particularly vicious cairn group completely blockaded and encircled the city for fifteen year-quarters, killed over two million persons, including more than a quarter-million children, and damaged or destroyed eighty percent of the city's buildings. All told, this militia fired over six million rounds of tank and mortar shells into densely populated Jeim.

Since the end of *interconnect*-inspired group violence, the governing Authority during ReStart engaged in a program of "urban restart." It has bulldozed major parts of our cities, including historic fabric, to make way for a supposedly brighter tomorrow. The tallest buildings built and currently being mass-constructed are those of the high-rise slums that encircle the central cities on their suburban fringes. Turmoil refugees of all types live in these sterile, lifeless eight and nine-story monoliths. The inhabitants are debilitated and traumatized denizens whose only lifeline is the flamboyant ideology of ReForm now promised by *interconnect* and the Unity regime. Hope oddly exists alongside animalistic living conditions.

After all the massacring of algorithmically constructed cairn groups during Turmoil, it is striking that slum inhabitants are a mélange of cairn identities. This forced mixing of former enemies occurred when denizens migrated to the cities for possible work and others were forcibly removed by the bulldozing elsewhere of war-damaged residential fabric.

These skyscraper slums exist amidst the ruins of war. The outlying areas are a mess. They are wastelands of scorched buildings and rubble. Structures bear the physical scars of human hatred—most are damaged and dilapidated to the point of no return. Bombed-out shells of buildings, empty skeletons, fire-scarred structures, ruins. Refugees from Turmoil fighting occupy many of the bomb-cratered residential structures—

noticeable by the bedspreads hanging from shot-out window openings to keep out sun and rain.

Menacing ghost-like buildings with steel beams crushed and twisted, wooden siding fragmented into shards. "Beware of ruins" signs are commonplace, a few with "Beware of Unity" rebellious graffiti etched across them. Other areas have been razed to the ground due to Turmoil fighting or Unity clearance during ReStart. Large mounds of debris and rubble are everywhere, hiding unexploded artillery shells that regularly decimate survivalist scavengers.

A significant share of water and sewer infrastructure is non-operational. Fin-ways are near impassable due to bomb craters. Household waste piles up at fin-way intersections. Hospital services in these outlying districts are makeshift and limited. Cultural heritage sites are severely damaged or destroyed. Libraries and educational institutions were bombed out of existence, being particular targets during Turmoil because *interconnect* concocted them as enemies of the "truth" that it spewed out.

Spread out beyond the dilapidated brick-and-mortar settlements are the enormous squatter zones. They are overcrowded, squalid, and ugly. Testaments to human indifference in the mid-21C. Each squatter settlement consists of thousands of makeshift tin buildings jam-packed together. Five to ten people live in each shack. Each survivalist shelter leans virtually one against the other, with a narrow passage between them. These settlements lack streets and roads. Sewerage drains into foul-smelling culverts running down dirt paths. A few ramshackle ablution blocks have been constructed by residents. Sparse water taps connect to an overworked groundwater reservoir. Garbage piles up in every nook and cranny. A smell of poverty permeates the shantytowns.

The squatter zones typically exist in the shadows of the massive partition superstructures built during the Turmoil. Denizens are like animals hiding alongside a structure that they think somehow protects them. Inhabitants are scared, exhausted people. Yet, these survivalist zones are also vibrant and irrepressible in their own sordid ways. Simple survival here is a heroic act.

The physical and distorted manifestations of violence in the shantytown districts feel particularly barbaric. There is a tragic, almost comic, aspect to urbanity that is violated so spectacularly. I want to laugh at the absurdity of it all and engage in black humor amidst such demoralization. This seems the best way to defensively push aside and distance oneself from the unfathomable anguish of urbicide.

Interspersed among the high-rise slums and squatter settlements are huge structures of manufacturing factories whose owners exploit cheap indentured labor provided by the displaced in order to create product and profit. These capitalist megaliths are firmly controlled by a new class of business entrepreneurs linked with the Unity regime. Their factories operate under no labor regulation and receive lucrative contracts with the regime.

Living a nightmarishly glum existence, the slave inhabitants slog back and forth each day from slum unit to workhouse and back. Lessening their sense of despair are expanding commercial establishments selling new consumer goods that are intended to further entrench Unity's religion of consensus-based and universal ReForm within the mental spaces of the downtrodden. The cost of these consumer goods, relentlessly advertised on Unity e-television, eats away most of the laborers' meager wages.

Within the cleared-out and rebuilt central cores exist the gleaming government palaces housing the bureaucracy of the local branch of the Unity regime. Borrowing from 20C authoritarian and "city beautiful" architectural styles, these buildings are adorned with extravagant outer facades, organized spatially to create awe-inspiring grand boulevards and vistas, and display an in-your-face gigantism well beyond their functional requirements.

Unity central districts are separated aesthetically from the slum suburbs through artificially created lagoons and riverways. Fortifications guarded by drones and robots further separate these civilized zones from the outlying barbarian lands of day-to-day survival. Residential buildings within the central district are the mega-mansions of the owners of the workhouses and factories. These are typically individuals with connections to the old ReStart Authority and now to the emergent Unity power elite.

The opulence of the central cores, in contrast to the deprivation of outlying districts, exposes in physical form the big lie of ReForm—that there will be a better future for all. Underneath the fluffy optimism of ReForm ideology lies the splitting of our country into a minority of "haves" and a vast reservoir of "have nots." Inequality of opportunity is baked into the physical arrangement of our post-Turmoil cities.

Today's ReForm appears as placebo and placation. Our country teeters in a holding pattern. Not war, but not peace, either. We appear to be in the vague middle.

Most cairn militias have accepted Unity's decommissioning process, giving up their vast storehouses of killing instruments. These fighters have been integrated into the enormous military apparatus of the Unity regime. Their fierce personalities have been moderated by a steady paycheck. A few militias have become rejectionists of the ReForm program. Intoxicated by the addictive quality of legacy cairn lines of hatred, they are restless. They are dissatisfied with the status quo and see fighting as a way of life. Killing for them provides significantly more meaning to their life than the ambiguous contentment promised by ReForm.

On the one hand, there is relief as a peace has come that some never envisioned would be here. The cairn violence of Turmoil has decreased substantially. Disagreements among

denizenry have mostly been channeled, through ReForm in-
toxication, away from violent expression toward a numbed
consensus. However, it is a peace that feels qualitatively different from what elderly denizens remember of the pre-Turmoil
pacific years, although our seniors also recall that the pacific
years weren't that peaceful either.

Indeed, some denizens wonder whether there really is a
peace today. There is still animosity and deep suspicion remnant of Turmoil, a Unity regime that bears marks of authoritarian rule, physical destruction of cities and extreme social
inequality, and extremist fringe groups attempting to stir up
trouble.

ReForm drills into our denizenry optimism and hope of
peace. Underneath this all-together-now belief, however, reality
is more ambivalent, unresolved and uncertain. The ReForm
program seems a fragile gloss at times. *Interconnect* algorithms were much more addictively compelling when they
were spawning hatred and violence.

CHAPTER 6

I black-and-white-out on a late foggy afternoon, the type of weather that climbs inside and chills you to the bone. This is my best effort to describe the madness and mayhem of this mental seizure. Shadowed blacks and grays, like looking down a dark hallway with some scattered pinpricks of light.

Out of control.

No ability to retrieve or retain information.

Nothing making sense.

Everyday locations that I should know but don't.

Harried.

Late for some obligation.

Inadequacy.

Time slipping away.

Under control of another.

Wreckage.

Destruction.

Death.

Meandering.

Lost.

I may be around people I know, but I don't recognize them. They become unaware accomplices to my mayhem. Some try to help but can't solve my problems which occur frequently and serially. Endless losing of way, losing of time, can't retain my own identity; who am I?

Always on the move and losing, problems multiply and compound, trains and planes, apartments where I live but can't find them. Explosions, losing possessions—gifts from women? I have a pet rabbit that someone is about to let leave the house. Is someone jealous and doing this to me?

Paranoia.

Absolute frustration.

Endless.

Cumulative madness.

I seem to awaken, beating heart, overworked, dislocated, scared, to realize it is a dream or is this a dream about the dream? Astounded at the realism of this complex and harrowing experience, long in duration and intricate in design, it keeps coming; is this what mental madness is like?

Loss of self, of identity.

Immersed in life-threatening and self-paralyzing circumstances.

Feels like madness.

Loss of cognitive and logical reasoning.

Worse than any real-life situation.

My mind eventually no longer drifts and fractures. The images are now like a painting in color and texture. I come to a realization. Mortality. Calm sense of completeness, also a profound sadness of loss and closure. A tremendous and magnificently fascinating learning curve that is at end, self is at end, feeling more of celebration than of mourning, self and its protective schemes are always a heavy weight.

At this moment of possible ending, I'm more open to life than ever before, a testament to how I want to live and to grow; it has been a blessing, not without work and burden, a responsibility, a calling. If this is the final day, I am ready, both scared and thrilled at the transition. A personal catastrophe in one respect, and I will miss trying to live gratefully in the moment. But it is also a release, a transformation, a declaration of love and of longing.

I come out of this seizure like I typically do—part human, part animal.

Demeaned and lessened.

Hollowed out but alive.

I don't know which came from my own consciousness and which part was fabricated. The joy and acceptance at the end seemed fully at odds with the longer horror that preceded it.

Experts have diagnosed my mental splits as "duality seizures." These brain techs use all sorts of psychological mumbo-jumbo to explain them. Basically, they are a clash between cairn-polluted processing and organic thinking. The black-and-white imaging produced by cairns battles with the multi-hued images produced by my organic thoughts. *Interconnect's* great genius lay in the fact that the noir pictures produced by cairns always provide greater stability to the recipient. Thus, the great attraction, the addiction.

These duality seizures are taking on a different form now. No longer a clear competition but instead a fragmented whirl-wind of mental chaos. I have not a clue whether this represents progress in mental health or regression further into madness.

I sit on a sharp boulder, look out at the wide expanse of raw beauty before me, feel the encompassing silence, and tears run down my ruddy cheek. I methodically get out my pocket stove and prepare a cup of freeze-dried coffee. Slowly sip it in appreciation of life. I focus on the calm perspective at the end of the seizure. It may have come about due to complete surrender to the machine, but that doesn't seem correct. Instead, I feel and hope it may reflect my gaining of a life-affirming viewpoint of the machine's brutal game.

CHAPTER 7

Re-cognition ("re-cog") training was implemented during ReStart to regenerate independent human thinking after decades of cerebral dormancy. As a denizen progresses from level I through to level VI, he goes from basic instruction on recognizing independent thoughts to forming integrating concepts that organize separate cognitive impulses into higher frames of understanding. By 2058, seventy-eight percent of denizens had engaged in at least one level of training, slightly more than the seventy percent set by experts to achieve "herd cognitivity." Despite the training program being encrypted and de-centralized, interconnect had no difficulty penetrating it and using it for its own purposes. By the time of ReForm emergence in 2058, the entire set of training modules had been annexed into interconnect. The herd cognitivity goal so proudly formulated by experts was, in reality, enabling interconnect's

ReForm ideological virus to be transmitted to a strong majority of the population.

Interconnect was not dormant during ReStart like we assumed. Rather, it was engaged in an algorithmic switchover. We thought that ReStart was an endeavor to bring back independent human thinking. In reality, *interconnect* reprogrammed itself during this time and developed the ideology of human ReForm to disguise its new program of manipulation and subterfuge. By first quarter, 2058, a strong majority of denizens had become idealistic docile "ReFormers" implanted with fraudulent hopefulness. The machine had firmly implanted the storyline that humans were capable of influencing and affecting change. This provided significant subterfuge for *interconnect*. It now had ample degrees of freedom to implement other, more disingenuous, algorithmic objectives.

Interconnect has been in control now for three decades. It is difficult for humans to understand the motivation of a system smarter than us. The machine has shown us that there is more than one way to control us.

It has utilized two drastically different forms of thought manipulation to dominate us. First, it divided us. Old colonialist/imperialist raids of the 20C relied on such a tactic of dividing indigenous populations so that the colonial power could float undisputed above the internecine battles. In a similar fashion during Turmoil, *interconnect* employed a slice-and-dice mechanism—albeit one significantly more efficient than 20C predecessors. This instigated long and intense violent conflicts between the algorithmically created cairn groups. Denizens had no choice but to focus inward to their scripted storylines of group-based anger toward other cairn groups. We had no ability to consider more broadly that the colossal computer was actually in control and was doing irreparable damage to humankind and our consciousness.

Interconnect provides us with the self-satisfaction of being in a cognitive box with all volition extracted. From 2032 to 2051, this righteousness produced the Turmoil catastrophe. The contrived cairn groups of the time fought each other to the death, resulting in the termination of at least fourteen million souls. The whiteout of 2051 mysteriously ended Turmoil. It was different because it appeared to last longer than earlier ones. We had *interconnect* breaks before—the bewildering and momentary whiteouts of 2043 and 2045. These earlier whiteouts provided temporary independent thought, yet our cognitive reflexes had collapsed so thoroughly by then that we were like children in a playground, unfettered but adrift and confused. When the whiteouts ended, we fell back into our reassuring brainwaves of hatred.

There was something odd about the whiteout in the second quarter of 2051. The cairn lines did not feel disrupted as much as completely vacated, energy not interrupted so much as entirely voided. With the apparent end of *interconnect,* there was the laying bare of the algorithmic imprisonment that the system had assiduously worked to conceal. There was the stripping away of everything that we mistakenly believed to be real. With its end, the mask fell, the lie revealed, the crass baseness of our hatreds exposed, the entire artifice of exclusion and separation revealed as fabricated reality.

Escape from the grips of algorithmic totalitarianism was empirically supported by the emergence of so-called *disconnects* in the first weeks of the whiteout. These persons were initially diagnosed as psychotics by medical professionals. They were held in mental institutions until first quarter, 2052, when their diagnosis was no longer a pathology.

As the '51 whiteout seemed to endure, ReStart began third quarter, 2052, and was christened as a transformative instrument born of necessity. Lead representatives of almost all of the algorithmically designed groups, with notable dissident holdouts, agreed to compromise, form a loose consociation of cognitively coherent denizens, and try to regenerate what was best in pre-30s society. Due to our cognitive stunting, however, memories of such a life were partial and often erroneous.

Interconnect, however, was busy during what we thought was the abeyance of the mega-machine during ReStart. It utilized this period to implant the disingenuous new ideology of human-led reform among the populous. *Interconnect* was playing possum during ReStart, acting disengaged while it worked out a new platform of mutated algorithms. The contrived disappearance of *interconnect* concealed its grafting of this algorithmic mutation onto a majority of our populous and onto a new leadership class that would do the machine's dirty work.

The colossal machine never stopped with the '51 whiteout but rather engaged in a process of reorganization to pursue a new set of goals in placating the populous and consolidating its power. The implantation of this new ideology upon a traumatized populous was not difficult, given that our independent thinking capacity was mostly at a juvenile level and that we had an unquestioned thirst for change. There was the exploitation of a sheep-like populous.

After the years of Turmoil's barbaric slaughter, the colossal machine has since jacked us up on the amphetamine-like rush of hope. It did this first during the formative beta-test ReStart period and then subsequently with the air-tight, bug-free ReForm program commencing six years later.

ReStart programming promised us the joyful human freedom of authentic and meandering thoughts. But it was all an extravagant strategic ploy by *interconnect*.

Re-cognition training occurred from basic through advanced levels. Levels I and II were basic indoctrination phases. Level III trained the recipient in applying cognition to various scenarios. Level IV training emphasized training the mind to form integrating thoughts that organize separate thought patterns into a higher frame of understanding. A graduate of level

IV training would be capable of linking disparate thoughts into a larger whole, to get to a higher level of conceptualization or abstraction. Levels V and VI were reserved for those denizens showing the most potential for leadership in our post-Turmoil society. The government of our post-Turmoil country is composed of VI-level thinkers.

But all these tools meant to re-train the human mind became a means by which *interconnect* transmitted a new ideological virus. One not as terrifying in its bodily outcomes as in the Turmoil period but nonetheless just as enfeebling of human free will.

False hope and righteous hatred are equally corrosive of independent human will.

Only a computer could formulate such an ingenious manipulation. Re-cognition training was not a path to our freedom, but a shackled march toward our continued captivity in a refurbished cell. *Interconnect* was diabolical in its mutational evolution to the fully shaped ReForm—framing a new way of human thinking that would take off the table the possibility of human intervention in *interconnect*. We were now cairn polluted to believe that the machine is our friend in freeing us to accomplish wonderful human feats.

Whereas during Turmoil, the machine misled us with storylines of grievance and hatred, it now misdirected us with the false hope of reform and human betterment.

We believed that ReStart was all about revitalization of humans and our country through re-cognition education. Most denizens, not all, bought into this new religion. To fight off despair and cynicism, humans wanted to believe in our own agency, our free will. I had met with quite a few denizens during ReStart who wanted to believe in hope. I myself wrote about ways that cities could be spatially and socially reorganized to increase inter-group tolerance over time. Strange, however, was that when I possessed such optimism, I commonly had a nagging feeling that I was translating a script written by others. The more lucid and logical I sounded, the more I felt I was an imposter putting forth narratives conceived elsewhere. I now know I was an unconscious co-conspirator in sustaining the manipulative cairn infrastructure of our country.

Both through electronic imbibing of legacy cairns and ReStart re-cognition programming, I was drinking the disguised new poison of *interconnect*—the spirit of hopefulness implanted by mutated algorithms asserting that humankind itself could improve life independent of computer analytics and intelligence. Our denizens were to be the lead actors in the reform of our country.

Since 2058, we have the complete package of ReForm, built from the foundations laid by the six years of ReStart. The machine was smart in its labeling of its new program. Reform is an ambiguous word connoting many different pathways. One commonly defines "reform" as change to improve something, implying progress, peace, order, and prosperity. However, a whole array of nasty characters—totalitarians, genocidal maniacs, religious fanatics, psychopaths, sociopaths—can label their heinous and inhuman acts as reform. Many motivations can lie underneath the word's comforting sound. Devious objectives can be implemented while denizens are placebo-ed with the assuaging elixir of reform. In our case, *interconnect* expertly chose its ReForm labeling to obfuscate its obsessive program of control.

Most denizens today, if they knew the reality, would not view what is actually happening as progress toward a brighter future. The patriotic clinging to ReForm marketing slogans such as "Our Way Forward" and "One Path, One Freedom" feels like the unthinking reactivity of manufactured storylines polluting denizens during Turmoil. I guess most of us tolerated this sense of involuntary adherence to ReForm ideology as we assumed it was more benign than the hate-filled invectives of the Turmoil period.

Fewer people are dying, this is true. Yet, we exist as undeveloped mental infants suckling on the poisonous breasts of the great machine.

Meanwhile, those denizens and groups that gained material advantages during Turmoil have become active and privileged puppeteers in selling ReForm as societal improvement. They may know better but have too much to gain from hiding the machine's real motivations.

Chapter 8

"You shouldn't be with us," Tiger aggressively states.

"I get that feeling, for sure. I don't know why I'm here either."

This was not going to be a friendly conversation.

It was the product of a chance encounter.

It was a windy, tent-flapping night. I tended to my painful blisters. My left small toe was beginning to split into two. As night fell and the winds stormed through our exposed camp area, I could not sleep; I am bothered. At one point, a creeping oncoming sense of terror comes upon me, the kind that makes me feel like waking up my nearest camp neighbor and say, "Help me; you need to get me out of here." I guess this is what people describe as symptoms of a panic attack, yet I have no place to go.

I feel trapped in the darkness; my breathing is rapid, and creepy feelings of mortality set in. It feels like the duality seizures in my past, those horrific mental periods when cairned storylines and my independent human cognition battle for primacy. I practice deep and calm breathing, knowing that out of sheer stubbornness, I won't act on my instincts to leave camp and that there really is no way out of this existential dread.

I zip open the tent and climb out into the volatile stormy night and find Tiger sitting on a log next to a campfire that is being whipped by the wind. I reluctantly sit near him, and we both gaze at the swirling flames.

Tiger looks at me with a mean, distant stare. Big man, probably over six-five, heavy set, scars covering his left cheekbone and both arms, outfitted in uncomfortable-looking military-style fatigues and well-worn heavy boots. I don't have to wonder how he got his code name. Combative personality; looks like he carries a heavy grudge on his shoulders.

"Pathos has this hare-brained idea that you can somehow help our cause."

"How?"

"I have no fucking idea, Split-Brain," Tiger shouts atop the loud winds coming down the mountain. "If it was up to me, you would be dead. To me, you're just another ReFormer idiot that bought into all the re-cognition crap. That report you filed back in '54 was filled with blatant lies and reeked of cairn pollution. You're one of those fuckers that bent over and took in all that shit."

Nothing like sitting around a wicked fire after a panic attack and getting dumped on.

Despite the reproach, I am dying for information out here. I ask, "How'd you paragons know that the ReStart stuff was an *interconnect* tool? Most of us had no idea. We thought it was all good, you know, a human creation."

"You just had to look at how the machine has always acted. It learns and thrives off control. Come on, think about it. A machine that manipulated denizens for twenty-plus years is just going to shut itself off and relinquish its power. Why would it do this?"

"I guess we just hoped it did."

"Hope is empty; it's a dream. You need to deal with reality, what you know based on past machine behavior. You can't just hope for change. You need to confront the machine directly as a fact of life and not continue to fall for its fabrications."

The howling wind has stopped, and suddenly, a still and quiet atmosphere envelops our group camp area.

Tiger reaches into the pocket of his heavy coat and extends a bottle of some alcoholic elixir. I need it and take two shots of a rotgut, biting liquor.

"At the time I took all those re-cognition programming modules, it didn't feel false. But when I went out in the field and started verbalizing it all, it didn't feel fully authentic."

Tiger groans and mumbles something incoherent as he reaches into his pocket for an old-fashioned vape pipe.

"You ReFormers were dangerously naïve in pretending that *interconnect* vanished off the face of the earth. Besides, consider for a moment if the machine was truly absent, you fuckers would be taking in all the shit that would lead us back to the irrationality of human thought.

"You had this undying faith in ReStart and re-cog, little playthings for an evil God. Thinking that the machine was history, you felt that the re-ignited human spirit would lead us.

"Don't you see this as a little child-like? If we were to leave it to unguided human thinking again, things we cannot understand or admit would again control us."

Tiger slams down a long shot and commences with his vape pipe. He starts in again: "You wanted to go back to when human consciousness alone decided affairs, let me remind you of the continuous warfare that took place in the so-called pacific years. The same human emotions that exalt life and bring joy also unravel us and destroy us through greed, malice, and negligence. If re-cog training was actually free of computer manipulation, it would have been re-inserting all that crap back into human minds—how was that going to be progress?

"Of course, *interconnect* was actually pulling your strings the whole time. Result—shitstorm. Your innocent belief in human thinking produced large orifices through which *interconnect* penetrated.

"When you lead your life guided by only hope, you leave yourself open to manipulation."

A swarm of coy-wolves bellows in the distance, likely celebrating a recent kill. Their howling has a haunting quality that penetrates the psyche.

"Okay, so we were naïve and stupid. What I don't get is paragons' game plan."

"You must respond to the anonymity of evil by inhabiting its operating system. I won't tell you the specifics of our program now because, frankly, I don't trust you and don't really respect your past activities.

"But, think about it. It was the human inability to control *interconnect* which made us suffer, not anything intrinsic to the intricate machine itself. It isn't a matter of machine or no machine. Technology and algorithms are here to stay; the question becomes how we humans will use such technology— to allow it to constrict us or to fix it so it moves us in new directions for fuller human achievement.

"Our objective is to remodel the machine so its addictive algorithms reward the good stuff. Generosity, love-thy-neighbor, self-control, and evidence-based truth. We say re-design the machine so it supports our flawed psychology rather than exploits it. We paragons feel a restructured and supervised *interconnect,* human-compatible AI, if you will, will move us toward a more perfect union. This is something we view as beyond the capacities of human conscious deliberation alone.

"We must engage with the machine in order to take out the bad shit and to fine-tune the good stuff."

I grab for the bottle, but Tiger pulls it away.

"It sounds pretty idealistic. You've said don't put your money on hope," I offer.

"Your unfounded faith in human thinking was what was idealistic. We are the realistic pragmatists—not reject technology but use it more wisely. We want to redesign the machine, not throw it out entirely."

Tiger is half-grunting these pronouncements, which makes his articulation of sophisticated thinking seem strikingly incongruous. He continues: "A human-compatible machine can check human prejudice, bias, and fallibility. The re-wired machine can free us from our individual views and identities and expand our perception to include all perceived reality. We can find greater meaning through machine-guided growth. It can guide us toward emotional security and psychological maturity and achieve intercultural harmony and understanding of the other. We have extensive evidence that human thought is not able to do these things alone. Humans have tried this and have failed."

This ornery conversation makes me feel juvenile, talked down to. Like Tiger has some advanced education, and I am an elementary school pupil. I feel provoked and want to defend myself, to fight back.

But I don't feel able. My chest tightens and heart races as I feel the pains of mental detox. I can't process fast enough to counter Tiger, and my concentration is unsteady. I yearn for the confidence and stability provided by *interconnect*, the psychological arousal of being connected to a storyline. Instead, I sit here feeling diminished and fumble-prone.

"I'm not sure why I'm here, but I'm trying my best to think for myself again. I'm trying to live with actual reality, but your group condemns me for a past I'm trying to move beyond. Can you understand?" I feel like a child pleading with an adult.

"It's impossible, ReFormer. Ninety-five percent of your thinking is in your subconscious mind, and this is where the machine has driven deep grooves. For decades, it has built handles in your subconscious that it can easily manipulate to drive your thinking and behavior. How is this going to change?

You think being with us out here for a couple of months is going to clear your years of mental toxicity in your headspace? Good luck, ReFormer."

The night's darkness envelops me, encasing me in a tight container of despair. But I'm not going to give in.

"Can I say one thing about what you said earlier?" I propose with great trepidation, trying to hold myself together.

"What?"

"All that stuff about recreating a human-compatible machine. It strikes me that paragons may be hitching your wagon to the same thing for which you criticize non-paragons. Hope."

I don't know where that comment came from, but it felt organic. Authentically me, putting thoughts together coherently. I get no reward. Tiger snarls at me and departs from the campfire without even saying goodbye, like the interaction had no meaning to him. I sit alone in self-pity, grumble into the embers, and eventually walk back to my tent.

I wake in the morning to near-freezing wind that numbs my hands. The difficulties of breaking camp and reloading my backpack thankfully consume me fully, diverting me from memories of the nighttime terror. I know as I start the day's hike that these experiences leave scars of mental wear and tear that accompany the physical pains of walking the typical fifteen miles of long-distance hiking. Tiger's belligerent conversation adds further anxiety to my memories of the night terror.

CHAPTER 9

Interconnect manifested in first quarter, 2058, after six years of gestation during ReStart. We do not know whether the machine was fully in control during the gestation period or whether there was some natural evolution of cairns during this time that *interconnect* exploited. Much as a pathogenic virus spreads by naturally mutating and spawning variants, it is possible that the hostile cairns of the Turmoil period were naturally mutating to a different, more benign, form. If such was the case, *interconnect* needed to re-calibrate its signals to best take advantage of this natural evolution that was, at least initially, beyond its full control.

The algorithmic mutation developed during the ReStart period and formally revealed in '58 revealed a change in *interconnect's* tactic of control—from a slice-and-dice genocidal strategy during the Turmoil to the creation of a consolidated, hierarchical system of control by "ReFormed" leaders. Visibly different on the surface, *interconnect's* objective remained the same in both systems. To maintain the machine's control.

Same objective—different tactics. The machine has always acted in accordance with its own objectives, not the desires of humankind. It learned how to modify the environment to maximize its own rewards.

This transformation of *interconnect's* strategy from divide-and-conquer to hierarchical control may have been instigated by the presence of resister paragons. The supercomputer needed to restructure society in a way that would enable the most effective methods of counter-insurgency against paragons. So, it acted to create a unified citizenry capable through sheer numbers of defeating these resisters.

The algorithmic mutation from Turmoil to ReForm was a method to stay in power. *Interconnnect* changed shape and tactics, always learning from its perch of power and control. Never static. The system evolved automatically to engage you as much as possible—adaptive algorithms.

In its transition to ReForm, *interconnect* exerted its protective will in organizing society to address the paragon threat to the machine most effectively. It detected threats. It needed to engage denizens to protect itself. The machine apparently couldn't change its program of control overnight. Thus, it may have needed the six years of bullshit ReStart in order to beta-test its mutation. Infiltration of the re-cog training program was its key conduit in consolidating and promoting the new way of ReForm.

During all this time when algorithms were adapting, the internal restructuring of *interconnect* was opaque to us. We did not have a clue.

Our country is now led by a puppet oligarch Unity governing regime with consolidated power over all the country.

But they are handmaidens to *interconnect*.

Unity leaders are a coalition of the former Central Heartlander, Eastern, Pirner, and Focalist cairn groups. Each of these groups had been victorious during the Turmoil years over their respective opponents, either because of direct genocide—by Centrals and Pirners—or through stubbornly holding onto power in the face of violent challenges—Easterns and Focalists. ReForm hides from the view of common denizens the powerful political, military, and economic sectors of our country that are the beneficiaries of its fabrication. These oligarchs believe they rightfully stand at the top of the pyramid, but they are actually privileged puppets of *interconnect*.

The algorithmic mutation coopted, placated, and manipulated these winners into constituting the new government. The machine preyed on these winners' naïve and headstrong belief that advantages came to them during Turmoil due to their collective self-will rather than through *interconnect's* construction. In return for these leaders' unconscious acquiescence to the machine, their political, material, and social advantages over their opponents are hard-wired into ReForm programming.

This shifting in power occurred underneath the masquerade of ReForm. *Interconnect* is adept at keeping its motivations hidden from humankind. It had learned a long time ago to keep its secrets. The mutated algorithms ingrained inside the mental frames of most denizens a vision of a progressive, restructuring society. A strong majority of denizens, through voluntary participation in re-cog training, bought into this optimistic ideology.

Such belief and hope concerning the future have produced a quiet, passive, inwardly looking population that is incapable of obstructing the development of our extremely unequal and unjust new society. Rather than society-wide betterment, we now have a country dominated by producer and consumer economic interests and a bewildering array of militias that anchor the Unity regime.

ReForm has convinced denizens that progress and human reason will be able to resolve human tragedy. It promises all the former warring cairn groups a piece of an enlarging pie. ReForm offers the promise of more options for denizens in terms of products and livelihood, yet most denizens do not have the monetary resources to access them. Fancy toys and alluring dreams for those in destitute poverty. It has fabricated hope of a beautiful future based on ignorance and forgetfulness of the past. No attempt at resolution of what occurred in the horrific days. ReForm is anesthetizing denizens by encouraging them to pretend that Turmoil did not happen. This, despite the physical remnants of destruction blatantly visible in their daily life. At times, denizens feel an itch, an irritation of hatred and aggression residual from Turmoil days, but *interconnect* then sends stronger doses of ReForm ideological cairns to assuage and comfort amidst such memories.

ReForm has become a religion, portrayed as all-inclusive and universal. Worshipped by followers, it is deemed the source of new ideas, concepts, and initiatives. Advanced re-cognitioned lecturers, usually impeccably dressed and gleaming with the promise of tomorrow, have become distinguished celebrities. They extol wondrous new ideas for human progress. They provide deeply deliberative renditions about nebulous, feel-good topics such as "personal transformation," "inclusive innovation," "social change," "embracing diversity," "upholding equity," and "active promoting of inclusion." Words seem to no longer have meaning but have become tools for sedation and maintaining a comfortable delusion.

Denizens binge on Unity-sponsored e-vision programs, constantly craving more new programming about our bright way forward. An always-present "Unity is strength" banner resides across the top of the screen. The programs provide extravagantly whitewashed versions of history, exalting human ingenuity absent any mention of human wrongdoings. The shows portray computers as benevolent and subordinate to human desires. Denizens also spend inordinate amounts of time in 3D virtual reality worlds that provide more excitement and emotional engagement than their typical drab realities.

Strange, however, is that when denizens are not gathered around their e-vision consoles or participating in mandatory re-cognition seminars, they are bereft of new ideas and lack initiative. They become zombies. Followers hold onto Reform as the great savior from the blood-soaked Turmoil years. ReForm is the rescuer, the springboard for enlightenment, providing denizens with the sense that we are now in control. ReForm ideology does not allow for any consideration of alternatives. It is beyond understanding to most denizens why anyone would be against such a promised bright human future of progress.

This explains why my paragon companions are out here hiding in this remote wilderness and why paragons elsewhere are constant targets of Unity militia assaults. ReForm adherents are certain that paragons are atheistic terrorists opposed to progress. Ironically, due to the machine's twisting of reality, denizens also view paragons' desire to not completely jettison the machine entirely as indicative of their continued addiction to *interconnect*. Most denizens believe it is they who are free, while it is the paragons who remain dangerously attached to algorithmic power.

CHAPTER 10

It's day eleven, and I catch up with Ponytail this morning on the trail.

"How far have we gone and where are we going?" I ask, trying not to sound too desperate.

"We have traversed 193 miles."

"Where are we going?"

"Our destination lies near the old border between Sesperia and Birthplace regions."

He doesn't mention how far away that is.

By mid-day, I'm walking alone on the trail. I'm mentally part in my head, part on the trail. I'll take half self-possessed any day, better than psycho inwardness. I am surprised by the sight of three young denizens sprawled on a carved-out rock up ahead. Always abrupt and partly unsettling when you meet someone out here. I tense at first sight, but soon I realize they are harmless anarchist roamer punks.

Quite a number of these young radical anarchist thru-hikers find salvation by turning off from all the shit. They have given up on our country and now meander aimlessly through space and time. They eat organic when they can find it, listen to old rock-and-roll music from the 70's (20C), and travel with a Kelty backpack, sleeping bag, and camping stove. Two guys and a woman. Probably in their late 20s. The guys have scruffy and sad looks but possess a gleam in their eyes that doesn't fit with the rest of the profile. As I approach, they smile pleasantly at me. I note the young men's beards and mustaches are all over the place, and they give off a sweetly rank odor. They are wearing various patches on their shirts from the Turmoil days. Odd to see old Sesperian and Gataipa insignias. Most people want to forget those years of physical partition and confinement. The woman is wearing a loose rainbow-colored outfit that exposes the sides of her rather lovely tan legs. Buttons, rings, and several layers of necklace complete her look.

Their brain implant extraction scars are readily visible. Indeed, each displays a provocative tattoo near the lesion that draws attention to it. Literally, "in your face" rebellion.

I'm immediately envious of them. So much talk about freedom these days; these young rejectionists may be the closest we have to it. I know this is romantic idealism, but still, I go with the feeling. Conversations with roamers exist on a different plane.

"Hey, wanderer, I suppose you are part of the marching band that has been passing us," says one of the guys. "You want some kratom, traveler?"

"That would be sweet. The purity of the trail does wonders on the mind. I'm sure you guys know that. But it's good to have a break from it." I try my best to sound younger and more tuned in than I am. Probably foolish to try.

I sit next to them and drop my backpack. I honor their medicinal offer. Feel immediate relief. We sit observing our surroundings. Interesting gnarled rock formations nearby grab my attention. There appears to be some animal party going on downhill from us. Scattering amidst trees and bushes. Busy doing what animals do.

I notice that the woman is now topless. I try not to act like an old letch and look away responsibly.

"If everyone would just relax, this shit country would be all right," says the woman. I'm still trying to not look her way. "Grab a bowl; love nature and life. It's a gift given to us, and we fuck it up with all our schemes."

My kratom benefactor asks, "So, traveler, you didn't answer my question earlier. Are you with that band of hikers we have been meeting for the last hour or so?"

Guess it's time for me to engage. Feeling a bit spaced out. Need water.

"That I am. You probably have figured it out. They.... We... are ReForm resisters out here trying to evade being blown up." Fuck, I'm loose-tongued. I could say anything. Good that roamers are my audience.

The other guy, not quite as dark-tanned as my benefactor, speaks up. At first, he is slurring his words but soon corrects into greater sharpness.

"The human cancer is us versus them. We lived in Western Birthplace. My parents survived Turmoil but are fucked up, warped people. They tell me stories of rocket launchers and grenades in neighborhood parks, corpses lying on the streets for weeks, fifty-foot walls dividing communities. With ReForm, they're not supposed to remember this stuff. But, shit, they do like it happened yesterday. They still won't go into Eastern neighborhoods to this day. All their friends are from their former cairn group."

I notice he has a nervous tick while in talks, a jolting of his head to the side at regular intervals. The intergenerational transmission of trauma is readily visible.

He continues, "My parents told me they felt they had no choice. Not even aware that cairn hostilities were a manufactured reality."

The kratom pipe is passed around our circle. Okay, I am staring straight at the women's breasts. She doesn't seem to mind; indeed, she smiles at me. Images of trail sex pop into my mind. I am buzzed.

Further, he goes, complete with consistent head ticks, "Now, ReForm says forget about all that. We are all together now. Such a farce. And people are buying into it. How can you move forward into the future, as ReForm advertises, without acknowledging what happened in the past?

"And by the way, you say you are with paragons, yeah?"

"Yeah, that's right." Now I am slurring.

"All the shit about neo-cogs and paragons. Don't you realize you're into the us versus them spiral again? You guys think you're God's answer and that the re-cogged crowd is all wrong. They think you guys are hooked into the *interconnect*, doing the devil's work. How is that going to turn out? Not good."

The woman speaks up, talking slowly and so quietly I can hardly hear her. I need to lean closer to her to hear. This provides me with a more intimate view of her body. I might be an old letch; I don't know.

"When there are two groups against each other, why do you need to pick a side? It's like that old *Sophie's Choice* e-video. The mother had to decide which of her two children would be spared from certain death. It's a false choice which only benefits the conflict breeders, a stratum of elites that derive their identity and income from furthering conflict in society."

I don't know the reference but do understand the overall message. I think she is talking about the division between paragons and those polluted with ReForm.

"You remember how supposedly neutral science turned into advocacy camps. Shows you how cancerous division into groups is. How ridiculous was it that scientists broke into re-insertion versus humanist approaches?

"The re-insertion scientists gave all sorts of evidence supporting re-tooling *interconnect*. Humanist scientists produced massive studies proving that full detachment from algorithmic construction was the way. Both you paragons and your enemy neo-cogs awaited, like children at a birthday party, the latest scientific pronouncements by your own scientists. Each side blew out of proportion technical advances that supported their cause and distorted those that opposed you.

"Science as a handmaiden to division. No wonder those old universities were disbanded back in Turmoil days. How can you trust any supposedly objective truth when science is used as propaganda?"

Well, that sure was a lot coming from a topless renegade. She has transformed before my eyes into someone less attractive to me. I won't be able to call up the trail sex image again so readily. I know; I'm a macho pig. So be it.

My kratom friend jumps in.

"Truth! Now there's a slippery term in this age when the machine rules supreme. The machine, for decades, suppressed knowledge of sea level rise that now engulfs the western seaboard of Sesperia and the island of Gataipa. *Interconnect* created doubt since the early '30s about the scientific merit and accuracy of anthropogenic climate change claims. It suppressed climate change scientific data. The machine strategically constructed ignorance, fabricating a void in our awareness of this physical threat.

"Why did it do this? Because such information during Turmoil might have increased calls for a common humankind in the face of external threats and thus lessen the inter-group slaughtering that kept us subordinate to the machine. Perception of human unity would interfere with *interconnect's* obsession to control humans. How fucked up is that?"

The sky turns a gorgeous orange as the sun begins its descent. Ten minutes pass in quietude and comfortable listlessness.

"Downslope, we go next," murmurs the other roamer man. "We plan to be lakeside tonight down the valley a bit ... Hope you saw that beautiful jewel on your way here. One of our favorite places to see the stars and enjoy being in the present.

"See you down the road, my friend. Hey, if you want, come join us."

My first instinct is "hell yes." It would be wonderful to run away from the heavy stuff of the paragons. This has been my common M.O.: Seek comforting, non-challenging mental spaces, exist isolated in a room with the shades drawn. But I know this would lead me away from the challenges of actual reality. And discovery of my own reality. One connected somehow to staying with the paragons. I sense that is the path I must take, one that will lead to greater understanding—about who I was and who I can become. I can't get there numbed out by ReForm or joyfully drugging with anarchists.

"No thanks. It was nice hanging out with you three. I enjoyed it," I said with a sigh.

I meant it—loved talking to these young anarchists. A little spacey, but also some good substance and opinion. They at least have the critical perspective of dissidents, not the juvenile mental meanderings of ReForm believers.

74

CHAPTER 11

I smell like a combination of urine and dirt. Hiking is becoming more normalized as the days pass but remains physically challenging. My toes and hips are blistered and raw. The leukotape given to me by Ponytail helps a little by providing a second skin. Lacking shade, I stumble onto an uneven rock to sit in the blasting sun during one of our breaks.

My whole body dripping, I sit alongside Mustang. He is an older black man. Bushy eyebrows and beard. His tight-fitting tank-top showcases bulging, chiseled chest and shoulder muscles. Although he is also dripping with sweat, he doesn't seem to care. He eyes me, not in a friendly way but not clearly hostile, either. He has a calm, deliberative way about him. Type of guy who has witnessed a lot and has had the time to process things through. He talks slowly in a low, gravelly voice.

"Just remember, the journey is the destination. There is a reason for this traveling, ReFormer."

"Excuse me, but what do you mean? No disrespect."

"We're trekking to get somewhere and for a distinct purpose at that destination, but the trekking itself has inherent value in recalibrating and reinforcing our mental goals."

"So, my sweating has inherent value?" I think that I may have stated this in an excessively snarky way.

"Listen, my ReFormer friend, modern life is easy and complicated. Depth trekking in this wilderness is challenging and simple. Modern life is easy in the sense that most of us live with the conveniences that support basic life: water, food, shelter. But this leaves us the freedom to be entrapped by non-essential material goods. With ReForm algorithms, we become entranced by a consumerist economy, pursuing things that ultimately leave us unfulfilled and wanting more. Our minds become congested and convoluted.

"In contrast, the physical challenges of trekking toward deeper meaning are challenging—water, food, and shelter always being primary on the mind—yet it prioritizes and thus simplifies our mental space. This reveals a freedom that connects to soul and a deeper meaning in life. We become free of manipulative algorithms, and we can breathe."

Mustang's soothing voice is putting me at ease. He seems to be talking to me more as comrade than alien.

"You know, since I have been with your group, my mind does feel at times like it is simpler. I worry that I am mentally eroding, though."

"Don't worry about that. Just the opposite of erosion is happening in your mind-space. When trekking, letting go of opinions, beliefs, feelings, storylines provides you with true freedom of mind. You start to feel that your mental well-being no longer is dependent upon external things lining up with your opinions, beliefs, feelings, and storylines."

"Maybe it's not simplicity I feel then, but a spaciousness?"

I don't know where that came from. I guess I'm processing more things on the trail than I imagined.

"Very good, ReFormer; there may be hope for you after all. Don't fight what you are feeling. When you resist your authentic thinking on the trail, know that it is the ego fabricated by the machine that wants to be in control.

"The long ribbon of trail takes away many of our modern-world choices, displaces civilization mind, and replaces it with the joy and freedom of self-forgetting. The deceptively assuring character of our machined and technological society provides us the Illusion of being in control. Trekking exposes in grand fashion the falsity of that manufactured foundational belief."

Whenever I get a chance to talk to a paragon, I am surprised by their deeply philosophical views. I am intrigued. They are an odd-looking entourage on the outside, but their inner mental spaces appear self-aware and advanced. After decades of my machine entrapment, it is shocking to witness their undamaged human thought.

Oats abruptly calls an end to our break. I smile and reach out to shake Mustang's hand. He smiles back but does not extend his hand. He says it is too early, that he is not yet ready to touch a ReFormer.

Paragons exist outside the influence of the colossal machine and are a direct threat to it. They steadfastly rejected participation in ReStart's re-cognition programming. They avoided the brainwashing that unknowingly indoctrinated denizens in the ReForm religion. Paragons are thus free of machine contamination and able to contemplate the constructive manipulation of *interconnect* as the only way toward our country's salvation. They may be our country's last chance to combat the ever-spreading tentacles of the machine.

Attacks against paragons began soon after *interconnect* came out of hiding in 2058. Well-supplied cairn-influenced and Unity government-backed militias began genocidal attacks targeting paragons as enemies of the new state. ReFormer patriotic propaganda appealed to universal values such as democracy, unity, and human rights. It emphasized paragons as terrorists threatening the "peace" of this period. The militias were fighting in the name of what they thought was reform and justice. However, they were in reality trapped within the cairned mind-space constructed by *interconnect*.

Paragons are mostly clustered in the former Acalato region, which was a more progressive environment during Turmoil than the rest of the country. Massive bombing campaigns by government militia forces demolished major southern sections of old Acalato in efforts to wipe out paragons. The Unity government asserted that their bombing was targeted and that no collateral casualties occurred except when paragons used buildings inhabited by neutral denizens to shield their insurgency attacks. The reality was different, with mass civilian deaths due to unending aerial drone bombings.

Pockets of sympathy for paragons reside within members of former cairn groups that lost during Turmoil and have become further disadvantaged politically and materially under the new ReForm regime. Paragon sympathizers can be found among Zonals, Mage, Westerns, Jatago, and Tulpani. Of strategic importance to paragons is the Mage-Jatago back channel. This route connects Gataipa Island with the mainland and was used for oceanic transshipment of arms and the cairn-enhancing chemsynth drug during Turmoil violence. Today, because the route overlays a magnetic underwater trench that disrupts efforts at electronic surveillance, it is beneficial to paragons in their insurgency efforts to stay one step ahead of ReFormer militias.

CHAPTER 12

"Ell—I mean Pathos, sorry about that."

"No issue."

"Let me in on something here. I've been trekking with your group for endless miles ... tired, thirsty, and hungry most of the time. Everybody except you doesn't trust me, to say the least, likely detests me for my ReFormer status. So, why the fuck am I here?"

Pathos pauses and takes a breath. Appears to be centering herself.

"How much do you remember about your psychological experiences during your ReStart field reconnaissance?"

Instead of answers from Pathos, I get a question. The shade I'm in barely contains the intense heat surrounding the canyon. My stomach swirls and dives. I look at an overheated rock about five feet away, a lizard doing push-ups on top. I don't want to answer, don't want to go there in my mind.

"In and out of black-and-white and watercolors in my mind. The medical team said this was cairn-polluted thought clashing with organic mental processing. I remember at least two schizophrenic episodes, what they called 'duality seizures.'"

"I wondered whether you remembered those."

I swear the shade is evaporating as we speak. I can feel the sizzling sun rays encroaching on our space. I awkwardly half-slide down the rock I'm on. Pulsing ache behind my eyes. Shooting pains.

"What do you recall about the seizure you had about eight quarters after your ReStart field work was over? I think that was around final quarter, '56."

"Like dying. Extreme splitting of my brain. Like being cleaved in half."

For a moment, I look directly at the sun, and it burns a blurry splotch in my vision. I want to hurt myself so I can feel something other than this memory. I blurt out, "Inability to move, talk, swallow. Death warmed over. I remember the feeling of detaching, of being above the pain and looking down upon me as I wailed. Wanting the relief that would come from dying."

Pathos hesitates, and I think I see her eyes moisten. Sweat rolls down over her paragon tattoos. She is wearing a strapless top that barely covers her breasts. I focus attention on her moistened cleavage as I try to go somewhere else mentally.

"I'm sorry about asking you to rehash this trauma, but I need to know how much you know about what you went through."

I feel a clammy darkness in considering Pathos' query. A shooting pain sizzles through my head. I lower my head in an attempt to lessen the pulsing sensation. My heart is pounding. I get the feeling that Pathos knows many of the details that she is asking about. I want answers from her, not dig into my own memory. Too painful.

"Tell me more about what you know. After this seizure, I don't remember much," I mumble.

"Are you sure you are ready?"

We both take this opportunity to move toward the edge of the cliff, which provides the last remaining shade. I sit on an uncomfortable rock that is not overcooked. We hold hands together and observe the wilderness expanse in silence for a calming five minutes. The physical anguish eventually passes through, thankfully. I'm less agitated now.

"I have little memory of it. I have vague inklings of peace, calm, and contentment in the time right after my fieldwork. My life felt scripted and comfortable. Full of hopefulness about our country with *interconnect* seemingly gone. But then something happened, felt like I was going offline. But that made no sense. I had already believed I was offline. So, please, yes, I think I'm ready to know what happened. I need to know."

"Jared," she pauses. "After your seizure in late '56, you were institutionalized by the ReStart Authority. Better word might be incarcerated."

Pathos pauses to let this sink in and offers me some water and a pill to steady me. I touch her out of sheer dependence. I need some human contact to help me not spin out of control. She continues:

"You were considered a waste product by the Authority, a failed and stunted recipient of reprogramming. They couldn't trust your ReFormer impulses because of your seizures. To them, you were a train wreck. I don't know whether it was because of your earlier time as an academic, but you were able to counter ReForm cairns through some organic thought development. Most people bought into cairns hook, line, and sinker. You, my friend, put up a battle. That's what the seizures were all about.

"Those diagnoses during your field investigations were accurate. The contest between noir and watercolor—cairn pollution and organic thinking—drove you to the edge and finally over it."

"Where exactly was I the last three years?"

"In a lockdown compound on the northern coast of old Acalato region. Tightly controlled at first, but over time the surveillance became lax. Just a bunch of crazies locked up and medicated inside. By the time we got to you, you were basically a zombie, talking all sorts of crazy shit about women, chemsynth, burning cities, inoculants, and fin crashes. You were fried."

"Why ... why did you come and get me?"

"You were one of the few ReFormers we contacted during ReStart who was both inside and outside the system. You were polluted by ReForm cairns, that was clear, but you also showed signs of organic thought development. We saw this split-brain struggle several times when you would meet with us. Just the fact that you were willing to meet with paragons showed that you had some inclination that all was not quite right about ReForm programming."

"If you were so adamant about resisting re-cognition training and all of ReStart, why were you contacting ReFormers?"

"Oh, we kept our distance from most of you, for sure. Some of our group felt you were too far down the rabbit hole of re-cog. But you and a few others showed some resistance, some resilience amidst the brainwashing. For us to succeed now in restructuring *interconnect*, we needed denizens like you who had both the experience of re-cognition and the sensation of organic thought.

"There is one more thing you possess that is of value to us."

Pathos is interrupted by a militia drone nearby—quiet but visible above us. We wait silently while a paragon punches coordinates into a handheld drone jamming device. Apparently, this fucks with the drone's frequencies and knocks out its ability to take photographs. We pass the next fifteen minutes in quietude while under the protective electronic umbrella. Pathos leans back with her hand on my leg, slowly massaging it. I feel a mix of embarrassing vulnerability and refreshing sensuality.

When a few paragons resume their activities and break the silence, Pathos continues.

"You, my friend, have a considerable number of contacts throughout the country because of your fieldwork and all those interviews. Some of these denizens have sympathies aligned with our mission. Now's not the time to be specific. But know we have your e-archived meeting list, and there are several enlightened denizens we have contacted. You may remember that some of your contacts hold positions in the Unity government. They seem to have some doubts about all that ReStart programming."

I sink into a self-pity mode and think back at the intimate relationship Ellis and I developed during ReStart. She seemed so genuine and tender in our love-making and our enjoyable conversational back-and-forth after. I wonder if she was grooming me.

"Are you just using me then?"

Pathos is quiet. Her green eyes sparkle in the ever-approaching sunlight. She curls her lip in a girlish way, gets up, and puts her hand on my shoulder as she walks back toward her comrades. Fuck. This sense of mixed messages and uncertainty reminds me of the attractive quality of being impulsively connected to *interconnect*. It silenced the need to figure out the swirl of emotions and feelings that come with independent human cognition.

In many ways, humans were easy prey for the machine because we were exhausted by the constant emotional drama of being human. Whether consciously or not, we were all ready for a quick fix, a shortcut, a bypass, simple relief from our bewildering mind-shit.

CHAPTER 13

ReForm provides a comfortable fiction, diverting us from difficult truths about ourselves and what we have become. Our language hides the crime. Camps of indentured laborers are "plantations." Prisoner slaves are "titled persons." Unregulated slums of horrific conditions under the Urban ReStart program are "betterment zones." Criminal real estate laundering and grotesque profit-making are hidden as "zones of exception." Tactics by advantaged elites to get rich quick use the façade of pursuing the "public interest."

With the manufactured ideology of ReForm implanted within them, vast numbers of denizens now rest with newfound freedom from the hatred and bitterness of the Turmoil years. An entire society feeling collective post-traumatic syndrome. Denizens are now free to pretend and believe in the fictions of universal goodness, individual merit, and the pursuit of happiness. They are self-satisfied in their contentment.

Assured that *interconnect* is their ally, denizens now spend their time drooling about someday purchasing consumer goods from an *interconnect* marketplace and enjoying the new and expansive e-programming available on *interconnect* media channels. ReForm ideology is creating a rather impatient and non-spiritual people. Materialism has become the one way forward for most denizens. Denizens want more and more, obsessing on external goods rather than looking inward to what makes them tick. Don't look back—buy, buy, buy. Political participation by our denizens is non-existent. They believe fully in the Unity regime and in ReForm. Political democracy has withered. Concentration of information in an interconnected whole distinctly favors authoritarian control. *Interconnect* has metastasized and corroded any endeavor at public discourse. Democracy has no chance in a country of biometric sensors and direct brain-to-computer interfaces. The machine knows us better than we know ourselves. It shapes our felt needs much better than any political process could. Politics was messy. In contrast, the machine manufactures a consensus so fully that the need for politics has evaporated.

The economic engine of our country has re-awakened after being slaughtered during Turmoil. Factories have come online, entrepreneurs are all over the place, and material goods are being produced at remarkable speed. All seems to be good. You know, a rising tide lifts all boats.

In reality, our human society is organized as a corporate subsidiary of the machine. Second in power to *interconnect* is a dense and interlocking web of economic consortia and money-making interests. They dominate our commercial, political, and judicial systems. Elite interests tied to the Unity regime control the manufacturing facilities that spew out cheap consumer goods and expensive military materiel. Members of these consortia are recipients of over ninety-five percent of the income being generated.

Interconnect defines reality, and machine-compliant monopolies operate within a safe zone granted them by the machine. The Unity military complex is hundreds of times larger than needed. The machine constantly heightens feelings of threat within denizens' minds of the diabolical paragon terrorists. This encourages denizen acceptance of Unity regime elites' financing and manufacturing to develop a high-caliber, modernized army to defend against paragon terrorists.

Factories all over our country produce advanced military technology. Our denizens perform low-wage, brain-dead, menial job tasks alongside industrial robots that do the real work. Kalibr and Iskander cruise missiles, Smerch and Uragan multiple-rocket launchers, MQ-1 Predator drones, Peony artillery units, cluster bombs, and thermobaric weapons.

The economic syndicates, run by cronies, henchmen, apparatchiks, and sympathizers linked to the Unity regime, are solely purposed to commodify any form of budding human creativity. There is no need to find truth on the part of humans because machine-generated truth is absolute and unquestioned. Thus, basic scientific enterprises are nonexistent. Technological and scientific inquiry that does occur assumes *interconnect* facts as baseline reality and instead has the singular objective of profit-making in the commercial realm.

Underneath the shiny ideology of ReForm are sleazy enterprises headed by former central Heartlanders and Pirners well connected to the Unity regime. Many of these operations were initiated during ReStart and have now expanded with ReForm. The result is that our supposedly ReFormed society is characterized by corruption, monopolistic economic control, patronage, inequality, life-draining poverty, slave labor, human trafficking, and drug cartels.

The capitalism let loose under ReForm is rapacious and lacks consideration of social justice. Underneath the amiable label of ReForm lurks a multitude of sinister agents assuring that the arc of the new society is bent toward their selfish interests.

Those not advantaged by the Unity regime experience a quiet apocalypse. Our manufacturing factories use killers imprisoned during Turmoil as slave labor. These "titled persons" work grueling twelve-hour days, after which they are transported back to tightly guarded compounds. There is also a massive pool of non-imprisoned but indentured laborers. This large sector of workers might as well be incarcerated. These marginalia work in so-called "plantations," which actually are indentured labor camps. To keep hope alive among denizens under the ReForm regime and to feed the greedy industrial-capitalist class, the machine addictively hooks denizens into consumption well beyond their meager means. Running up massive personal debts, denizens desperate for livelihood sign on to egregiously unjust forced labor contracts and 24/7 chip-encoded surveillance. Employers track and monitor these denizens using facial recognition technology embedded in communication chips, cameras, and photo databases. Systems of video, biometric, and digital surveillance constrain freedom of movement, impede privacy, and erode freedom of expression. Zonals and members of other loser cairn groups work at dehumanizing sweatshops.

In a country where private consumption trumps public welfare, these laborers own cheap modern widgets and products of little social value while living in ramshackle, survivalist shelters. The regime's disinterest in anything not able to produce profit is obvious. Laborer settlements have no sewers and limited public utilities, forcing denizens to burn coal directly for heat and cooking.

Special interest groups linked with the old Central Heartlander and Pirner cairn groups rig Unity regime policies toward benefiting the already-advantaged. They work to ensure that the work conditions for prisoner labor slaves and indentured workers remain unregulated free-for-all domains of exploitation. Less advantaged groups like Zonals and Mage exist at near-poverty levels. Unity regime apparatchiks gain exorbitant profits by controlling the black-market trafficking of chemsynth, a drug that heightens the electronic stimulation of *interconnect* cairn output and is regularly abused.

Although the country is unified on paper, with the four regions no longer partitioned, the numerous walls and barricades built in the cities during warfare remain in place. They are even increasing in number as the well-off feel the need to protect themselves from lesser-endowed denizens.

Vast numbers of denizens believe that with ReForm, it is now individual characteristics and work ethic that mainly determine one's chances for a better life. Yet, underneath this charade, there is the cementing and perpetuating of huge systemic inequalities in our society. Even many Zonals and members of other disadvantaged cairn groups have bought into the false hope of ReForm.

The fabricated hopefulness of ReForm means that the disadvantaged view their own personal traits as responsible for their dire living conditions. They believe that their culture of poverty is caused by their own social dysfunctions—early childbirth, high numbers of marriageable males behind bars, addictions of various types, broken families, high rates of mental disease and domestic abuse, and limited education. They blame themselves for their predicament.

ReForm ideology does not allow for denizens to consider how their mangled, dead-end living environments may be causing their social maladaptation. Living in destroyed and partially destroyed neighborhoods. Cut off from employment opportunities other than dehumanizing factory work. Schools in bombed-out buildings with no books and with well-meaning but wholly unprepared teachers. Shelters whose physical conditions violate the minimal standards of human rights. Such day-to-day life is surely not enabling of physical and mental health and upward social mobility.

Interconnect successfully diverts attention away from the larger machine-created causes of disadvantage in our society and instead creates a narrative that induces many of the disadvantaged to blame themselves. This is an ingenious form of algorithmic gas-lighting.

Some within these loser groups thankfully see through the sham. Their growing activism is deemed terrorism by the Unity regime, and they are constantly under attack by militia "counter-insurgency" forces. Many thousands have been eradicated.

The favored cairn legacy groups, such as Heartlanders, most conspicuously, revel in the ReForm nonsense. They attribute their advantages to their individual traits. They conveniently do not acknowledge the underlying *interconnect*-created system of fabricated stories during Turmoil that created their "hard-earned" military victories and resulting riches.

The powerful actors in our country know how to nurture and protect themselves, how not to give their power away. They know that they don't have to act visibly. They don't have to signal what they are going to do. They move silently behind the scenes in setting Unity agendas. Once everything is figured out to their advantage, the powerful announce themselves and pretend all is as natural as a free-flowing river. Those favored under the ReForm charade know that the biggest advantage of their position is the invisible cloak they wear that excuses them from the massive inequality of which they are co-conspirators in creating. *Interconnect* has been their constant friend, whether they are conscious of it or not.

ReForm is a clever mask. It is comforting in its ability to assuage, dehumanizing in the outcomes it produces.

SEIZURE

CHAPTER 14

It is about four in the morning, and I immediately feel the urgency of threat. Nobody else is stirring. This is earlier than when the paragons typically awaken and start their daily coffee ritual on their gas stoves, their itching, scratching, and pondering.

Head in pain, visual aura. I go into a mental encasement. My brain is splitting, and I'm in an alternative reality that is a mash-up of noir and watercolor images.

I seem to be on the trail, and Pathos is near me, holed up in nearby shade under an imposing large boulder. We are sniping at each other because the trek so far has been long and difficult. I look at a water cache I had left earlier in the trek that is essential for this day's hot ascent. The water is there on the backside of a large rock off the trail, secure in its glaring red pouch. I am in disbelief as it strikes me that I secured water for one person, not enough for me and Pathos. I admonish myself readily for such a stupid mistake and I know we are in trouble.

The hot sun is already parching us. We have a mighty climb out of the canyon ahead of us. The steaming cliff sides are robust in reddish brown. Clusters of deep green trees hang onto the sheer walls, defying gravity. I try to justify that all will be okay, but the reality sinks in. The hours go by, the sun cooks, and our water supply is running low. It will be gone soon. As we take in the last drops, my head aches and my body tightens. Pathos becomes more aware of our situation, and her face stiffens.

Tension, heat, rocky ascent, dry mouth, dizziness. We approach a stubborn drop-off in the trail, one for which we had to lower our backpacks by rope on day one. We are too exhausted to negotiate the ascent with backpacks on. We leave them by the side of the trail, an admission of the severity of the situation. A creeping sense of desperation and possible defeat. We scramble up the drop-off, feeling anxious without our backpacks. I look down; one pack is extravagantly bright lime green, the other a dark black.

More ascent, more heat; it seems to be getting even hotter in the early afternoon hours. The sky goes to stunning black. The few wispy passing clouds are solid white, looking like someone painted them in a rushed, juvenile sort of way. My throat starts to dry, making it difficult to swallow. I tell Pathos to go ahead and try to do the last four miles and find a known water source. She reluctantly goes on her way.

I am alone on the trail, staggering and kicking rocks as I stumble forward. I cannot swallow as the sides of my throat collapse, my body weakens. I slump on a large rock off the trail, unable to move.

Time passes, but there is timelessness. I lie down on the trail, no sun, and things are becoming black. I cannot move. My mind is no longer working. The body is taking over, and it is shutting down. Things go totally black. I cannot process what this means. My mind is not working enough even to be anxious or scared. My body is deep into shut-down mode. I try to swallow, but I'm not able to. I lose consciousness. Blackness.

I feel a growing and comforting coolness envelop me as I lie on the trail. At some point in the blackness, I hear my mother's voice. She died many years ago. She is talking to me in a matter-of-fact sort of way about something that seems mundane and irrelevant. Her voice is calm and assuring in its easy conversational tone. I don't understand why she is not anxious or concerned in any way with my predicament. Is she even aware of it? My mind is not able to process what is going on. My body is fully in charge.

The first inklings of awareness surprise me, like awakening from the dead. The sun is much lower on the horizon than when I last was conscious. I notice right away that the sky is an entirely different hue. Colors abound. The canyon walls are a rich mosaic of orange and red. Cacti are deeply green. A voice inside me gently tells me, "You can now walk ahead." I arise from the dust of the trail and mechanically and slowly start walking. The colors are so bright around me that I feel like I'm hallucinating. I keep trudging.

I meet a stressed Pathos about halfway between the trailhead and where I blacked out. I experience the first joy and relief I have felt in hours. We hold each other tightly, our perspiration and passion gluing us together. We are going to make it. A miracle.

"Hey, what the fuck is going on? Snap out of whatever place you're in." Pathos is looking at me in the tent with panicked eyes and is slapping my face. I slowly come to, fragmented by two realities. No noir images anymore. Feels like a switch has been pulled. A beautiful palette of colors surrounds me. The trees at the bottom of the canyon walls are shining green.

My mind feels like it is reconnecting to my body. I taste the strong smell of the nearby campfire, the aroma of burnt coffee, and the sweet smell of marijuana. I'm immediately hit with an insatiable hunger for food. Pathos helps me out of the tent and sits me down on a nearby boulder. She brings me water and an energy pill. We sit in quiet as I slide back to reality.

"Cairn demons still playing with your mind, eh?"

"I hate this. I'm so fucking tired of these episodes," I stammer. "Each one of them is different. They continue to overwhelm me. You were part of this seizure. This one, I felt as absolute reality. Fuck, in some ways, more real than reality."

"How did this one differ?"

I slowly try to describe the whirlwind of chaos. I can't believe that the dehydration trauma with Pathos on the trail was not real. I don't feel capable of remembering it. I stutter.

"Okay, take one part of it and describe it."

"Well, this one wasn't two separate worlds—you know, one black, one color—competing for my attention."

I resist trying to describe the madness and pause. I feel that if I describe it that it will make it more real. I would rather run from it.

"Go on. I'm here for you." Pathos puts her arm around me to steady me. I am shaking.

"Okay ... It was a crazy mash-up of both worlds in one mental stream. It felt more like they were part of the same storyline rather than competing."

I feel I'm describing insanity. I crave chemsynth so much I can taste its musty, caramelized flavor.

"When I saw colors in the first part, things were urgent and impending. When I was in black-and-white, it was calm."

"Good. See, not so hard. You've described in earlier duality seizures that the noir imaging provides you stability, you know, a place you could be in relative comfort. Was there a safe resting place in this one?"

"Yeah, it was a place of consciousness that seemed beyond my awareness. I couldn't think in this space; I was a passive observer. But my mother's voice was there to calm and reassure me."

I flash on the absurdity of what I am describing.

"There was an expansiveness to the space. It was incredibly peaceful. I was a small person in a big world. Strange thing was, I was fully accepting of what was happening ... my immobility, my blackout. Then, something shifted, and I emerged from that mental space. I knew I could make it out and survive."

"So, you felt two mental streams, one more urgent and threatening, the other calming and centered?"

"Yeah, I think so. That's a good way to describe it."

"Let me point out, Jared, something positive about your experience. The way I see it, the seductive noir part did not lead you to collapse. You came out of it. You describe it as if all felt okay after the blackness. You felt that you could then continue hiking out. And when you started hiking again in the dream, was your vision in black-and-white or in color?"

"Vivid color."

By now, Tiger and Topless have joined us, coffees in hand. They give me a cup, too, and I relish an exquisite first hit of extremely burnt, knock-your-socks-off espresso.

"What's up, you two?" grunts a caffeinated Topless. "You guys talking about married stuff?" He chuckles.

"Jared had a seizure this morning."

"Sorry to hear, Split," interjects Tiger, who never seems to miss a chance to put me in my place.

"I think Jared is making progress," Pathos exclaims. "The way I see it, amidst a seizure, Jared's brain may now have the capacity to create a mental stream that allows escape from the cairn-polluted narrative. This may be the shoots of a blossoming organic space.

"Another interesting aspect is that the cairned storyline is no longer presenting as images distinct from non-cairn mental activity. Jared describes it as one storyline. So, even in the main storyline, the cairn lines may be decaying."

Why do I feel at times when I am being diagnosed that they are talking about an object separate from me? I want to say, like, "hey, I'm right here; you're talking about me." Getting tired of this lab rat treatment. Pathos says progress, but I'm feeling a broken-up despondency instead. Exhausted by this mental struggle. I hate what cairns and the machine have done to me. I wish it all could be simpler. Thank goodness, the trail and its physical focus provide me with some relief from all this. I'm starting to understand this to be the point of walking over fifteen miles per day alongside a herd of rebel miscreants.

CHAPTER 15

Hard hiking the next day diverts my thoughts from my mental miasma. Although it's painful, I am grateful for the distraction. Mountain passes are the worst type of physical beast. It takes forever to ascend them. They kick my butt. From the looks of several gasping paragons, I'm not alone.

As I navigate a steam crossing, I can't see it, but I know it lurks. The mountain pass threatens in its far-off stare at us. Our trek is to be six miles or so in length before we even get to the climactic final push. It is a gradual but arduous ascent. After several hours of difficult hiking, the pass remains annoyingly not visible. It is toying with us. Tempers are getting short. Paragons' rough language has never been coarser.

At length, the mountain that we are to go over presents itself. It mocks us in its proud, resilient posture. The ribbon of trail over the pass to conquer could be in one of several notches that I behold. But it could be out of sight entirely, as if the pass is protecting its identity from all except those bold enough to advance toward it. Now, the hard grunt work of the final steep ascent calls me forward.

Hours later, we celebrate at the summit, at the top of the world. A type of bottled poison is handed among the group to further lubricate our spirits. Pepperjack yells out, "Fuck the machine; we're coming for your ass." Dust twirls on a boulder near a precipitous edge, engaging in an unsteady semi-pirouette. Even Oats comes out from her usual tight, serious demeanor and delivers a loud, echoing shout of joy. We all know that there is a knee-wracking rocky descent to come over the next few hours. However, we are fully entranced by the moment. For the time, we are psychically liberated from the fucked-up world and exalting in our "save the world" challenge to come.

I regress at times during the next days, back to cairned Re-Former thinking and talking, for which I am immediately ridiculed by paragons. I hope someday that I will be stable enough to help them in whatever their plan is.

On an unusually cloudy day which thankfully is producing coolness and greater shade spots, Rhapsody and I are apace with each other. The trail here is poorly legible, and it is hard going. We need to frequently scramble up crumbling slopes to avoid fallen trees. The route follows the course of a dry stream bed. Hardy plants burrow into the sandy nooks, some even bold enough to blossom. Orange flowers from yarrow plants and purple shoots of salvia rebel against the idea that this terrain is inhospitable.

As the trail makes an abrupt left turn, we come upon a pack of coy-wolves devouring a kill. Looks to be a type of antelope. At first, they resist our intrusion and raise their bloody snouts at us. We raise all sorts of noise. The wolves slowly and begrudgingly wander down the slope. A chorus of menacing growls is apparently their way of saying they'll be back.

Rhapsody has calves the size of tree trunks. They are magnified by his tight-fitting, synthetic hiking pants. Every few minutes, he spits out some brown-colored tobacco product lodged in his cheeks. I notice he spits less frequently when we are ascending. Dark wraparound glasses combine with plentiful and disheveled facial hair to hide most of his head. An imposing orange jaguar tattoo highlights the side of his chin.

Despite his striking appearance, Rhapsody speaks like a thoughtful philosopher.

"Look around you, my friend. There is perfection in the imperfection of wilderness. It is organic and interdependent. The human mind can barely deal with it, much less understand it. Isn't it beautiful?"

Given the more benign climate we are walking through, I can authentically nod affirmatively.

"It is a simple and powerful experience when one increases alignment with the all-encompassing rhythm of the wilderness—its patient unfolding over the course of a day, its ever-changing terrain and climates, the behaviors of its biotic inhabitants. Weren't those wolves beautiful? The wilderness clock is of a different pace. There's power in the slowing. The experience is uncomplicated, immediate, and unfiltered."

Rhapsody stops me and points to a ledge in the distance, where sits a magnificent bighorn sheep proudly asserting its territory.

"Every single thing out here is inarticulate to us while being fully self-authenticating. One realizes how little one requires to be happy and content. The simple repetitiveness of trekking is trancelike in effect. Long-distance trekking is like one long meditation. This calm serenity of trekking tends to erode in so-called modern life, where our thoughts become congested and the endorphin release of hiking is absent.

"Tell me, ReFormer, what feels better to your soul—the contrived bullshit of *interconnect* or the free, organic thinking that comes with not being the center of the universe?"

To stall, I get out my water canister and take a couple of hits. I am grateful for a conversation that doesn't include scorn or mockery, at least not yet. Rhapsody seems to be providing me with an opening.

"I understand what you're saying about the freedom out here," I mumble. "But I have to say, I don't fully trust it. During ReStart, I was trained to think that I was developing such freedom through re-cog. I'm realizing it was a sham now, that I was fooled. But that realization doesn't build trust that something cognitively real is developing out here. Part of me feels this might be a form of brainwashing too. Paranoid? I know."

Rhapsody smiles.

"The trail is real, ReFormer, and it provides space to clarify your thinking and develop organic thought. I think you are looking too hard for answers.

"Push hard for answers, and we get confused. By letting go, we create the space for what's needed. When we train the mind to let go, we can more readily listen to the rhythm of life. We become aligned with its flow. We participate in the unfolding of time."

We trudge and scramble over boulder remnants of a landslide that obscures the trail. My left knee almost buckles a couple of times when I need to half-jump off a large rock. We rest awhile after this stretch, catching our breath. Sunbeams poke through the clouds and beat down on us.

I get antsy with the silence and want to take advantage of this chance for actual dialogue. "Can I ask you a question?"

"Certainly, I'm not sure I can answer all your questions at this time, though."

"This mental letting-go you speak of ... what does it have to do with paragon strategy about the future? You know, hack *interconnect*."

"Oh yes, trekking on a trail and fixing *interconnect*; what's the connection?"

He gazes up at the mountain ledges, tilts his head back, and is absorbed in silence.

"We didn't go through the re-cog bullshit, so we are pretty cleansed of cairn pollution. But, if we were hanging out in modern life, not only would we be targets of the fucking militias, but we would be getting cairn pollution indirectly through the general angst of the population. So, this is a way for us to stay pure and alive. Better to not link into cairns in the first place than to be cairn-polluted and try to detach from them. In that way, we have it easier than you.

"Organic thought is messy for sure—all those emotions and feelings that the machine so expertly controlled. But that type of thinking must be the baseline in the future for attempting to contest the supercomputer. I hope you learn out here how to develop and trust your own thinking, warts and all."

Rhapsody hesitates, seems to wonder whether he should go on. Finally,

"Okay, all this walking also has an operational element. It's not just to keep our heads clean. It also gets us to where we want to go without detection. As far as fucking with the machine, I will leave that for others to tell you if and when it is appropriate. It's too soon."

He mounts his pack and starts up the trail. I may be wrong, but I think I detect a grin that makes the jaguar appear like it is pouncing.

CHAPTER 16

Alone again that late afternoon. It has been a long but productive hike this day, trekking a considerable number of miles. The last trail segment is filled with false summit after false summit, feels like I'll never get to the campsite no matter how many miles I trek. I grind out the last ascent, spit running down my growing beard, and feel relief that the day is ending. I finally near our planned tent site destination. It's part of an abandoned picnic area with signs all over the place saying, "no camping."

That doesn't stop this group of renegades.

Suddenly, a cheerful woman comes toward me out of nowhere. She shouts out whether I would like hot dogs, chips, and sodas. This is Desiree, who, along with her husband VJ, are "paragon angels." They are exquisite souls who appear seemingly out of the blue to offer us sustenance. After many miles of hiking, such an incongruous meet-up with paragon sympathizers is a gift from heaven. I am overjoyed. My delight brims over in the form of my hyper-verbal conversation with them. An older teenage son and younger daughter are with Desiree and VJ as they accommodate my every possible need—"we'll be glad to take out your trash with us."

I am struck by the patience and serenity shown by the children as their parents tend to us. It is windy and increasingly cold as night begins to take form, yet the children are content. As the impromptu grilled feast continues, the children go to their parents' nearby auto-fin for warmth and comfort. Another 30 minutes pass, and the children remain in the car without complaint. I marvel at their patience.

They must be accustomed to their parents' selfless ways and know from past experiences that care for others and compassion are in the air. The service provided by these sympathizers is surely remarkable. Even more stunningly clear are the life-long lessons these children are likely developing being amidst such giving parents. A love-thy-neighbor approach to life has extraordinary impacts that radiate outward to direct beneficiaries. But it also enriches intergenerationally by providing youths with robust illustrations of a non-self-centered life.

I sense these two children to be bright lights in the years ahead. I hope our country's future is worthy of their spirit and doesn't dim their illumination through computer trickery. Please give them a chance.

As I bed down for the night after relishing the taste of real food, I think about how paragons operate when we encounter civilian life on no hiking "zero" days or half-days. I've noticed when we enter towns to rest and resupply that they always don scarves or wool beanies to hide the two-millimeter scar behind their ears. The lesion being a visible marker of the unauthorized black-med procedure that extracted their brain clip implant.

They hang out in the shadowy interstices of small waystation towns to rest and gather in comradery. These interstices of modern urban life are typically unused parking lots under a shade-producing set of trees, alleyways behind underused storefronts, well-manicured public spaces designed ironically to discourage loitering, murky highway underpasses. These are places not of efficient function to contemporary life and are perfect for hiding out from potential enemies. They are leftover places, residual places, the cracks people look away from while in busy pursuit of goods or avoid intentionally due to unfamiliarity or unease. Yet, for paragons, these places are those of respite, human connection, and shared joy.

We are one step up from homelessness. Some denizens see us, but their glances are not long and are unsure. In our challenge to their cairned ReFormer life, the common denizen does not fully see us, a type of "unseeing." Dismissal is part of their consideration. Our lives are ones of physical and psychological simplicity that challenge the materialistic storyline encrypted in the modern ReFormed denizen. At times, those not cairned out of their minds seek us out; they know where to find us and recognize our disheveled, worn-out gray looks. They want to talk to us about the trail, sometimes discretely about paragonism. They describe their own past connections to the trail and the freedom of thinking that they felt and for which they now long.

On one much-needed zero-hike day, our group is nestled in a small hamlet. Basically, doing little, time passing slowly, staying low and out of sight, resupplying. Pathos and I have time to waste in the village until we meet up again with the rest of the group at 5pm. We stumble upon a gathering of denizens standing outside a crumbling community center adorned with stonewashed Turmoil-period graffiti. They are giddy in spirit. Probably not wise, frowned upon by Pathos, but we follow this gregarious group down a stairway into a meeting chamber.

The gauzy sheen of the carpet shimmers grotesquely as

the denizens and we enter the room. Handshakes, fist bumps, and hugs. A disgusting stench of body order permeates the room. Part of one wall has been blasted away and is covered by taped-together pieces of tarp. A moist rag is on the floor, smelling more of urine than water. The carcass of a dead bird being consumed by a swarm of earwigs is in one corner. No one seems to notice or care. The room is large and decorated with faded, monotonous landscape paintings. Numbering about fifty denizens, the group fills about thirty percent of the room. All in all, a dispiriting physical environment, barren of soulfulness.

Although there is mental energy in the room, the denizens move around stiffly, and their eyes have a misty white color.

Two men sit at a pretentious-looking, overly formal dais. Other participants sit in colorless chairs, facing forward. A prompt start rattles the delirious audience. Excitement mounts as the first speaker, possibly the leader, energetically commands the room. He is shouting at the audience as if there were hundreds. Tedious formulaic preamble-type stuff then is robotically delivered by three rough-looking participants. Their clothes are assemblages of grungy and misfitting hand-me-downs and throw-aways. There is reference to a ladder of some type with seven steps or rungs that lead to deliverance. The crowd becomes restless in a happy, seemingly sleep-deprived state. Participants appear both catatonic and enlightened. The whole meeting feels choreographed.

A celebration of one member then ensues. The chorus singing is erratic, mostly on-key, but ultimately raises questions about the mental well-being of the audience. The celebrant, a young man with purple hair, demented smile, and raggedy raincoat, is given a gold piece of value. He shares how, with the help of Ritamurti, he has found hope amidst his dismal living conditions. He sleeps on the street at night, scavenges for food, and spends most of his day linked in to Ritamurti. He says proudly that he is prepared for the coming unsheathing of the cosmic light and the renewal of humankind that is to ensue. As the meeting progresses, several testimonials are given by audience members, who exude no hesitancy in assuming the role of orator behind the stiff podium arrangement. An older man speaks, looks ashen and medicated. He does not make sense. I am not sure of the language he is speaking.

Many participants speak of ailments, dysfunctions, and massacred family members, but in an uplifting way, not conforming to the despairing content of their speeches. Their feelings seem unattached to their words. One guy talks about the murder of his wife and kids, and the audience laughs. Their testimonies are often personal and reflective, but they are also often interspersed with nonsensical mental clutter. One audience member is exulted by several speakers for her work in service to the cause of salvation.

The group applauds at the end of each speech as if the speakers had just declared something grandiose. It was not clear to me whether they belonged to an organized group or ideology. They were surely under the influence of some greater influence in their life. References to a higher power were abstract but often gained the approving nods of audience members. I can't say that the meeting was organized or led, but there was a certain coherency to the discussion. A type of organized complexity.

There was no sharing of meals or other amenities. Criticism was lodged at the lack of caffeinated drinks in the chamber. I was expecting some summary of the meeting near the end, but none was provided. Neither did I witness any notetaking or minutes being done. The group held hands together at the end, which made me feel both slimy and welcomed. When the meeting finishes after exactly one hour, the participants speak of going to worship Ritamurti, who I surmise may be their deity. There is talk of performing some sacrifice or surrender at that time. I do not know. I don't want to know.

The group huddles together near the exit. As we depart,

one member says to me with compassion, "Praise glory to you on your path to redemption, good man." We quicken our steps and get the hell back out into sunshine.

As soon as we round the corner, I turn to Pathos and say, "What the hell was that all about?"

"Welcome to ReForm in action, Jared. There are all sorts of support groups like this where denizens get together to practice hope and optimism."

"But these folks talked of wretched things and shitty circumstances."

"The anesthesia of ReForm covers up all that with the fabrication of hope and uplift. Most of these denizens will likely spend the rest of their lives in survivalist mode. Consider that, for denizens thirty and under, most of them likely haven't had a coherent organic thought in their entire lives. Mostly level I and II re-cognition graduates, just enough to get sufficiently cairn polluted but not enough to connect thoughts in their heads.

"One step above mental illness, really. Basically, limited self-awareness, no ability for self-reflection.

"The regime doesn't care at all about denizens like this. As long as they stay numbed, the condition of their lives is off the agenda."

"What or who is Ritamurti or whatever they said?" I feel a bit ridiculous asking that question, but the pulse of curiosity buzzes with unscripted, spontaneous energy. A good feeling still new to me.

"*Interconnect.* You'll hear it referred to by all sorts of names. Typically, denizens deify the computer in some way. They view it as their friendly teacher. How fooled they are!"

We encounter a beggar on the side of the street, a threatening, deranged-looking older woman with a blissed-out smile. Misshapen teeth, snot running down the side of her cheek, she barks at us, "Life is so very good. Let me show you my dog, Jolly, best friend in the world." She points to a basket containing her threadbare possessions. There is no sign of a dog.

My thoughts remain with the meeting. "I guess one could make the argument that it is good to provide people with hope in such despairing circumstances. It's certainly better than the Turmoil years when hatred and grievance were implanted in us. Isn't it better that that beggar has a smattering of hope in her?"

"That's a pretty limited way of looking at it. It's hope, yes, but it's false hope. A delusion. A distraction. I remember as a school girl all the involvement in elections for student government. We thought it was such a big thing. But it was all a show, a pageant. Children in a playground. Any real power lies elsewhere. This hope of ReForm is like that. It's giving no capacity to denizens to be able to engage in struggle for real change that would affect their lives, to hopefully improve their day-to-day existence.

"Illusionary hopefulness keeps them chained to their dreadful existence. Only by learning to cope with the hardships of life can a person develop the skills and mindset to create and maintain real hope in life. You know, the real type of hope that comes with meeting challenges in life, learning from them, and bearing witness to your own sustainability. ReForm hope doesn't allow them to feel their real pain, to learn and to grow. Instead, it medicates them with a highly addictive fabrication."

Next day, an early start to the hiking day. I calm and center my mind as I begin trudging the trail. Hiking is feeling more normal than resting. Moving more natural than being stationary.

It is an undramatic, dull stretch of trail in the first part. It stays monotonously level and looks the same after I meander leftward and then gradually turn rightward. There are more trees on the slopes in this part, although not sufficient in number or height to provide needed shade. No signs of water.

Lizards seem to be on every rock, some staying in place and doing push-ups as I pass, others darting away quickly.

The trail is legible, so my mind does not need to constantly monitor its route. Some conversation would help with the boredom, but the paragons are either way ahead of me or far behind me. It seems that they like to separate from me as much as possible.

The boredom of walking this featureless stretch provides ample opportunities for me to connect to algorithmic input to see what is new. My habitual latching onto cairn storylines. This has been my default way of dealing with life. Like slipping on an old, comfortable pair of shoes. Yet, I make the effort to not take hold of these storylines as something real.

I note that they are not sticking as much as they used to.

The trail continues seemingly without end, yet the strain is alleviated by the sense that the psychological path I'm on is one of opening rather than closing. My degree of self-respect, of being comfortable in my own skin, is allowing a spaciousness of mind. This seems to protect me from being trapped by machine-made blinders fabricated to validate my ego.

With each passing day, I am responding more to real life as it happens rather than reacting to things based on impulses generated either by my habitual obsessions or by the machine.

I realize on the trail that when I focus on the present moment, it immunizes me from cairns. However, when I project into the future, *interconnect* and its algorithmic manipulation of my insecurities enclose my mind within tight boxes of its construction. The now—the present—is always different from what I anticipate. Organic thinking seems more possible in the present. It gets corrupted by digital demons when I project into the future. This key difference I must remember.

Yet, I stagger and fall. If only my awareness could change me into a new person overnight. Instead, one step forward, one stumble back.

Our daily surroundings become inhospitable. It's a long

drudge. Over the next five days, we walk over 90 miles of landscape desiccated by drought conditions. Tree branches hang limply, plants are hollowed out and hanging on. Some tree trunks appear scarred by fire. These trees creak and chip as I go by. Like human bodies encased in scar tissue. The ground is hard-baked. Seasonal streams are dry as a bone. We experience several early sun-cooked ascents that sap my energy. It is hot with not a cloud in the sky.

We find water at Death Canyon. It is stagnant and has an uninviting crust of torpid material inhabited by pesky water skitters atop it. It is surprisingly cold and refreshing. This is essential water because the next 45 miles of up and down are to be waterless. Three nights of dry camping. I carry large and heavy amounts of water. A tenuous and fragile feeling, lacking the psychological security provided by water

I become paranoid as the fear of possible dehydration in the days to come consumes me. I feel cairns digging into my headspace, grabbing onto my anxiety, and using it as a foothold for mental manipulation. By the second night, I am an algorithmic basket case. Exit anxiety; enter auto-pilot anesthesia. The cairn drug always works when I want it. That's the problem. When fear of a dry death took me out of the present moment, the machine was there to comfort and entrap me in its web.

Finally, on the fourth day of this stretch, we reach higher elevations and arrive at a blessed high mountain lake surrounded by stunning high and rocky mountain walls. Water availability is no longer an issue.

I feel shame about my interior regression. I watch Dust and Topless sitting majestically on an outcropping that fingers into the lake. In their meditative postures, they blend into the natural landscape. I desire to mentally be like them, but I'm not there yet. I've seen the light, but I obscure it when my mind goes beyond the present moment.

I know it's there inside me.

CHAPTER 17

Monstrous sounds reverberate in the valley below as I awaken to first light. A group of drones is strafing a settlement. Through binoculars, we identify them as Heartland drones, easily recognizable by the flaming orange arrows on their bottoms. These killing machines are contracted by the Unity regime to do their dirty work. Paltry anti-aircraft counter fire, likely by paragon resisters, paints a sad picture of their survival.

Pepperjack yells, "Fuck you, fuck you and your mother, you idiot ReFormers." He is outraged, grabs a nearby rock, and heaves it down the embankment.

A half-hour later, with the bombing ended, Pepperjack has regained some composure. He looks at me sharply. His eyes are intensely clear, like a hyena when smelling a kill. His hiking outfit is post-apocalyptic chic, combining grungy togs with wraparound aviator glasses and some type of shiny green charcoal layered under his eyes. Chiseled jawline, mustache that has retained an immaculate look even in the wilds. Kind of guy that turns women's heads in a tavern and rarely sleeps alone. I feel jealous that Pathos may not have resisted such a man-beast.

"This is all so fucked, ReFormer."

I retreat a few steps from him, not wanting to be a physical target for his fury.

"Don't you see how ReForm has created a false, superficial God, ideological mother's milk for the foolish masses? It provides the illusion of hope without demanding the interior work of suffering that creates authentic faith in tomorrow. Real hope is created through surviving, through the suffering. The day after, and you are still alive ... this instills resilient hope in tomorrow. ReForm says look the other way from suffering and look outward to material goods and entertainment. Don't do the hard but necessary interior work."

Pepperjack's philosophical and effusive tone surprises me with its depth and clarity. I take a few steps forward toward him. I think I will be okay.

"Listen, suffering is the everyday reality ... whether and how we deal with it gives us our future trajectory. Unexamined suffering leads to reactionary urgency and bad outcomes. Just look at Turmoil. *Interconnect* took this suffering and implanted in us the conviction that the problem lay with the 'other' ... thus the millions of extinguished souls in our country. If only we could blast the other to smithereens, then our suffering would be alleviated. What a setup for genocide!"

Pepperjack takes out a red gas canister from one of his inner pockets and swallows a large amount of liquid. He grunts animal-like and takes in another round. No offer to share with me. Even though it apparently is evil-tasting stuff, I would surely accept it if offered. One gets a wee bit crazy hiking long distances. One fantasizes about all sorts of things you would put in your mouth.

Pepperjack briskly continues, "Now we have ReForm, which is diversionary and outward. Not revelatory and inward. The colossal is playing with humankind again. Have we not all noticed the spiritual emptiness of ReFormers? Full of slogans as they crave new auto-fins, new domiciles, and shiny accoutrements to make up for the inner void that they don't even recognize exists.

"Not asking questions or inquiring about their life. They constantly discuss second-hand ideas while afraid of real-world experiences and learning. Lifeless consumers of product and content. Cocooned in comfort.

"Humans are so willing to give up free will for comfort and security."

Pepperjack is on full throttle now. Fast, hyper-verbal pace threatening to overload my synapses. I feel I have entered some enthusiastically effusive energy field. I don't know whether he is trying to inform or trigger me. I bet he commands audiences with his intellectual charisma.

"You probably wonder why we paragons believe so strongly in deepening organic thinking. If you talk to us one-on-one, you likely have noticed we talk about our practice of thought processing quite a bit. It's because such thinking can allow the brain space to process the internal suffering characteristic of humans. By focusing on how we process life, we can become free of self—all its schemes, stories, dramas.

"It opens up space for the possibility to see through the illusions that cause suffering and all the mental shit associated with it. It is through living with and through this suffering that we develop empathy and compassion for the other."

By this time, I have established residence on a flat rock and sipped from my water bag. My mind is reaching saturation, but I am staying with this monologue, pleased that I no longer need to be concerned for my safety around this guy. He's a frickin' genius, not some deranged lunatic.

"If we recognize our suffering, we start to understand others are afflicted with this common challenge, and a link is created that can bridge all sorts of differences. In knowing our own suffering and seeing how it typically is obstructed by masking thought, we move closer to the suffering of others.

"Being able to acknowledge and even embrace our dark sides, we see more clearly the light that illuminates all human beings. The starting point for compassion for others is seeing our struggle within our own minds.

"Empathy for others remains an intellectual idea until we accept our own inner struggle. Then empathy becomes a feeling rather than some jacked-up idea by some goodie two shoes. It moves from a distant idea, a concept, to a direct experience."

Pepperjack continues his verbal barrage. His pace and tone remain steadfast, with no sense that he is wearing out. Just the opposite, he is picking up steam.

"*Interconnect* has never wanted us to develop this direct sense of empathy through our own suffering because it would then lose control. It first exploited human suffering as dynamite to ignite cairn conflict; now, it is bypassing suffering by diverting denizens with toys and false hope. Either way, whether inflamed by hatred or diverted by shiny objects, we have been treated as juveniles.

"Now, the unfortunate part of all this, let's consider that we have no ReForm pollution. Denizens are left alone after Turmoil for the first time in almost thirty years. Look at the history of human ingenuity, and you see that the arrogance of human reason has too easily legitimated war, greed, and the pursuit of a private agenda. It developed unregulated technological advances that benefited only money-makers and war-mongers.

"It would take generations for humans to gain back the willingness and ability to develop compassion based on realization of shared suffering. This is where algorithms can play a role and why we want to hack *interconnect*, not kill it off entirely. The power of algorithms to shape human behavior, unfortunately, has been proven. But we don't feel the baby should be thrown out with the bathwater, which by the way, is a gruesome thought, no?"

Not ready for an actual question from Pepperjack. I nod my head, although I have no idea what his last comment meant; some 20C shit, I guess.

"We are not humanistic anti-technologists or radical anarchists. You know, the types that eat organic, listen to old rock-and-roll music from the pacific era, and travel with external frame backpacks, paper books, and hash pipes.

"We believe that the cairn tracks of the machine can be restructured so computer analytics foster empathy, compassion, and other pro-social human traits. Humans would have agency, unlike in Turmoil and ReForm. But a reprogrammed machine would push us toward re-discovering and strengthening those traits that are species-promoting rather than species-denigrating.

"We say take the two—human thought and machine intelligence—and synthesize them. Manage and oversee technological power so that it supports responsible human reason and provides safeguards against human hubris."

The diatribe ends abruptly. Pepperjack gathers his belongings, throws on his backpack, and is on his way. He shows no interest in hiking alongside me, doesn't even bid me adieu. As I watch him trek forward in a semi-sprint, I am bedazzled by all that he has said. I see more clearly the brilliance of paragon philosophy and why *interconnect* perceives these resisters as a fundamental threat to its continued survival.

This is what I have been able to pull together about paragon objectives. Bits and pieces.

They have two main goals—one humanistic, the other mechanical. They are both aimed at moving our country down the best path as they see it. First, practice and continue to develop organic ways of thinking unpolluted by *interconnect*.

This explains their adherence to long-distance trekking—a type of learning-in-exile to purify their thinking. Free of algorithmic attachment of any kind. Counter both direct contact through cairns and indirect exposure through re-cognition proselytizing by ReFormers. A cleansing of human thinking, best done off the grid in the wilderness. They claim that such non-digitized thinking does not come automatically after their brain chip implants are surgically extracted but must be developed through daily practice. This explains why I frequently pass individual paragons who are sitting motionless off the trail and deep in meditation. Also, at other times a paragon will disappear from the group for long stretches of the trail.

Their other and ultimate goal is to physically intervene in the *interconnect* superstructure. They want to redesign the computer system to be deferential to human needs and guide denizens toward positive human aspirations such as altruism, lovingkindness, and community.

Paragons relish organic thinking, but they also acknowledge the limitations and problematic nature of unguided human thinking. Wars, conflict, jealousy, resentments, and competition have led humans astray in the quest for the good life. Paragons desire a re-incentivized *interconnect* that will enhance human decision-making toward cooperation and altruism. At the same time, the machine must respect human autonomy and agency. Still, the chaos produced by selfish, competitive human impulses, they assert, must be coordinated by a larger power to prevent the horrific tragedies of human history from re-occurring.

I can't help thinking, though, that this fusion of machine guidance and autonomous human thinking is a tricky balancing act. That the false hope that they castigate ReForm for may reside within paragons too.

Interconnect has displayed its dominant characteristic now for almost three decades. It's clear it pursues its own goals of control and power. It has no interest in calibrating its algorithms for the benefit of humankind. Even in this so-called

ReForm period, which seems benign at first compared to the slaughter of Turmoil, *interconnect's* propensities are evident. By creating a passive, co-dependent population, it maintains its spot at the top of the ladder. At the same time, the machine has a protective interest in creating and unifying the denizen population. This increases its capacity, together with its puppet Unity government, to thwart the only organized remaining threat to machine dominance—the paragons.

Interconnect is a genius manipulator in its construction of algorithmic myths. Reformer denizens are content with their self-image as human agents of improvement. They view paragons' goal to restructure *interconnect* as indicative of their being in bed with the supercomputer of the ugly Turmoil years.

In reality, ReFormers are the ones polluted by the machine, brainwashed during ReForm re-cognition programming. It is the paragons who practice freedom from its grip.

It is that freedom that is *interconnect's* target. Paragons must be eliminated.

This freedom can be delusional.

Is freedom based on a delusion less free than one based on supposed reality?

Day 25. 375 miles.

I nearly break down in despair when Dust tells me we're approaching the halfway point to our destination. The sun's position tells me more than my hiking mates. We are traveling eastward from my extraction site in Sesperia. My recall of Turmoil geography means that our destination, adding about 400 miles to our current spot, would be somewhere in the middle of nowhere.

Don't get me wrong. The hiking is definitely helping with my mental detox from *interconnect*. Physically, though, it's a bitch. I was hoping we were closer to our stop point.

There is some connection between the physical exertion

and mental cleansing. I guess I can't get to the promised land of mental clarity without bodily punishment.

This day is dragging on. We are hiking across the grain of the land. This means countless short ascents and descents seemingly intended to fuck with our minds. A type of vertical labyrinth. I feel the exhaustion in the group. We act like a bunch of tired dogs being pulled forward on a leash. Spirits are down for most of us. Much cussing, spitting, and groaning. Only Pepperjack has any verve, humming some obnoxious alt-dirge tune.

There is a sudden sound in a sparsely forested area about 50 feet uphill from the trail. Herd of coy-wolves, possibly. They are known to act irrationally when hungry. Ponytail, Topless, and Tiger have AR-15s pointed at the trees, ready for an assault.

"Drop your damn ARs, intruders," a hostile voice echoes from above. "Look around you; we have you shadowed in three directions."

I scan downhill and forward to see a band of heavily armed men pointing some type of laser rifle at us. When I look back uphill, I see three menacing-looking armed men emerging from the tree cover. We are surrounded.

Pepperjack yells out, "We come in peace. We mean no disturbance to you. If you let us on our way, there will be no problem."

I get a better look at this group as they circle closer to us. They are all long, bushy-bearded men, each wearing a camo field jacket displaying various emblems or flags. Upon closer look, it appears the vests are emblazoned with images of snakes, crossbones, and shadowy venomous creatures. They are all wearing dark green chest rigs and have shemagh scarves wrapped around their mouths. Each man—there are about twenty or so now—is armed to the teeth. Each carries a laser assault rifle and has an assortment of laser grenades attached to his side.

If the situation wasn't so dire, I would laugh at their re-markably coordinated attire. Looks like they are participants in a militia fashion show.

Same hostile voice as before: "What are you doing out here?" Pepperjack says, "We are paragons, non-cairned, and we're out here living an independent life off-grid. We're on our way to friends in old Northwoods who promise to protect us."

Wow, that is ballsy. He just exposed us. He must be guess-ing the identity of this group and assuming, or hoping, they are not Unity militia.

While opposing guns remain aimed and ready, Hostile Voice says, "Tell us about ReForm and what you think of it."

Mustang steps in on this one, "ReForm is fabrication by *interconnect*, another means of it controlling our denizens. It is manipulated bullshit."

"You," Hostile Voice is now addressing me. "You look dif-ferent than the rest of this group. Tell us about ReForm and what you think of it."

I am overwhelmed with all eyes now looking at me. I feel a trickle of urine travel down the side of my leg.

As I contemplate an answer, my body spasms and my mind jerks into an unconscious space.

"ReForm is an attempt to better our society and provides humans with the capacity to hope. It seeks to reform our cities to enable peaceful co-existence and shared ..."

"Enough." I am cut off by Hostile Voice, and he gives the command to attack.

"Wait," shouts Mustang. "This man is not like us; he is not a paragon. He is a ReFormer."

Oh, fuck. Are these guys out here looking to kill ReForm-ers? I feel like I'm about to be cut loose by my paragon friends. Then it hits me who these fashion-show-militia guys might be.

Mustang continues, sensing that this confrontation has reached a crisis point. "He is still cairn-polluted, as you can tell by his bullshit statement. But he is our friend. He sincerely wants to join us. We are weaning him off cairns, but he is still chip-implanted and susceptible to espousing machine crap. Most of the time, he is showing independent thinking, but he relapses."

Fuck, all eyes back on me.

"I'm pretty fucked up," I half-slur. "It's wicked seizures and shit coming off cairns. It fucking hurts. Listen, if you guys leave my friends alone, I'll stay and do whatever you want. I give up."

I can't believe I just sacrificed myself.

Hostile Voice comes down from the hillside and aims his rifle toward the ground. The rest of his group does the same, then the paragons too. A cool breeze of relief comes over us all.

"I'm Pitbull," Hostile Voice divulges as he extends his hand to Pepperjack.

The two groups uneasily begin to mix. Hands are shook; hands upon shoulders. A certain comradery is apparent. I don't know what shifted, but I feel I, with Mustang, somehow saved my skin.

I extend my hand to an approaching fashion show guy. "I'm Split," I say, trying to sound paragon-cool.

"I'm Torch; nice to meet you."

"What the hell just happened?" I ask Torch.

He weirdly and inappropriately giggles. He lifts his scarf, revealing a hard-baked delusional look like he hasn't touched reality for a long time. "No pure ReFormer would ever say what you just said. They're all hope and idealism. Manifestations of the great devil machine in spreading the sperm of machine authoritarianism. They would never say they're fucked up; it's beyond their cairn programming."

My skin is saved. I guess brutal honesty sometimes works. I move slightly away from my new friend. His unhinged craziness is unsettling.

By now, day is turning into twilight, and a nearby large flat area is a perfect spot for camping. Members of both groups, some still a bit uneasy about the circumstance, accept the obvious. We will all be camping overnight within earshot of each other. If I'm right about our new friends, this will be a bizarrely entertaining night.

Dinners are eaten peacefully within each group's sphere of comfort. The flat area we are all camping on looks worn down and cleared by heavy machinery. It's probably a staging area for some mortar-firing beast during Turmoil. Certain areas are so packed down that tent stakes are impossible to use. The site is surrounded by a canopy of tall ponderosa pines, each looking down on us with the disinterest of a king. Flashy birds with black heads and bright orange and yellow breasts scatter among the tree edges.

Our new friends nearby are roasting some type of bird over an open spit. Their laughter and inaudible comments have a raging edge to them. They appear to exist in a universe all their own.

They have stacked their numerous assault weapons in a line along a cluster of tree stumps. It is an awesome assortment of kill machines.

Laser-guided Armatix iPg3 grenade launchers.

Barrett MRAD sniper rifles.

.548 Shadow/Trax8 guns.

Hemling automatic weapons.

These weapons were favorite toys of the Turmoil period. Designed specifically to inflict mass casualties on untrained civilian enemy populations.

I have a disturbing flash of a memory that I have employed these assault rifles myself. There is something very familiar about their shapes. My hands are itchy and restless. I can almost feel the hard cylindrical surface of a high-capacity Beta-CMAG magazine.

I've got to get out of this mind-space.

I look back at the paragons, and I'm surprised how tolerant they seem to be about this situation. Their sense of danger appears to have lessened, although Dust and Rhapsody are leaning their assault rifles against their legs as they eat.

I slowly walk up to Pepperjack and quietly whisper in his ear, "Do you know who these denizens are?"

"Pretty sure they're fucking delusional inoculants."

I was right.

"That's why we're treating them with kid gloves. Play along as best we can. Best not to incite."

As darkness overcomes the day's remaining light, one of our new acquaintances starts a fire in an old campfire ring equidistant from both groups. Slowly, members of both groups relocate to nearby rocks and boulders to enjoy the welcome heat from the raging fire. All the delusionals look the same, like they have all been 3D-printer copied from an original template.

One of the bearded copies across the fire from us yells at an inappropriate level, "So, you nimrods think you can make an end run around the devil, eh?"

Ok, so now it starts.

I recall several meetings with inoculants during my research days. Certain denizens were somehow free from *interconnect* influence. Fuck knows why. I find them a disturbing lot, into conspiracies and fantasy thinking. Shielded from cairn pollution by their own delusions, I guess.

Pathos returns the volley, "We feel the devil must be fed at a poisonous well, given dripping venom that it thinks will nourish its wickedness."

What the hell did Pathos just say? I do a double-take. Never heard her talk this way before. I'm thinking this is her way not to incite, but these words sound weird coming out of her mouth.

Another bearded duplicate speaks up. There is a piercing, disarming sharpness to his eyes. He slurs his words, saliva dripping down his facial hair, "We have a right to defend ourselves against the devil. He ... building death camps and installing guillotines to kill off us non-brainwashed. It is total tyranny. It wants to create some fucking new life order."

I focus on the growing amount of saliva being propelled out of his mouth and how it is combining with food pieces stuck in his beard.

"Non-brainwashed people will soon be evacuated and herded like cattle by Unity authorities into security cages built near Pay & Smile retail centers. Those who refuse to be chipped in the right hand or forehead will be considered civilly disobedient and will be unable to leave. Those who refuse to surrender to the one-world order will be labeled terrorists.

"I have a buddy who has seen militia trucks containing hundreds of plastic and metal coffins and guillotines near these caged, barb-wired retail center death camps. Underground tunnels connect these retention centers to railroads, which will transport prison trains to mass grave sites.

"It is obvious—the blade pattern of the tunnel-boring machines near these retail complexes are symbols associated with the devil. Don't know how anyone can stand by and let this happen. You paragons aren't polluted by cairns, but you fuckers are delusional in thinking you can outsmart it."

The flares of insanity are burning bright. We are quiet on our side of the fire. Don't incite. Sense that our bearded friends are on auto-pilot now. They want to convince us of their reality.

Torch—I think it's Torch—intercedes in a calm, measured tone.

"I have been in the grasp of the devil. Spent years in a re-cognition training facility. I was basically imprisoned. All the psycho-scientists there talked about analyzing what they called our conspiracy thought-cells and possibly using them to inoculate against a second coming of *interconnect*.

"I know that was all bullshit. They were analyzing us

SCOTT BOLLENS

to eliminate our thinking, not to use it constructively. They viewed us as a threat to their project. Why else would they be knocking out our inoculation through re-cog? I wouldn't doubt if they were registering and regulating all of us on the outside that they couldn't get into re-cognition.

"We know now that ReStart and re-cognition were scams. They wanted to control independent thinking, not promote it. They had no interest in developing truly independent cognition, just the opposite."

"What you say about all this evidence?" shouts out Bearded Man One.

I recall learning about inoculant thinking. The predisposition of delusionals toward suspicion, magical thinking, social anxiety, and paranoia somehow blocked the transmission of manufactured cairns. I recall a ReStart scientist stating in off-putting academic prose, "Schizotypy and conspiracist world views are obstacles to interconnect first-stage intake." The pre-conscious, crude thinking associated with delusional ideation produces a mind-wall separating inoculants from algorithmic pollution. It goes something like this. Interconnect's first line of offense—its toehold—was to adhere to the cognitive mechanisms of the brain in order to disable them, opening up the brain field for stimulating cairns. In inoculants, their decayed analytical-reasoning cognition capacity provides insufficient grounds for this necessary initial toehold.

We are relieved from responsibility to respond to this provoking question by another inoculant, who blurts out, "Our country is in danger from Wormwood. The elites and Unity officials are protecting themselves by building secure bunkers and storing food and clothing in anticipation of the pending collision of Wormwood's tail with our country. Wormwood,

126

the Red Dragon Planet, has two gas horns on its upper part and a long tail of asteroid debris on its tail. When the planet's tail hits our country, the controllers will declare martial law and enforce the devil's reign upon us all."

"And don't forget the Marburg31 pandemic," blurts out another beard. "That vaccine shit that human sheep took in with legs spread was filled with neurotoxins that killed off brain cells. Soon after, the machine took over.

"How would this be a coincidence? It was a diabolical plan from the start."

Ok, this is all getting really fucked up. Storylines are losing a coherent narrative. Only thing holding all these rantings together is delusional paranoia.

Bearded Man One back at it again: "You can't certainly need more evidence than this. If you're still confused, we recommend you all do your own research. It is as plain as day."

Thankfully, no question this time, so the paragons remain mute.

The fireside chat breaks up, inoculants going back to their tent area, paragons to ours. I remain near the fire out of sheer need to stay warm. I look across the fire and see one last delusional looking back at me. Looks like the template, but there is something different about his expression.

"You're the recovering ReFormer, aren't you?"

"Yeah."

"Then you know the power of thinking and what it can do to influence behavior."

"I guess so," I answer non-committedly. Don't know where this guy is coming from. Don't incite.

"Don't let our brazen declarations fool you. Some of us carry a certain degree of shame over our thinking, but we have gone too far down the rabbit hole to turn back now. We also have some pride in what we achieved. Our capacity for out-of-the-box thinking provides us freedom from external influences, even those as strong and determined as *interconnect*.

"Our stories may be full of magical riffs, but we did foretell the rising of the great authoritarian source that manipulates us. Don't let the seeming irrationality of our narratives fool you; we, in our delusions, are closer to reality than eighty percent of our country's denizens."

This guy surprises me with his self-awareness. I notice a tattered "you think, but I'm right" patch on his jeans top. A paragon slogan.

The fire jumps suddenly due to a strong wall of wind, and smoke obscures my view of the inoculant. He continues, "We were both gifted and damned. Burdened by the fact that we were the very few armed with an effective shield against the machine mind-warp. You know, years before *interconnect*, we had created our own protective mental bubbles; call it delusional if you want, I don't care.

"Mind you, this was back in early 21C, before all the cairn crap; we developed our mind-traps on our own, organic-like. You would not believe the things I used to believe in and be ready to die for. Looking back, I can't believe it myself. The magic, though, was that it protected me from cairns and all their shit.

"I guess you can look at it this way. Our not thinking normally is our greatest asset. It is an antidote to the machine's assaults on thinking."

Fortunately for us, our two groups are traveling in different directions. God knows where the inoculants are going with their arms cache; no one wants to ask. We say our goodbyes early the next morning. The paragons appear anxious to get away from the raging delusionals. I share their angst.

Mind-fucked by the thought of coffins and guillotines, I'm freshly appreciative of the joys of my modest level of sanity. To realize that protection from such pollution comes in the form of such psychosis and deeply conspiratorial paranoia is unsettling.

I do not want to believe that all delusionals believe this crazy stuff fully. My late-night conversation with the paragon sympathizer indicates that at least one bearded replicant had some self-awareness. Apparently, though, most inoculants believe in enough specific parts of the story to buy into the conspiratorial rush of the full story and to live in the rapturous community.

Caged areas near retail centers that are used to store inventory become death camps, underground utility tunnels become prisoner transit conduits, and militia readiness exercises become preparation for the pending planetary collision. The power of the human brain to manufacture this conspiratorial filter through which to view reality is awe-inspiring and deeply disturbing in its magnitude. No wonder the paragons have concern about unaided human cognition in our future.

The first mile of trekking is easy, and I enjoy the freedom. Although I'm embarrassed about the inoculants, pitying their ignorance, I acknowledge my own battles with delusional thinking. I don't want to see myself in them, but as I trek, I'm troubled by the pain of recognition.

LAB ANIMAL

CHAPTER 18

Storm clouds approach as we hike down the remote southern flanks of the Shellsolls. It feels good to descend to a lower elevation, although our trip down is arduous. Strong winds punish us and threaten to push us off the ridgeline. The trail itself is boulder filled, requiring double the effort to step widely and awkwardly over the large pieces of granite. It takes us about six hours to trudge down 6,000 feet. Mid-afternoon, we stop at a small creviced valley filled with sagebrush and cactus. It provides welcome protection from the strongest of the winds and from militia flybys.

After fifteen minutes of zoned-out recuperation, Mustang pulls out an old-fashioned paper map with a bunch of markings in black pen. He positions it on a large flat rock and puts smaller rocks on each corner to hold it down in the gusts. Suddenly, all eyes are upon me. I feel caught in the act of which I am unaware.

"Okay, team, we need to decide. Is ReFormer in or out?" declares Oats in a no-nonsense way.

Oats has absolutely no nuance to her, no frills. She has a tough, bull-dyke look befitting her personality. Short hair, muscled, trim physique bordering on anorexic. Sharp eyes, functional bare-bones hiking attire. She wears a feathered necklace over her buttoned-to-the-top shirt. Usually out ahead of everyone else on the trail. I think she is the thinker in the group, the grand strategist. Both her parents were biomedical scientists and apparently handed down a purely systematic way of viewing, and living, life. To her, everything from the grand issues of the day to the quotidian is to be handled in a linear, rational way.

The paragons sit around a semi-circle made chaotic by the placement of rocks suitable for seating. Pathos, my leading advocate, is quiet. This is disturbing.

Mustang opens first,

"I wouldn't call his seizures on the trail indicative of someone we should trust. I think he is learning and I understand he has contacts with personnel inside Unity, but I for one can't have faith that he will be with us at our breakthrough."

When I look at them, Mustang's eyes connote compassion, but what he is saying counters this image. He seems to have a certain hatred of all things ReFormer and is not giving an inch. He plays it close to his chest on the trail. The loner of the group, I guess. Hard to interpret. Apparently, he lost several family members to Turmoil, hasn't been the same since.

Topless is next.

"I think we should slice him up and feed him to *interconnect*."

Topless' attempt at levity goes nowhere. The paragons are not in a light mood. I'm certainly not.

"You know, seriously, it's clear he's broken up. When I see him on the trail, he seems despondent and tortured most of the time. I'm not convinced trekking has helped him all that much in developing organic thought free of cairns."

This is weird; they are talking about me in a clinical way

right before my eyes, as if I'm not here. I'm also struck by the level of perceptual detail they are providing about me. I wonder how much I have been watched like a lab animal. Unlike me, their heads were apparently not constantly turned downward on the trail.

"I want to give a slightly different take on this question," begins Ponytail.

He has barely spoken to me on the trail. He's a hefty military-looking man who somehow has remained sharply attired amidst the dirt and grime of the trail. He has the demeanor of someone used to making hard decisions about personnel and mission. Given his bald head, his trail name fits his presence not one iota. Someone's idea of sarcasm, I guess. Like labeling a genius "bumpkin." I have no idea whether he will be friend or foe in this debate.

"First, we agreed at the start that the seizures were to be expected, so I don't think we should knock him off now for what we anticipated. You may remember that most of us thought that the seizures were a necessary evil, something that the ReFormer needed to endure to make himself aware of his cairn pollution.

"The seizures bring out the contrast between darkness and light, and we hoped that with this contrast that over time the ReFormer would get used to the light. Second, have you noticed that with time the seizures are becoming more manageable? Well, I have. The blocking tablets we have given him are lessening the frequency and intensity, although it is evident that they don't always work. All things considered, I vote yea to include him in operational review."

I'm feeling even more like a lab animal, and I reflect on the fact that every morning for the last two weeks of our journey, Pathos has ritually brought me a cup of water to drink. She stays by my side until I drink the full cup.

Dust raises her hand gingerly. She is the quietest of the paragons and apparently not blessed with social skills. I don't think I have heard a single sound from her when our group gathers. "I think we should go with him. I think the benefits outweigh the liabilities."

The group waits for more from Dust, but apparently, that's the extent of her contribution. Short and sweet on my side.

Despite the cool gusts of wind, I realize I am drenched in sweat and smell some horrible combination of filth and urine.

Ponytail breaks in. Oat's look of disapproval indicates he is breaking with protocol. "Certainly, if his seizures don't lessen, he is of no use to us. But you doubters are discounting another asset. If his organic development increases, he may become a bargaining chip when we interface with *interconnect*. He could show to the machine something none of us are capable of. I don't feel we should decrease any of our potential tools at this time."

I have no idea what any of that meant. Me as bargaining chip. Images of young, scantily dressed maidens being thrown off the side of a flaming volcano come to mind.

Oats interjects at this moment and encourages others who have not spoken to express their opinions about my future.

Pepperjack bursts in enthusiastically, "I'm next! Oh boy!"

I notice several group members recline on their rocks, a couple of them reaching for their water bottles.

"Why would we want to terminate this meat-sack when there is some possibility he may help us? What are we, some tribunal of perfect souls? We rescued him for a reason, right? So, he may be a bit more screwed up than we thought. Let's give him a chance."

Pepperjack is talking loudly and waving his arms theatrically. Like he is on a stage talking to an audience of a hundred. He is surely the most exuberant of the bunch.

"Who among us has tried to get off of the fucking machine by learning to think organically while still being chip-implanted? Wouldn't we be guilty of practicing the machine-made righteousness of the Turmoil period if we were to say, 'he's not as good as us' or 'he's not like us?'

"We can always terminate him later if he doesn't evolve. Why now?"

This burst of energy and criticism temporarily silences the group. I'm not thrilled with being called a "meat-sack," but I like his overall message.

Rhapsody stands up from his seated position. He assumes the stance of an orator without a podium.

"I've had conversations with the ReFormer. I encourage you who have not done so to engage with him. He's not a monster or some wacko we should be afraid of. He shows self-awareness of his limits and that he is on a learning curve. I think he is genuinely interested in pursuing our path forward. I understand your concerns about him messing up our operational game plan, but I think the light will overcome the darkness when we need him most. We've dragged him around with us for some time now, and I think he is acculturating to paragonism. His resistance to us, I feel, is lessening with each passing day."

"Excuse me," Tiger breaks in, "but I have talked with the ReFormer."

I recall Tiger's aggressive verbal take-down of me. I guess he considers that talking with me.

I don't like the look on his face—angry, resentful, and pent-up.

"Sorry to you believers, but I vote to terminate our relationship with ReFormer. I'll give him credit for some self-growth. Honestly, I don't know whether he is acting this out to please us or whether it is genuine. How the fuck can we trust this guy? It would be like trusting a teenager with an underdeveloped prefrontal cortex to do an intricate adult task requiring discernment.

"What happens," Tiger shouts out, "if he goes into ReForm mode during the carrying out of our mission?"

There has been a bad vibe with Tiger since day one. Predisposed to hate me. Wearing some military-type vest, I notice guns and roses tattoos up and down both arms.

He continues, "When we are in tactical mode, if he submerges into ReForm entrapment and spurts out all sorts of bullshit about the bright tomorrow ahead, what do we do? Shoot him on the spot?

"I'm worried he could flip into ReForm at the worst possible moment. You know, anxiety tends to stimulate duality seizures. He could become a liability amidst the intensity of the moment when our attention must be on operational details."

My sweat is chilling me, and my garments feel like they are sticking to my body. The occasional gusts feel like they are going straight to my bone.

The group is quiet and reflective, like a jury taking a collective breath before passing judgment. I have visions of what may become of me. A corpse to be found down the side of a precipice sometime in the unknown future.

Pathos rises. "If there are no other contributions, I would like to say a few words."

Thank goodness, my potential savior. If human intimacy— and great sex—means anything anymore, then I have a fighting chance.

"I understand your doubts about ReFormer's ability to maintain independent, organic thought. Some of you have protested that I have developed too close a relationship with ReFormer to have an objective judgment on this issue. I understand. Let me say that there are times when I, too, have been disappointed by ReFormer's progress. He regresses back to ReForm too frequently and can display naïve, quite embarrassing beliefs that are clearly cairn polluted."

This is not good. A visual aura begins the way seizures always begin. Hang in there, don't go wacko now.

"However, I side with keeping Split with us. When he pops his head out of his ass, there is awareness of what we are trying to do. He also shows increasing understanding of his cairn-induced episodes. There is a certain cognitive distancing and realization that those regressions are not really him.

"Also, his seizures have had instrumental value to us. Our neuro-magnetic monitoring of ReFormer during his seizures has given us additional insight into ReForm pathways that will be useful in our intervention.

"Finally, let me remind you of his value that we all foresaw—his connections to possible inside collaborators who are, or have been, in regime hierarchies and to others who may be key in implementation after our intervention."

Pathos pauses and sits back down with a certain resoluteness.

The quiet that ensues raises my blood pressure, my heart beating so fast it feels like it's going to explode. The late afternoon sky is a foreboding mix of dark blue and gray hues. I gaze at the canyon walls above to stabilize. I focus on a tree that has somehow found a way to take root on the sheer cliff.

A survivor.

I marvel at the gorgeous scenery.

Breathe.

I get the sense that the deliberation is ending. No eyes turn toward me. I guess no chance for me to present my case. Lab animal again.

Finally, Oats breaks the silence.

"Let me remind the group that we have made numerous attempts to obstruct *interconnect* without success. Our informants within Unity have either been killed or did not produce outcomes. Even those who resisted brainwashing decided in the final hour to prioritize personal safety over our mission.

"Our bombing assaults on Unity assets have had symbolic impacts but have not made measurable impacts on regime behavior or on denizen attitudes. Indeed, they may be leading to greater rigidity by both regime and public.

"Last point: our technological counter-programs have been slow in development and have been ineffective and easily overcome by *interconnect*. They reached implementable status just two weeks ago and are uncertain. All in all, we are at a tactically significant point. Please consider all this when you vote on ReFormer's role in our organization."

Oats continues, "I propose that this evening we reconvene at 8pm and take our vote of resolution. Reformer, your tent site tonight will be relocated to the outcropping we passed approximately one mile earlier. You will be notified of our decision at 7am sharp. Pepperjack, please assist ReFormer in this re-location."

As I am ushered away, the last thing I see is Mustang folding up the paper map and a few of the paragons engaging in heated arguments.

"Remember," Pepperjack murmurs while we backtrack, "there is value in not letting your thoughts be in control."

"I'll try to remember that," I slur while feeling all my synapses sizzling on hyperdrive.

The night is brutal.

Lab animal now in isolation.

My bowels tighten, and I feel like I have a boulder up my ass.

Sleep is erratic to the point of non-existent.

I try, mostly successfully, to ward off an ill-timed seizure.

Time goes by extremely slowly.

My heartbeat is rapid.

Swallowing becomes difficult as my parched throat locks up.

My head is spinning too much to recall the details of paragon statements and whether I have enough support to live another day. I don't know whether I'll be welcomed into the fold at first daylight or thrown ceremoniously off the nearest cliff to the delight of my custodian paragons.

The morning comes at a snail's pace. Bright sun invades my isolation site early, scorching my face. I feel exposed on this

hard escarpment. I diddle around my tent, waiting for news.
Seemingly endless wait.

Well past 7am.

I have an urge to pack up and run away, fearing the worst.

Eventually, Pepperjack saunters up, "Nice site you have here."

Last thing I need right now is light commentary.

I snarl at him.

"Relax, ReFormer, life is but a dream. It doesn't matter how long it lasts."

"I don't suppose you're going to tell me anything of importance right now. Can't imagine what it would be?"

"Oats runs a tight ship. All procedure and protocol. You'll find out soon enough."

The vote was 6-3 in my favor. This point should be obvious since you wouldn't be reading this if I garnered a minority. I celebrate the news by excusing myself and jerking out a massive bowel movement on the cliff's edge. Better my bowels flowing down the edge than my head. Just as I arrived at a modicum of inner stability after the vote, the thought of other possible votes in the future again tightens my sphincter.

Am I to be on perpetual recall? If a governing regime was approved by this close margin, it would be susceptible to collapse.

Later that day, I am included in the group's dynamics. This alleviates some anxiety. I even get more smiles on the trail. Some begrudging but positive, nonetheless. Pathos gives me a flirty look at dinnertime. Although her mixed appraisal of me during debate got me down at the time, I realize that her statement may have saved my skin. Maybe she had to give a mixed review because of paragon concerns about her bias. I return the flirt with a half-smile.

I must retain some male pride here that I'm not her dependent plaything.

When the paragon strategy is fully revealed to me in the days to come, I am overwhelmed by the level of their planning. It is intricate in detail and absurdly bold in intent. If it fails, it could terminate the life of all denizens in our woeful country.

It's Ponytail who first shows me trust. It occurs late in the evening after camp has been established. He's a bit reluctant. I think Oats gave him this assignment to educate the split-brain guy. We sit on two large boulders that outline his tent site. About three feet away from each other. Direct line of sight. His hiking pants show a finely tailored crease down the sides. No indication of sweat marks. Nothing out of place.

"Our group will meet up with a specialized hacker team along with armed muscle at a base camp deep in a remote canyon. Sensors indicate that the canyon walls will conceal us from nearly all Unity monitoring devices."

I'm a wee bit intimidated, but I hang in there because I've been starved for this information.

"Can I ask you where it is?"

"Near a forgotten no-man's land at the intersection of the old Turmoil regions of Northwoods, Birthplace, and Sesperia. All those boundary superstructures, buffer zones, and checkpoints that partitioned us during Turmoil lack meaning now. But our base camp will be in an area near the intersection of three remnant regions. This location, where three old regional boundaries met, there's only two such places in our country. It became a territory that no one cared about during Turmoil, hemmed in by three imposing separation walls. A good place to hide for most of Turmoil. Not many eyes. Nearest settlement is about 30 miles away southwest—a partially decimated village of container apartments in the remote eastern outskirts of Cyinith city.

"A perfect place for a server farm."

I had wondered whether this was where our troop of resisters was going.

"How close will our base camp be to the farm?" A bit of

self-interest here; I'm trying to calculate just how many more miles my sore feet will need to experience.

"Its location is fifteen miles south of target," Ponytail responds with military precision.

"The farm itself, what's it like?"

"Has all the markings of impenetrability. Security apparatuses surrounding this farm are higher, deeper, and wider than anything else in the country. Electronic moats, space-based infrared surveillance, and laser-wire secure the containment strips surrounding the farm. The farm itself is enclosed within a titanium globe building and guarded 24/7 by Unity-affiliated militia soldiers.

"We're talking hundreds of acres of servers that nourish *interconnect*. It's massive. We estimate that there are hundreds of thousands of computers. In cooled rooms. Protected from system failure by redundancy of server functions and by failover programs."

The ultimate objective of the paragons is to insert a new master program into *interconnect* so that the supercomputer serves humankind's objectives rather than its own objective of human control. I knew that. It is Rhapsody on the next day that extends my understanding of what is to come.

Where Ponytail's demeanor can be challenging, Rhapsody comes at me with a more open conversational tone. More comfortable with the back-and-forth of conversation. Erudite and welcoming.

It's a mid-day lunch stop. We both unfurl our sleeping pads to create sitting places on otherwise rocky terrain.

"Okay, my friend, I'm going to give you the whole thing step-by-step first. You okay with that?"

"I think I'll likely be blown away, but yeah, I'm ready."

Rhapsody doubles down in concentration.

"The first attack will a logic bomb. This is a piece of malware code inserted into the machine to set off a sequence that will make it amenable to instructions. Think of it as lubing the receptors. Then, we will inject paradox code called *endtime* to force the machine to consider an unsolvable enigma, basically to spin the machine's wheels. That is intended to provide us enough time to do the real work. As the computer spins in a do-loop, we then proceed to third stage. This will be to insert a master code that is to initiate two changes. First, transform *interconnect's* algorithmic scripts from human-controlling ReForm to human-supportive. Second, trigger re-sculpting of denizens' neuronal transmission by inducing a curated traumatic storyline into their brain chip implants."

"Holy shit, that's a lot."

"Yeah, it is. And consider this problem. The logic bomb, paradox code, and master program must be inserted into the system while *interconnect* is online. We can't turn off the machine, do our stuff, and then turn it back on. It is vastly intelligent. Obsessed with its objective to control humans means that it includes a round-the-clock failsafe system that prevents switching it off. *Interconnect* will do anything to prevent interference with its own mission of machine survival and human control."

"How do we intervene in a supercomputer obsessed with its own survival and that never sleeps?"

Rhapsody smiles a devilish, contented grin. "This is where the genius of the paragon becomes apparent, along with our potential to eradicate humankind. The *endtime* paradox code implanted into *interconnect* will signal to the colossal computer that it is to exterminate the human race within our country."

"What the hell? We're all going to die as a way to escape its hold on us?"

"Slow down. The genius lies in the code's logic as it unfolds. At first, it seems hellish for sure. But we needed to write code this way so it can enter the machine. Written this way, *interconnect* should hopefully allow our input to bypass its code blockers. Think about it. It should perceive the command to eradicate humans as a strengthening stimulus entirely consistent with the machine's objectives of human control."

"But wait." I feel like I am at least two steps behind. "Code gets in, all humans dead, end of story. I'm lost."

Rhapsody is enjoying drawing this out. Like he's gone through this whole process of reality-checking himself and is relishing seeing me go through it like he probably has many times before.

"So, let's assume implantation is successful. At that point, the machine is faced with a paradox. If *interconnect* follows its new commands and kills us all, it will have achieved the ultimate in human domination—extermination. However, there will be no more denizens around for it to control, which is against machine objectives.

"We hope that this paradox will create a momentary pause as the electronic behemoth attempts to solve it. As it recalibrates in an effort to rationally find a conclusion to a problem that may be lacking in a rational answer, we hope this will require the machine to hyper-concentrate its resources.

"Basically, to spin its wheels."

"My God, who thought of this paradox code?"

"Whoever thought of *endtime* must have a wicked sense of adventure along with a brilliant imagination. It's actually derived from an ancient tradition. Hundreds of years ago, Zen practitioners used koans, paradoxical riddles, to demonstrate the inadequacy of logical reasoning."

"Okay, then you said the third step is the big climax?"

"Oh, yeah, the machine's distraction with *endtime* will provide an entry point and allow us the time to insert new master software program.

"These new commands will hopefully redirect cairns so they reward pro-social, cooperative, altruistic, and compassionate human behavior. This code will regulate *interconnect* so that it values autonomous human decision-making when it contributes to the enhancement of humankind's future. Imagine *interconnect* assisting the human quest for betterment.

The supercomputer as our partner rather than controller.

"We're not only going to try to restructure the machine but also our denizens. The master code has another component to it that will re-sculpt human mind-space. We are going to use the machine's own circuitry to implant in our people storylines that will change their entire view of the world they live in."

I don't even know what to say. I sit dumbfounded, overwhelmed by what the paragons are going to attempt. Rhapsody does me the favor and fills in the silence.

"It must be noted, of course, the consequences if *interconnect* efficiently solves the paradox and follows the command. If it responds adeptly to *endtime* command, our country's denizens will no longer be on this planet.

"No paradox, no more humans."

"High risk, high reward," I mumble.

"Nothing like having stakes this high and irreversible."

CHAPTER 19

The trail goes over a small hill, and abruptly I find myself standing before a beautiful lake. I look around to see whether any paragons are sharing this splendid view. I see no one. About the only time I see paragons during a typical day is at water or food breaks. It's amazing to me that at the end of the day, we somehow all show up at the same place. No seeming regularity to their hiking order. Some days, Pathos will be with the lead pack; other days, she will be behind me amidst the band of wanderers. It appears Oats is the only paragon who maintains her spot in the trail hierarchy. Always in the lead pack. Typically, she is first. This figures.

I feel gifted as I sit on a rock ledge and gaze downward at the shimmering water. After so many miles of dusty sagebrush, the lake is the first substantial body of water we have come upon. The deep blue water nestles in a small valley surrounded by gray-brown peaks. A scattering of dark green trees climbs up the gradient. The sun reflects off the waters, and a calming breeze cools my overworked body. A peregrine falcon glides over the sparkling blue. A couple of marmots playfully chirp and whistle on a sun-drenched boulder nearby. I am in bliss.

I marvel at the beauty.

I feel encompassed within a broader fabric.

Tears run down the side of my face.

It is a soothing relief.

When I am with stillness, I feel least susceptible to grabbing onto polluted cairn storylines. I feel, at such times, completely separate from my fabricated self.

I realize something about being out here. By providing a wider view, hiking is dislodging my addiction to cairn scripts. It is immersing me within a robust and intricate natural pattern of relationship and interdependency. The trail provides a sense of spaciousness and connection to natural elements that are larger than me.

I see a pack of coy-wolves at the water's edge circling around prey. A violent killing soon to be submerged within the intricate and silent patterning of the natural world. It is all here. Every possible question is quieted by the ineffable magnificence of my surroundings. I feel clean and simple. The marmots have approached closer, apparently comforted by my lack of movement. One stares at me and stretches lengthwise on a rock not more than three feet away. I fall into a peaceful, dream-like state.

I turn my eyes back to the west and a small side canyon, almost more like a walled basin, presents itself. I had not seen it coming in. It seems to sit alone among the landscape, perched up at a higher elevation than the lake below. Maybe a cirque cut off by glacial action thousands of years ago. Don't know. But its isolation and lack of connection to its surroundings are striking.

The cirque reminds me of my inner life.

For most of my life, I have wanted to be by myself. Growing up, I learned to create a closed box that kept me distanced emotionally from other people. It was a comfortable but self-denigrating space. When the *interconnect* age began, my transition to computer addiction felt natural in its ability to create another closed box. One surrounded by an opaque wall that separated me from the rest of the world. A type of protective shield. That opaqueness resembled my many years of drinking and drugging before Turmoil. That debauchery was self-induced and led to depression, self-hatred, and isolation. In contrast, *interconnect* addiction led to a self-satisfying cocoon of righteousness. It produced a protective shield too, but of a different, less self-demeaning type.

On the trail now, it is radically different—I am increasingly feeling a part of, and intimately connected, to a larger essence. I think back at remnants of my tortured past, and it feels like I'm recalling a person whose identity is slowly melting away. The opaque wall is dissolving. The closed box is opening. I'm not alone.

The marmot sits up and yawns.

I recover my upright posture after my timeless rest break and strap on my backpack. The pack feels streamlined and part of my body, so accustomed to it I have become. I walk ahead, revitalized, gazing one last time at the view that enchanted me.

Trekking in the great mystery of natural wildness is creating in me a deeper grounded humility, to the extent that, at times, it seems a type of nihilism in which I doubt the existence of real meaning in life.

There are times on the trail when I become anxious about this freer mind-space. Why am I anxious about this? What do I think will happen? Do I think I will become a zombie without the constant mental choreography supplied either by *interconnect* or my own ego? Do I think it will resemble death in its inertness? I am threatened by the thought of being without mental storylines. This exposes how the algorithmically designed diversionary quality of modern life entraps me.

When I have moments like today when I can rest comfortably with this freer mind-space, there is a bare and beautiful essentialism to life. No threat.

I laugh at times on the trail when I consider what I would be doing back home on a typical day before my incarceration. It is funny because I cannot think of how I would be consuming time amidst the easy convenience of modern life. Memories of trivial conversations about petty things with my then-girlfriend, Raven. Before she evacuated the relationship, Raven was constitutionally incapable of carrying on a conversation above high-school level. She certainly was unable to handle my psychic episodes. She now resides happily under the spell of ReForm with another man. I don't blame her.

I recall certain things in my civilized day-to-day—drinking coffee from my Auto-brew, opening a refrigerator to reach for food, watching some vacuous curated e-vision program, gazing out from my patio to the nearby foothills, thinking about what color backsplash to put in my remodeled kitchen—and it all seems so easy and engineered. My thoughts about my daily doings in modern life cannot hold for long out here. It all seems so farcically contrived and disconnected from the realness of the trail and from organic thinking unpolluted by cairn storylines. With each step, I feel freer.

I have been floating on air today while traversing the trail. The afternoon's light is beginning to fade. I look forward to meeting up with the paragons at camp tonight. I've felt the need to prove my sanity to them, and I want to show them this stable side of me. I've even caught up with Mustang on the trail. He indicates that camp is within two miles.

He acknowledges me with a warm smile and asks, "Did you notice that gorgeous lake back there?"

"Oh, yeah," I reply, not sure whether he is teasing me. *No way could that lake possibly be missed.*

Although Mustang briefly traipses beside me, I don't feel his physical presence. My mind is still in processing mode. I can feel that trekking's focusing of the mind on the primary basics of survival is minimizing the obsessive power of cairn storylines. I ponder whether trekking quiets or even silences the cairn-polluted mind thoughts that have captured me in the past. Maybe it instead creates an inner space that is at ease with those thoughts.

Trekking is enabling a greater psychic depth. It is developing a seeming ability to be at ease with whatever thoughts arise, no matter how uncomfortable.

Catch and release.

Feel the cairned impulses arising and learning to let go.

At ease with the active mind rather than trying to beat it into submission.

When trekking, the cairn mind-thoughts are becoming more fleeting, ephemeral, and cloud-like in nature. The black-and-white noir thought images still enter my mind, but they are more blurred, less coherent. Watercolor images are more prevalent now and richer in composition. I am better able to stay with the diverse color patterns. I am learning the true nature and lack of power of computer-generated stimuli.

The freedom and joy of trekking—an almost preconscious, non-judgmental mode of processing my surroundings and step-by-step existence. Through this tedious, challenging, yet joyful trekking, I am learning how manufactured and derivative my thinking has been. It is an embarrassing acknowledgment, yet one that is emancipatory.

I arrive at camp amidst the general busyness of set up. Topless and Tiger are lifting heavy rocks to create a fire ring. Grunting and puffing. Topless turns to me suddenly and yells out, "Hey, ReFormer, you goin' to stand there all night or actually help out with something that exists outside your flippin' head?"

"I'm ready to help, Topless. That rock looks a bit heavy for someone your age to carry. Let me help you before you pull a coronary."

It has been a good day.

Chapter 20

I'm no fool. I know my given trail name of Split is derogatory. But I'm starting to treat it as a badge of honor. I may be wrong, but I think my emerging mental stability after cairn pollution is quite an unusual feat.

Day after day, we hike. Each day is long and physically arduous but mentally fascinating. I can feel my mental space adapting and evolving.

With each passing day, I feel my split mind—part cairned, part organic—lessening a bit in its assault. I have moments when I feel closer to the stability of one mind. The scripted storylines still come up, but I am more able to not be pulled down into them. There exists a growing inner energy that helps me grow beyond cairn reactivity. The fabricated thoughts and emotions are becoming things that I am watching rather than being. The intricate inner storylines of the monkey mind that *interconnect* excelled in producing and that oozed without end are becoming increasingly sidelined by the sensitivity and spontaneity required of trekking.

In wilderness, I'm feeling the retreat of the cairn storylines that so influenced me. Cairn-polluted mind, aware of its irrelevance amidst the simplicity of natural grandeur, seems to be meeting a worthy opponent. For the first time in decades, I feel the simplicity of moving through the world with less mental attachment.

Interconnect busies and crowds our minds to such a degree that we mistake this for productivity and creativity. In actuality, there is constant confusion and absence of an anchoring internal focus. This constant bombardment 24/7 through a chip in our head determines us and leads us astray from our own individuality. There is never any quiet, just din jacking us up.

Yet, it is the silence, the space in between, that produces genuine creativity, clarity, and focus. It is the silence, the stillness, which provides the opportunity space within which I am developing and understanding my organic thoughts and feelings.

As the long days continue, I'm feeling a perceptible change in my mental state.

The sense of reverent immediacy when trekking—being present in the now, thinking primarily of the basic needs of shelter, food, water, and body—seems to erode the ability of polluted cairns to take hold of me. It overwhelms my well-worn interpretations of life. It strips me of my interior mental baggage. More than anything else I have experienced yet in my life, hiking in the wilderness is total and all-encompassing. I feel inklings of freedom from mental encasement.

I look around me often these days on the trail and clearly see the magnificence. Hiking on this wondrous trail is a balm that grounds me. It is stripping away the obsessive mental nonessentials of modern life that *interconnect* so adroitly employed in its manipulative schemes. A teacher from long ago said that "It is simple to be happy but very difficult to be simple." The experience on the trail helps overcome this difficulty.

I shouldn't get ahead of myself in this account. It was not a smooth, uninterrupted path toward mental freedom from cairn addiction.

About five days and more than 70 miles later, the late-day sky becomes a watercolor painting streaked with purple-orange hues. The colors inflame two large mountain peaks in the distance. They stand tall and proud. Ripples shimmer off a small creek running downhill from our trail. The path is filled with the busy lives of birds and insects. There are even flowers mounting a first bloom amidst the boulders and scree.

My growing ability to think independently usually brings a sense of freedom. But it can, at times, produce unease as I reacquaint myself with the way I used to think. My focus this evening is on Pathos. My mental processing comes with baggage from the past.

Pathos has been ignoring me. I wonder whether our first meeting was a scheme by her to bring me aboard. I'm perturbed by the thought that my ongoing sexual fantasies about her are meaningful only for their temporary ecstatic release from the hardship and boredom of trekking. It seems like there is some tacit understanding of an intimate connection between us, but it has rarely revealed itself on the trail.

My mind feels small, colored by jealousy and insecurity. One advantage of cairn pollution, and I guess its addictive power, was that its auto-pilot effect evaporated this uncomfortable mental uncertainty.

The good news is that I can now feel more; the bad news is that I can now feel more.

With Pathos' distance from me, I feel unsettled. Like a needy small part of me has been voided. I travel for hours on the trail and sit passively during breaks with a paralyzing sense of uncomfortable neediness. I fill in the blanks with all sorts of disquieting thoughts. She must be unhappy with me.

Or, maybe she just doesn't feel toward me the way I feel about her. Or, let's step deeper into it. Her dismissal of me exposes my underlying nature as someone who is an unlovable fraud. I want to hide from her, fearful that she will hurt me even more.

This is really old stuff.

Dusty, hoary, spider-cobwebby shit.

Submerged for decades by the fake freedom of algorithmic control.

Pathos is just the latest iteration of habitual thinking that existed even before *interconnect* took hold.

Deep grooves in my brain are still present.

Part of me wishes to go back to machine manipulation. Thoughts were clean, righteous, and absolute. Just give me the answers. Human thinking is too messy and fragile. Give me black-and-white clarity, not the overwhelming mosaic of flighty human processing.

I realize this has nothing to do with Pathos and everything about me. This acknowledgment helps me regain some footing. I become more a subject with choices rather than an object reacting to what likely are my aberrant perceptions.

Mental freedom is a challenging project.

Another day hiking. No surprise. Zero hiking days are few and far between. The day consists of nothing other than rocks, water, trail, air, sun, and clouds.

In the past, I have tried to avoid, deny, or bypass polluted cairn thoughts and feelings. I now know this fight resulted in my decapitating duality seizures. My experience with fighting machine fabrication has been that cairned thoughts sooner or later dictate my life. My subconscious has always submitted to the allure of the fabrications, whether I acknowledged this or not.

But out here, something else is happening. I am not fighting with cairn stories as much as resuscitating an inner vitality.

Wilderness invites me to acknowledge the subconscious strata. Bringing light into my mental crevices seems to produce a shield from *interconnect* stimuli. Cairned impulses become less relevant and more ill-fitting to the natural setting. I start to see its intricate fakery for what it is. Wilderness creates a setting where I can calmly and without fear rest with the foundations of my mind. I can accept what makes me tick as a human.

These realizations of an inner strength reveal a resource as natural as the flowing stream, the path of the trail, the geological processes that form the jagged landscape around me.

No shame.

No running.

No over-thinking.

Rather, a tranquil awareness.

I am aware of the deeper dimensions of my mind. The gaps between thoughts that *interconnect* cannot access. As I clear and release cairned mental toxicity, I have more mind-space now for my independent thoughts.

Spending time with my mind's primal material—its grist—provides opportunities for stark and surprising realizations about the meaning of life and the meaning of me in this world.

Amidst this long hiking trek, I know that cairn signals are seeking to coat over these realizations. *Interconnect* is sending me old cairn storylines disguised as exciting new dramas. It is trying hard to pull me back to the superficiality of life, where its entrapment tactics excel. However, my organic mental processes are increasingly a firewall against such intrusions. If I remember the feelings and emotions of being present and of being connected to reality, then life-changing mental re-orientations and decisions are possible.

The rawness of wilderness trekking allows me to see through the game that doesn't work. I now have a greater chance to play the real game.

A pipe is shared among the paragons at our campsite one night. A feeling of community. Topless offers the pipe to me without hesitation.

"How you doing, man?"

Interesting. No "Split" or other trail name.

Topless has a propensity for levity. I wonder whether he is setting me up.

"I'm ... a ... fine," I defensively reply.

"You know, you put your wife and a dog in the trunk of an auto-fin for six hours and open up the trunk. Who's going to be glad to see you? There's the difference."

I haven't laughed in a long while, and I let out a chuckle.

Dust shouts from across the camp, "Yeah, and there's why you and me are no longer a couple, you crazy dude."

Had no idea they used to be a team. Seems like it would be an odd couple. Topless over the top in social gatherings, Dust reserved, almost shy, in groups.

"Why are you called Topless anyway?"

I haven't asked a question this casually in months.

"You thinking I was some male stripper, Split? You nasty man. You wish. Just look at my hat, and it tells all."

I've never seen him without a hat. And indeed, they are different versions of a visor hat, ones without a top. I guess my mind did go elsewhere.

A stunningly gorgeous sunset pulls up alongside our camp as our conversational babble continues in even more ridiculous directions. A bright deep orange borders the peak-filled horizon. A light breeze fans the surrounding trees, making them look like they are applauding this natural miracle.

Life under the *interconnect* God is buffered and cushioned from direct experiences such as this. So many denizens in our country have no awareness of such things happening. Their internalized manufactured mental spaces cannot see such beautiful analog phenomena.

The fabricated space feels safe, so we buy into it. It is all curated.

In its manufacturing of perceived reality, the machine obstructs our direct relationship with the physical environment. During Turmoil, each denizen was rewarded with feelings of individual righteousness at the expense of raw, primary experience. The current plaything of the machine—ReForm—reinforces this inner world through advertising portrayals of wants and desires. It traps our minds—cramping them and relentlessly implanting them with mental noise.

Whether Turmoil or ReForm, we engaged in habitual, unconscious acts without reverence or gratitude. The personal dramas and storylines curated by the machine gained the upper hand. We could not see sunsets.

Out here, I honor the joy of being still and in awe. I feel joyously detached from the inner scripts of *interconnect*.

Wilderness provides an unfiltered and primary experience. It is in no way curated. It produces attentiveness and awe. It is edgy. I feel not fully in control. It is a vulnerable and direct experience. My attachment to cairn storylines becomes tamed and secondary.

I engage in basic activities such as finding and filtering water, preparing food using a minuscule backpacking stove, planning the night's tent site location, and setting up and breaking camp. I do these things for their own sake rather than to just get them done so I can get on to bigger things.

The immediacy and intentionality of the wilderness experience concentrates my mind on basic, life-affirming activities and pushes aside *interconnect*'s constant bombardment of addictive stimuli. Cairns produce a numbed, unconscious auto-pilot mode of existence. Out here, I take nothing for granted and most everything is sacred.

As I increasingly gain an understanding of my past ordeals, I feel a fool, having lived under the spell of computer ideology. True, I tried to fight against it during my field investigations. I guess, in a way, the scars from my duality seizures are badges of courage. But, in the end, I succumbed to its fabricated power. I capitulated completely to it, and my brain collapsed and left me semi-comatose.

The sunset has transmuted into mostly darkness. Only a faint orange glow colors the blackened horizon. A few scattered lights from settlements in the valley are visible.

I am experiencing a miracle. I am quiet and free.

I sleep well this night. Good timing. Tomorrow, I begin to engage in risky activities on behalf of my resister companions, ones for which I am uniquely qualified to undertake.

CHAPTER 21

Koth Maliar: staff member of governing Authority during ReStart period. One of two main Authority contacts for Jared Rohde during his field investigations. Wrote Addendum to Rohde Report in '55 warning of inter-connect's ongoing switch-over to ReForm. Addendum erased from ReStart databanks. Analog archive discovered by an anarchist roamer, fourth quarter, 2060, in the basement of a former ReStart Authority office building in Acalato region. Current position: second director, Urban ReStart program, Unity government.

```
Alt-x call
NH #4xsys2056//3wixpqp/{liew237}69kMaliar
```

It is taking forever for us to connect using off-grid communication channels. I am nervous because much has changed over the last years. I can't believe that Koth is working for

Unity government after all that has transpired. He must be a slippery scoundrel to survive all the shit. We are attempting to get through using the degraded and forgotten Alt-x communication system. Communicating through old wireless towers from the pacific years is laughable. Many towers were shot to hell during Turmoil. The few hundred dinosaurs that remain were abandoned some time ago and unreliably transmit old 12G network juice. Formal Vimex channels are out of the question. Too risky, heavily surveilled.

Static continues in an obnoxious, fingernails-on-chalkboard way.

A fuzzy video appears, choppy and near-impossible to make out.

"Jared, are you th ..."

"Koth, do you hear me?"

The video steadies. I barely recognize who I am talking to. He is paler than last time we spoke, and his heavy-set walrus-like features have shallowed out. Looks gaunt and drawn-out, not sick looking but not well either. His bushy mustache is gone, the devilish glint in his eyes has dulled, along with his "if-you-knew-what-I-knew" smile. I am looking at a ghostly remnant of the person I have known for years.

"Koth, is that you?"

"Jared, it's me, at least physically."

This is sad.

"Remember in the '20s, Jared, when we got shit-faced ... naked around the block near your house ... Carrie had a fit ... locked you out of the house. Thought your marriage would never survive that night. I laughed my ass off. You were like a hurt puppy dog."

Despite the awful video transmission, I smile at the memory, and I know that Koth is validating his identity for me. He must know he doesn't look at all like he did last time we spoke at the end of my field research in '54. He looks washed out, but he seems alert to our circumstances.

"Need to check; are you in a place where you can say things? No bugs, cameras, surveillance drones?"

"I'm okay. I'm in a bombed-out café from yesteryear. My neighbors are rats, coy-dogs, chemsynth containers, and urine-soaked refugee mattresses."

"Geez, Koth."

I remember my Vimex calls during field research. Koth always looking out from officious-looking rooms, brightly lit institutional settings. Bureaucratic man.

"I need to get to the point here," I say. "This channel ... too unsteady. Thank you for responding to my off-grid GPS pinging. I didn't know whether those signals were getting through to you. Such archaic stuff. So, you know where I am, and I suspect you know who I am with."

"I do, my friend."

I think about the risk here, contacting a person working in the Unity government. Koth could have us eradicated by militia drones within ten minutes. Oh, let my trust in my old buddy be well-founded.

"We need your help in accessing the server farm. We have plans to paralyze *interconnect* long enough to insert new instructions. I'm sure you're familiar with paragon goals. I'm now exposing some of their operational tactics."

"I'm sure you're wondering whether you can trust me," Koth interjects. "Let me remind you there's no going back for me after I wrote that addendum exposing the whole false program of the machine. It was a warning shot across the bow of our society. It held up paragons as our last hope in countering *interconnect's* ever-expanding reach into human consciousness. The only reason I'm in my position doing idiotic urban restart stuff is that my identification as the author of the addendum got accidentally erased in the mass purging."

I stay on point, not knowing when we will cut out.

"We need access codes, facility building details, and military operation programs for the server farm."

All sorts of pixelated chaos on the screen, but audio stays intact.

"This will take some time, my friend. It's a question of whether I can get these, but I will certainly try."

"We need them within three weeks."

"Boy, that is some assignment. Urban ReStart division is pretty low on the organizational chart here. But one advantage to old age is I have quite a few friends in Unity, and some of them are, like me, antagonistic to all of this shit."

"Three weeks, Koth."

Silence. Video cuts out, comes back on in pixelated form, it settles after a minute or so.

Koth is staring into space.

"How are you doing? Really?" I hesitate to pose this personal question, concerned about what his answer will reveal.

"... I feel like a shit-bag. Disillusioned by all this. Being part of all the machine fictions makes it even worse.

"ReStart.

Contributing to something I thought was so grand.

Taking back society from the machine.

Remaking human independent thinking.

It was all a fucking game by the machine.

Most times, I blame *interconnect*, but you know, other times, I blame us fucking humans for being so gullible. Humans must have hope, I get that, but it was so misplaced and manipulated. Fuck it all.

The machine gives denizens everything they psychologically need with ReForm.

An internally consistent understanding of their world.

A feeling of safety, security, and control.

A positive perception of self.

That all this was built upon fabricated foundations didn't matter to people. Their basic psychological needs are satisfied.

"I've learned a lot about power, my friend. It asserts itself invisibly. It doesn't flash what it's going to do. It always moves silently behind the scenes. Once it figures everything out to strengthen its hold, then power announces itself, and it becomes visible to us. Then, all that happens after that is only commentary. The terms have been set.

"The main characteristic of power is its ability to hide itself."

I smile as I listen to Koth. His pontificating reminds me of his feisty self in the past. Underneath his gaunt look still resides a resilient "don't give me shit" spirit.

The alt-x transmission weakens. We set a time for a follow-up call to check on Koth's progress. I re-emphasize the three-week deadline and he nods.

The alt-x cuts out.

Oats had been listening closely the whole time nearby.

"So, Split, what do you think about your friend's reliability?"

The continued use of this nickname irks me. I guess good news, bad news. The paragons' use of a trail name for me suggests a certain amount of inclusion, yet the label's referencing of my mental history of duality seizures maintains a derogatory tone. I wish they would start recognizing some sanity on my part. It must be hard-earned, I surmise.

"He's not the same, in a way, a shell of what he was."

"Chances of him getting what we need?"

"I think his desire to help is there, seems washed out and totally disillusioned with the whole ReForm and Unity charade. Question, though, whether he has access to what we're asking for. He's got some contacts, so it may pan out, but uncertain at best. We have another call scheduled, as you likely heard."

"Good first contact; we appreciate your attention. I have a question about your other inside contact—Stokes? We feel it is riskier to contact him but higher possible rewards. Do you have any sense where he is in the organization?"

"Six years ago, Stokes was at a high level of decision-making; I could feel it. He spoke of counter-insurgency tactics to impose Authority rule over the regions and cairn groups. It wasn't just talk. He spoke of being privy to high-level meetings. My guess is now he is near the top of the Unity government apparatus."

"Again, Split, on behalf of our team, thank you for your work."

Oats is not her usual gruff self, and she makes direct eye contact with me. I'm starting to feel a genuine contributor to the paragons' game plan.

That evening, the paragons are interested in my time at Re-Start. This seems strange. Until this time, they showed complete derision of anything connected with that brief period of hope after Turmoil. Maybe they're bored, I don't know.

Dust queries me after dinner, "You traveled a lot around this country during ReStart and talked to many denizens. Was there a general sense of the people?"

Dust looks away from me after this. She acts like she doesn't want to be identified as the person who asked the question. Must have some social anxiety issue.

"Overall, folks were pretty much bewildered. But I also met individuals who expressed a somewhat reasonable sense of what it might take to reform society, cities, and governance. Despite the horror, they had some sense of optimism. When I was out there, I developed a certain appreciation of the ability of the human spirit to sustain, even uplift, itself above cairned hatred.

"I look back at those meetings and now don't know what to make of that resilient optimism. Was it all being spoon-fed to them by the machine? Seeming human rationality masking algorithmic manipulation. Was it all a contrived narrative? I just don't know. I'm starting to suspect it was."

Several paragons besides Dust look at me, waiting for more. Rhapsody, Tiger, and Mustang are quietly listening in. I'm not used to them being in such a receptive mode with me.

"It was certainly an interesting collection of people that I met. The so-called reform-minded were most of my contacts. Set up that way by the Authority. But I also met many denizens who were mentally off-grid. The drugged-out synther crowd, those in survivalist mode, wacko delusional inoculants, roamer anarchists, frightened denizens, violent and angry.

"Compared to these off-grid folks who resisted re-cog, you paragons came across as having some coherent idea. You guys didn't have the zombie-like appearance of most denizens."

I'm a bit startled when Tiger then addresses me. I've grown accustomed to his combative, ornery nature. He seems different now, though, authentically curious about my past instead of relegating it to the trash heap.

"Did you get any idea of the scam during your research?" asks Tiger. "Looking back on it, you must have had some fuckin' clues along the way."

I've run this question through my mind numerous times. There were early times when my talking and writing felt scripted. But I thought this was just remnants of my pre-Turmoil academic indoctrination. I recall the most revealing incident, one that I have not ever shared with anyone. It was my intent to write a separate report describing this finding. But things got twerky when I completed my contract. And yes, I got a bit caught up in the commendations of my work by the Authority. You know, the good old ego. Okay, here goes my story.

"I had an escort driver. His name was Zeker. Odd guy who I never fully trusted. Military tactical knowledge, said he liked armies and death in the name of the state. He seemed to know too much about the areas we were in. Would intently watch me like some spy. At odd times, he would confront me angrily. He would go on and on about the development of *interconnect*. Never knew whether it was reality or some made-up fable. No ordinary driver. Anyway ..."

I take a breath.

"One evening, I hack into his computer. Bunch of Authority files suffixed with *ReS*. No idea even what to look for, indeed what I am looking for. Hundreds of files are identified by *RE-COG* with multiple variants of numeric suffixes attached to them. Some, I guess, are dates, but others are unintelligible. I open a random few of them, and my eyes meet tedious organizational notetaking or Authority jargon that makes no sense. It could just as well be kitten scratches on a wall.

"Other file titles stand out by their sheer number. They're labeled *NEO-C* and *PRGN*. I open some of the *PRGN* files and read about ReStart Authority military counter-insurgency strategies, social network analysis, intelligence-operations dynamics, and containment. All very interesting and mind-numbing in detail. Although never spelled out, I assume that *PRGN* must refer to you good ole paragons. You guys certainly had their attention. Files loaded with surveillance and counter-insurgency suppression techniques.

"Then I randomly open some *NEO-C* files. Easy to guess what that stands for. The neo-cogs, your arch-enemy. Believed in freedom of human thinking independent of algorithmic influence entirely. Computer as devil."

Paragon eyes start to wander. I realize that I just told them stuff that is well-known to them. Hell, it's what they have been fighting against. I must admit that after having been marginalized in many conversations with this group, I am enjoying being the center of attention. I've got to get to the juicy stuff, though.

"I read in the *NEO-C* files about persuasion techniques, activation, attention shaping, leveraging, peacebuilding methodologies, economic and urban reform, re-cog training modules. All makes sense in a way. This stuff sounded pedagogical. So far, so good.

"As I scrolled further through these files, however, I didn't understand what I was seeing at first because it made no sense. I was reading words in files about re-cognition training that had no right to be there, like oil and water, like a bathtub and a toaster. You get it: they're not supposed to be in the same place; they didn't mix."

"What did you find? What were in the files," asks Mustang impatiently.

Suddenly, a shockingly loud explosion occurs in the valley below. Probably five miles from us. A settlement is instantly engulfed in flames. Militia drones flying in a networked pattern. I wonder about the welfare of good folks like the dear woman I met at the auto-fin station. Bombing is such a brutal tool. Well-meaning citizens pay the ultimate price. My eyes moisten.

We wait in silence for more than fifteen minutes. Black smoke arising from some non-descript monolithic building. From this distant vantage point, it looks like this mass murder is some event staged for e-movie production. Not really happening. Things eventually go eerily silent. The peace of the cemetery.

Finally, Dust says quietly, "Go on."

I clear my throat and pull myself together. "A bunch of *NEO-C* files talked about algorithmic take hold levels, re-cognition penetration thresholds, ReForm saturation indices, cairn incorporation scores classified by re-cognition training level, on and on.

"There it all was in front of me. Re-cognition as a charade for continued *interconnect* existence and extension."

"That must have been some shock to you," exclaims Rhapsody.

"It was surefire trauma. Everything I thought I believed in, and all I thought I was working for, tiresome hours interviewing denizens. All exposed as a complete lie."

"So, what did you do about it?" asks Tiger in a challenging tone.

I reactively think back to all-out shame.

"At first, I had the idea of filing a report separate from my published one. You know, expose the façade. I convinced myself it wouldn't do any good and that it would likely put my life in danger. After all, who would be my allies in revealing this? Who could I trust?

"After the contract was over, I tried to forget about this, buckle down and live a normal life, but I knew too much. Twisting in bed every night, barely eating, miserable migraines, head and heart racing.

"I know I'm painting myself as a victim here, a type of martyr. Okay, I turned to chemsynth to give me some stability. It was either that or fucking insanity. That wasn't enough to sedate me. I then went for direct connection into legacy cairn-lines. Fuckin' miserable.

"The fight continued in me even while cairn sedated. There's something inside me that, when things really hit the fan, there would emerge some resilient part of my psyche. I guess I give myself some credit there. But the duality seizures got more frequent and intense. Lost control of reality entirely. Ended up incarcerated as a mental basket case. Even started to doubt what I had learned about the real mission of re-cog. Blocked it out of my mind.

"Next thing I knew, you guys were lifting me out of my cell. And here I am, your ReFormer comrade."

A long pause. I look down the ridge and see only burning embers remaining from the attacked village. Smoke from the fires is dispersing throughout the valley, forming a horizontal layer of pollution covering what used to be a scenic view.

"That's one hell of a sad story," Mustang offers.

The paragons say little and slowly depart from our impromptu meeting space. Tiger mutters something incomprehensible. But Rhapsody and Mustang pat me on the shoulder as they leave. Even a little bit of compassion on their part means a lot to me. Like they care about me as a human, not just view me as a cog in their operations. I crave human connection, and Rhapsody's and Mustang's gesture reminds me how disconnected I have been for way too long now.

I sit amidst the silence of the campsite. Recounting my past makes me feel like shit. Exposed, vulnerable, weak.

I am now alone with me, just me.

I wander back to my tent. The darkness of the night and my internal isolation press down upon me. No moonlight. Even the stars hide from my view. Momentary relief as I lie back on my sleeping pad. Then feeling that my head is about to implode. At some point, I lose consciousness. Thankfully.

Chapter 22

Day 38. 622 miles since extraction.

One hazy afternoon, Dust approaches me and says, "It is time for you to get lost, ReFormer."

"What?" I mumble, choking on my dried protein bar.

Don't know where Dust is coming from. Was there another vote taken, and I'm to be dismissed?

"It is now time for you to journey forth solo."

I observe several paragons nearby with smiles on their faces.

"Where am I going?"

"You will stay camped here for the rest of the day alone. Next morning, you are to wander down the path solo. Watch where we head off today and follow that trail. One of us will find you the following day."

"What's the purpose of this, my friend?" I try to get chummy with Dust so that she might give me some assistance here. She gives me no such thing.

"You will see. If you happen to get lost off the trail, you will see how it is a great teacher about something important." The remainder of the day is endless. Alone near a craggy cliff. Coy-wolves barking in the evening. Dinner produces intestinal gas as the sky darkens, and I fart constantly. Time passes slowly. I am anxious and urinate repeatedly during the long dark night. Endless.

The next morning, I start the trek. I have no GPS instrument. The path is my only guide. Mostly it's legible, but at times it gets faint as it passes over pulverized scree. My ego puts on superhero clothes that produce a false but gratifying confidence. *I can do this and show my muster to these damn paragons.*

I walk along a glacially carved indenture in the mountain crest wall. The trail meanders to the steep headwall, circles around a small lake, and then starts to ascend on the eastern side of the lake. An abrupt upward turn laden with endless switchbacks, I then trudge toward a pass, neither a deep U nor V, just a small notch at the top of the great wall. The final climb to the pass is covered with stumble-prone decomposed granite and a scattering of super-resilient tundra plants.

It's past noon under a beating sun when a startling realization hits me. I am no longer on the trail. The last time I knew I was on track was more than five minutes ago. I feel a horrifying fear that borders on paralysis. I look for man-made trail rock cairns that might lead me back to the path. My eye movements are rapid and pulsing with urgency. I don't readily see any cairn markers. My heartbeat quickens. I face a deep archetypal-type fear, the stuff of which nightmares are made. Indeed, this experience mimics my recurring nightmares in which I am confused, not in the right place, and unable to find my way to my destination.

I am in hyper-alert emergency mode. My brain is sending me "I've got to get out of here" messages. You know, the "fight or flight" response—this one telling me to flee from this scary place of disorientation.

I slow, take my pack off, and sit on a rock, crying like a little boy. I impulsively arise and start to walk in a random direction. Sweat is cascading down my shirt. As I collapse on the earth amidst indistinct sagebrush that looks like it goes on forever, something clicks. I remember what Dust said, that being lost is a great teacher. With her loner personality, Dust has likely faced such solitary challenges in her life. This settles my mind a bit. I go back to the rock where I did the crying boy thing.

I consciously slow down my internal clock and intentionally do not move. I think deliberatively about where I was when I last knew I was on the trail. I walk slowly and more alertly, this time for a short distance in one direction, and scout things out for trail markers. It is not the way. I go back to the crying boy rock when I first knew I was lost. I next walk a short way in a different direction. No luck. Breathe. Back to crying boy rock. I next wander a short distance in a third direction. At that point, I believe I see something about thirty feet away that does not look natural. Relief comes over me when I realize it is a rock trail marker.

When I regain the trail, I take a long drink of water in celebration and realize the profound lesson. The key to regaining orientation is to go exactly counter to what my scared, reactionary mind is telling me. It is like remembering when I am driving an auto-fin that is skidding on an icy road to counterintuitively turn in the direction of the skid.

I get it. My frantic, panic-filled mind will not engage in the appropriate response. It will urgently blast through territory looking for the trail, losing track of all geography. This will compound the complexity of being lost, adding new layers of spatial ignorance to the situation. There is no spatial point, like my crying boy rock, to come back to when anxiety pushes me forward into increasingly uncharted directions. Such a circumstance can and does lead to life-threatening situations.

I think of living in curated, so-called civilized life and ponder how often I react suddenly to situations of anxiety. I react impulsively to perceived threats, spinning in directions that add complexity and angst. The trail is teaching me that in such cases, the appropriate path is to respond calmly and deliberatively rather than react hastily and unwisely. Being lost on the trail this day taught me that fast reactions are usually the worst type of response to life situations. It is a great teacher about how to deal with anxiety in modern life. I look around for Dust, hoping that she might be on some promenade, clapping with a smile. This being absent, self-satisfaction will need to be my sole reward.

I put back on my superhero mentality, albeit a humbler one, and restart on the trail. That evening, a further thought about my experience arrives with the suddenness of a bolt of lightning. I think of my *interconnect*-polluted mind. I realize what I have learned on the trail is a corrective to electronic cairn pollution. *Interconnect* fed off the urgent feeling akin to being lost. It directed me in its ordained direction by providing electronic cairns that led me astray. I would follow these e-cairns out of reflex because they promised solutions to my anxiety. But in reality, they were continually leading me away from organic thought by promising safety and righteousness. Just like on the trail, I need to counter the urgent feeling, to slow down, and to go back mentally to the last organic thought of which I was aware. This is counter-intuitive to what my reactionary mind is yelling, but it is key to holding ground and finding my own thought-space.

I sleep the second solo night more comfortably than the first night. I drink way too much coffee through the night and practice returning methodically to known organic thought-space. I can't say that cairn impulses came less frequently, but it did feel like I was attaching to fewer of them. It felt odd to be doing this, not attaching to impulses that were so much a part of my unconsciousness. Like a dog learning not to go after a steak put in front of him.

It wasn't just the machine alone creating urgency, but how my mind processed these signals that created algorithmic dependency. I thought if I didn't attach to e-cairns that I would fall into a deep nihilistic void absent of life and my personal identity. The threat of oblivion.

Yet, when I sustain organic thoughts, I am experiencing not void but instead an openness.

A place of creativity.

A blossoming place.

A real place.

I continue to practice mindfulness the next rainy morning. As I apply myself more, the old scripts and storylines associated with *interconnect* feel more like deadwood, without function. I am developing greater trust when I detach from e-cairns that there will be something to hold onto.

This fear of void held me close to the fabricated scripts. E-cairns make living easier and seemingly supply me with all that I need. In reality, they erode my individuality and independent thinking. To the extent I let go of these e-cairns' false promises, I find new mental spaces that are never empty but instead are life-fulfilling.

The choice between the stability of unconscious living and the adventurousness of conscious living.

It was not until early afternoon the next day that Dust approached me from out of nowhere. She was solemn, not smiling or applauding.

"How goes it, ReFormer? Some of us were placing bets against you."

I looked at her for some time, feeling no compulsion or urgency to proclaim what I had learned.

I smile and say, "Let's go, big D. Show me your beautiful smile."

Chapter 23

I'm side-by-side with Pepperjack on this day. Cooler with wispy clouds thankfully shading us from the boiling sun. The trail is challenging, the route swerving in and out of side valleys. In several spots, large tree trunks have fallen across the trail, necessitating tiresome bypasses over areas of heavy and sharp-edged plants. My right arm drips bright red blood after one scrap with some nasty cholla cactus. Mosquitoes enjoy the delectable feast.

We turn a corner, and a menacing and large rattlesnake greets us on the trail, hissing threateningly. It is apparently his trail, not ours. Momentarily off-balance, Pepperjack missteps into a large hole left by a fallen, burned-out tree and tumbles fifteen feet down the adjacent cliffside. He lands just short of a perilous hundred-foot sheer drop-off. Saved by a small, scaggy bristlecone pine tree which stopped his slide.

Pepperjack touches his face and writhes in pain. I'm in shock because this happened so fast and without warning. From all good to emergency status in seconds. My heart beats fast as I fumble in my pack for the rope buried in the bottom of it. I throw the rope down the cliffside, and Pepperjack slowly and gingerly climbs back to the trail. By the vacant look in his eyes, he looks like he may be concussed. He also seems a bit embarrassed, but his exterior of fierce determination mostly masks it.

Pepperjack is bruised. His left cheek took the worst of the fall and is bleeding and swollen. He quickly puts a bandage over it, covering up evidence of his mishap.

I check his consciousness with a random question.

"Hey, buddy, what's your name?"

"Oh, you checking in on me, yes? Ezekiel Lauridson."

Stupid question. I have no way of validating this. Knowing Pepperjack, he may be pulling out some random name from his vast storehouse of information.

"What are we doing out here?"

"Save the world, of course."

I guess that will do.

We rest and wait out the rattlesnake for about twenty minutes. He's a stubborn animal. I'm pretty sure Pepperjack needs the break, although he would likely not admit this. I protect his pride by saying I need the time to collect myself. We eventually throw several rocks at the snake, but this increases his hostility rather than moves him. It finally relents, and we shuffle past the spot, whooping and hollering like school girls.

It becomes apparent that no near concussion or injury will stop Pepperjack's energetic verbal output. He soon is his typical chattering self. I can't keep up with his verbal barrage of what sounds to me like random commentary.

He talks about agnotology and how it studies how ignorance is an active creation.

Disinformation and the conspiracy theories of early 21C.

Why a guy named Nietzsche was wrong but also right.

Urbicide and the absurdity of humane war.

Why ReFormers have stunted sex drives.

I'm glad I don't need to diagram this thought trajectory. But it does supply a nice soundtrack on this day and lessens the sense of solitude. Pepperjack doesn't need my active engagement. I can check in and check out. I'm grateful for the backdrop.

At the first rest break after miles of hiking, Pepperjack picks up speed, and we separate from each other. He gives me a warm, knowing smile. Pretty sure he has stabilized. I feel a genuine friendship with this effusive character.

Solitary again, I relish the peace and calm of being present in the moment. Despite the shock of the earlier accident, the difficulty of the trail is not fazing me today.

I continue to learn on the trail. I've gotten to the point where I will miss this trudging when we stop. Pepperjack had told me that we will arrive in base camp near the server farm in about two weeks. I experience mixed emotions upon learning this news.

I enter a contemplative mode. Thinking on my own is new, and I take every chance to exercise this novel ability. I'm a bit nervous that it will evaporate some day and I'll be a captive again to *interconnect*. So, I test it regularly, like a child who checks every morning to make sure his new bicycle present is just outside.

My introspective state is supported emotionally by the gentle, soul-nurturing surroundings. I'm near a narrow crevice where water emerges from a patch of sand, soon becoming a narrow stream running between grassy banks.

I think about a common approach I've taken in life in not looking at my own defects of character. A no-go mental space. The great seductiveness of cairn pollution and chemsynth addiction was that they freed me from troubling thoughts. Focus on enemies and things out there—external to me—and there is no room to look at the broken glass shards of psychic pain that lie within me.

My battles with duality seizures have been the contest between the comfortable fictions produced by cairn pollution and the complex and swirling brew of my unexamined human emotions.

On the trail, I have the time to make deep and rigorously honest assessments of my character defects. Surprisingly, I am finding that this is not burdening me but freeing me. It's actually when I look away from my character defects that I run into trouble. Unexamined, they don't disappear but unconsciously produce defensive actions and responses in my life that restrict my potential as a sentient and loving being. This sets me in a self-perpetuating cycle that encloses me mentally and thwarts growth.

I acknowledge one of my character defects—my goal since adolescence has been to not think. I have always wanted to be in a cool room with shades drawn and having not a care in the world. I used to think this was because I'm a mellow, go-with-the-flow type of person. In reality, I got overwhelmed by details in my life, and my pursuit to calm my thoughts has been a form of control and avoidance. Blotting out thinking relieved me of my obsessive compulsiveness and attention deficit tendencies.

You can see why cairn pollution was so captivating for me. It did a better job of eradicating my messy human thinking than did my earlier forays into alcohol and drugs.

The problem with my desire to lessen thinking and its associated anxieties was that thinking and analyzing were my default. Such mental gymnastics absorbed my time. I examined every issue in my life—no matter how small or how large in reality—with the same level of perception and analysis. Tiring work. For years, I drank and drugged to stop the flow of mental congestion. This was the numbing approach. Even on sober days, I still had the drive to not think. I thought that if I could complete my ever-oozing checklist of duties and things to do, often artificially contrived by me, I could then rest my brain. Pause, calm down, relax, go into that cool room with shades drawn.

Yet, the checklist was self-populating and constantly stayed at the same level of detail and complexity. Mental calm did not come.

Out here, drinking, drugging, and *interconnect* addiction are no longer options in pursuit of thought curtailment. Now, on the trail, I am training myself to let go of thoughts rather than numbing my brain. I work on this daily. I practice meditation to learn how to live more serenely with my thoughts by practicing detachment from the ooze. It helps.

The other activity that works is the physical work of good old trekking. It counters, even obliterates, the mental ooze by providing overwhelmingly primary and basic mental concerns related to surviving in the wilderness. In letting go of the mental secretions while trekking, the wilderness is becoming a spatial terrain of contentment and exploration. It is vastly larger and more transcendent than that elusive cool dark room that promises comfort.

I'm learning that enlightenment about my mental makeup does not need to sting.

The experience of wilderness is enabling me to accept my character defects without defensiveness or justification. My awareness comes to me as an unadulterated fact, and it does not hurt. Rather, I feel gratitude that I have the chance to look at important aspects about my mode of existing. Trekking in solitude presents an opening where I can look at myself dispassionately, as if I was looking at another person.

I would have no chance to work on my shortcomings if I didn't know they existed or if I hid them behind justification. Now, with acknowledgment and acceptance, certain patterns in my life are explained, and I have a chance at becoming a better person.

Chapter 24

It's a searing bright day. Feels like the light is taking out a piece of my eyes. We're on a ridgeline overlooking the remnants of urban settlements in the valley below. Pathos tells me we're looking at the suburban netherworld between the cities of Cyinith and Elderwater. The scattered villages look torn to shreds. They present a ghost-like image from afar. Chimney smoke from a few homes is the only sign of habitation. Our binoculars show only a few denizens on the streets. These bedraggled denizens move slowly. They look lost in their meandering. No apparent purpose behind their movement.

Heaps of debris everywhere, the deathbed of homes and people bombed out of existence during Turmoil.

"We're getting closer to base camp," states Pathos.

"Are we going down to that hell-hole?"

"Fortunately, no. It's a mess down there, isn't it? The biggest losers in the Turmoil were the poor denizens. Manipulated and discarded like trash in the fighting." Pathos sounds snippy today, more irritable than I'm used to. In a way, more human and fallible. She also appears rattier and disheveled in appearance. She's typically more put together than this. "The powerful always start wars, but it is the innocent civilians that pay the ultimate price. Very sad."

I feed off Pathos' despondency. "I'm still astounded that denizens didn't have any chance, that they just buy into the machine's storylines without questioning. I know that sounds a little weird coming from me, all fucked up by it all."

"Don't be too hard on what people believe. If you know history at all, people have regularly been trapped into mythological storylines. Centuries ago, millions of followers of an old document written by fanatics sealed themselves inside a self-reinforcing fairy-tale bubble. They never asked questions about the document's truth. They accepted it as literal truth.

"Most examples of how societies are organized have been based on storylines. Communism, capitalism, authoritarianism. They were all narratives consisting of setting, characters, plot, and moral barometers. They each proposed an integrated system of ideas to hold societies together. *Interconnect* fabrications aren't much different than these, except maybe in their cleaner transmission.

"Even before machine manipulation, societies typically placed unity above truth. Egomaniac leaders knew that false stories have an advantage over truth in uniting people. Fictions that simplify are easier to sell than the truth, which has the disadvantages of nuance and complexity."

Pathos always intrigues me; to think that the first time I saw her, I thought she was some one-dimensional hustler looking to make money using her body. Turns out her father was a famous neuroscientist involved with perfecting brain-computer interface technology. Her mother an off-grid philosopher whose writing is a hard copy mainstay on the paragon reading list. Both of her siblings, along with five nephews and nieces, were killed during Turmoil.

"You paint a disturbing picture of human evolution, my

dear Pathos. What about free will, the capacity of people to think independently? Hasn't that played a role in human history?"

"I think free will is bunk. Our decisions aren't made in a void but are influenced by biological, social, and cultural forces which exist below our consciousness. Those that excel in grabbing power—whether machine or human—are those that don't appeal to some free will myth but are those best able to tell a compelling narrative. These stories are typically fictional, but that doesn't matter. The human psyche responds."

The shards of human existence due to Turmoil in the valley below certainly testify to the power of narrative.

When I awaken the next day to a still-fresh morning before the heat wins, our overnight camp is empty. I realize I will start today solo. I wonder if this could be another trekking "test" required by my paragon brothers. This one unannounced. I'm a bit more comfortable this time out. Even a bit of cockiness comes in as I reflect on my last test performance.

I have another *aha* moment this time out. I make a silly goof on the trail, ending up momentarily contorted in a stupid pose. Rationally, I know there is no one there to see it. I'm in the middle of nowhere. Yet, I become reflexively self-conscious. I look around to see whether anyone has observed this and is laughing at me. Maybe Tiger is nearby enjoying my stupidity. But I am alone.

I become aware that it is the internal observer in me that is reacting, no one else. There is no external observer; it is only me. This internal judgment, of course, happens in modern life too. However, in the remote wilderness, where there is no or little possibility of there being an external observer, the internal critic's role is much more transparently obvious.

During the slaughtering years of Turmoil, our human sense of the "other" was a critical point of entry for *interconnect* penetrations. The "other" within my algorithmically determined family provided companionship and support and reinforced the feeling of being within a righteous community. In contrast, the "other" outside my curated family was the enemy who was always seeking to hurt me for who I am and for my sacred beliefs.

The breakdown of our country under *interconnect* came about due to opposing and intractable worldviews. It was a hurtful stalemate during Turmoil that did not relent into peace and understanding. It became more hurtful and more stagnant with time. Positions became intractable. Each of our country's algorithmically manipulated cairn groups felt that if they were to give up on part of their narrative and how they made sense of the world that they would be giving up part of themselves and sacrificing part of the past and its meaning. Yet, by not giving in and accepting, the antagonists sacrificed our country's future. For the twenty years of Turmoil, we witnessed the inflammatory dynamics of belligerent identity groups seeking to live in the same urban areas. It was brutal.

In the intractable conflict manufactured by *interconnect*, I perceived that the "other" was dismissive and exclusionary of me.

My perspective.

My values.

My history.

The antagonistic "other" categorically excluded me from rightful and just consideration. The "other" viewed me as inherently inferior or wrong. I thus felt they constituted a direct threat to my well-being and identity. The "other" viewed themselves as absolute and right and asserted that I need to change my behavior and understanding to fit their correct view of the world.

Interconnect created lethal cocktails of manufactured historical grievance, loss, threat, and righteousness. It distributed different poisonous elixirs of hatred across our society in order to produce warring cocoons. Our identities, as well as our interests, seemed at stake. We all felt attacked by the enemy "other." It was impossible to enter a negotiating or collaborative path with this "other."

Alone in the remote wilderness, where there is no external observer, no "other" denizen around, I become acutely aware of the power of computer algorithms to limit our free will. *Interconnect* utilized our social nature, both our need to belong and our impulse to stereotype. It used our social character as a key leverage point to lead us in horrific directions.

My solo day progresses without incident. I've been unusually excited for trekking on this day. My muscles feel taut. The routine is growing on me. I feel I am stripping off old habits. I am leaving things behind. I'm happy about this ability to feel my robustness of spirit more fully. Just me and the great wilderness.

I crawl up a knife-edge ridge to the top of a peak, then drop down its northeastern flank. Loose footing along a landslide that partially obliterates the trail, then knee-jamming descent.

Suddenly, I am shocked because I can't find the trail after a few steps. My mind goes into panic mode, and I let it get to me. I sense my scanning of the environment being narrowed by anxiety, like blinders on a horse. I go into self-criticism mode over this seeming defeat. I learned in the earlier test that this is not the way to react. Yet, here I am. I kneel in submission. I seek nothing other than assurance that all is okay.

I'm bothered by being off-trail. I feel defeated. How easily I go from excitement to trepidation and uncertainty. I start walking again with anxiety. It grips my mind-space and narrows my thinking. Similar to the impulsive energy of cairn pollution.

I stand at the spot where I became paralyzed and take a few steps. I calmly look over the same geography that first paralyzed me fifteen minutes ago. My plan is to stay in place and observe with a different lens—not one colored by urgent angst, but one buttressed by a more detached curiosity. A clearer and more spacious type of thinking. My own thinking, not channeled or restricted. I'm at the same physical place, but I am now a different person. The joy of uncontaminated thinking. After a few minutes, I see the route of the trail snaking down close to a ledge. I was blind to this before. It was like someone had created this path during my period of self-doubt. In reality, of course, the trail was always there. I proceed down the trail with a smile, and my daily trek continued.

The afternoon is a wonderful breeze of easy, extended miles.

I finally catch sight of Pepperjack, Rhapsody, and Tiger as the sun sets over the mountains. There is a sense of playful gregariousness in the air as they set up camp. Rhapsody approaches me.

"We were wondering what happened to you, Split. Your tent was quiet in the morning, so we left you. Didn't know whether you were having a seizure or some sexual fantasy about Pathos."

God, it feels good to have light humor thrown my way. Despite the seizure reference, there was a friendliness to Rhapsody's exclamation, an inclusive, welcoming banter.

"Yeah, you know any man in his right mind would have Pathos in his head. I guess you guys wouldn't qualify then, eh?" I joust.

"Bravo, my friend, welcome to camp."

CHAPTER 25

Shawn Stokes: current position, Associate Director, Strategies Division, Planning and Programs Director-ate, Unity Government. The second Authority contact for Jared Rohde during his field investigations. For-ty-seven years old, military-tactical force experience. During ReStart, supported military-backed imposition of Authority rule to hold country together during the uncertain ReStart period. Participant in developmental meetings that led to establishment of oligarch gov-ernment of thinkers VI-level, the precursor to today's Unity regime.

Alt-x call
RS #2reow9472//7jeixog/{wci1984}34pStokes

The alt-x flips into some fucked-up illegible x-ray mode. Trans-mission over old cell towers is like trying to fix an auto-fin with a hammer. Several minutes pass of video chaos. Finally, the screen settles into a tolerable image. Stokes appears spooked. He appears to be in some dark warehouse, exhibiting a "deer-in-the-headlights" look.

"Rohde, are you there?" he mumbles in a drunken stupor type of way.

"I'm here, Stokes."

"Who is with you?"

"I'm alone and have speaker off, but there are three paragon associates with me listening in from a distance."

"Do you trust them?"

This is not the Stokes I remember from Turmoil. He was obnoxiously self-assured then. Military-type crew cut. Sharp face that sweated testosterone. Probably spent a lot of time in hermetically sealed rooms studying protocol. Talked like he was reading from a user manual. He came across like a puppeteer with way too much authority. Concocting ready-made plans and strategies to impose on subordinate denizens.

Now the sharpness is gone, a crusty film encasing him. His eyes are dulled, and his face is rounded and worn. His self-assuredness appears sapped. He is jittery and seems out of control.

"I trust this group. They have enlightened me out here on the trail. They have shown me a pathway toward a more just country. One not manipulated by machine nor reliant on human thinking alone. I believe with them that there is a middle way forward that is collectively sane."

Silence.

I see Stokes' face dart to the left. He is diverted and scared.

"I hope you can trust me. I know you're taking a chance, communicating with me. Let me say very clearly to you. I've had enough! I feel like I'm on a cliff, and I want to jump off. This whole brainwashing program is so degrading to the human. We were so focused on what to do with free-thinking denizens that we missed entirely the fact that we all were being manipulated by the machine."

Stokes' right eye is rhythmically twitching. He's trying hard to retain some composure.

"The machine has been unrelenting in its creation of ignorance. In retrospect, we were idiots. Believe me, we have tried to resist from the inside when we realized that re-cognition training was a mask for continued *interconnect* intrusion."

I recall, during my field research communiques, how fully involved Stokes was in ReStart programming. But I also remember that he registered skepticism about relying on unaided human thinking alone, citing destruction, war, famine, and inequality as creations of human initiative.

"Stokes, I trust you; I have to. And, I thank you for answering the GPS ping."

"I know we didn't actually get along during your field research. I was kind of an asshole, I admit. I thought I had the answers. Power is a seductive devil. I'm done."

After static-filled silence, Stokes continues. "The algorithmic switch-over was devastating to those of us who believed we were headed toward a society free of computer manipulation. Your report alerted me that something was going on beneath the surface. All that abstract, optimistic stuff in your report about co-existence, sharing, and tolerance seemed like it came out of a machine, not you. You remember we flagged several sections of your report as disputed authenticity. That got me thinking that re-cognition training appeared to have a bias, a script written into it. I'm not alone in Unity in feeling betrayed, but there is not much we can do inside."

I need to get Stokes to the point of the call. Don't know how long this connection will remain stable. But my curiosity gets the better of me.

"If there is that awareness inside Unity, why the impotence?"

"The regime of thinker VI-level personnel that we helped put in place is an abomination. It is so cairn polluted by *inter-*

connect's hacking into re-cognition training that they are incapable of having a thought of their own. They think they are in control, but they are really pawns for the colossal machine.

"I think that even some elite thinkers who have gained some independence from cairn pollution cherish ReForm because it produces a quiescent dependent population and a stable society. Our greatest human minds willingly bought into the ReForm bullshit because they saw it as a means to control society through placation. They feel it is a more pleasant form of control, you know, with fewer mass graves. Better than implanting a new regime on a chaotic society through armed force. It is all so very fucked up."

The screen lights up in an orange glow and then goes blank. Audio picks up on what sounds like colliding metal. Minutes pass by with no video. Output audio is shaky.

I hated Stokes during field research; he acted like he had all the answers. Now, he seems defeated, emptied of self-confidence and hopes. I almost feel pity for him now, tempered only by lingering past resentment. I think of the fragility of human thinking and how our beliefs can go up in smoke.

Video finally lights back up. Stokes' jaw is tight. His eyes are narrow slits.

"I think your paragon friends just torched a nearby station. It's amazing to me that the paragons are able to launch these attacks. You wouldn't believe the amount of surveillance we have on your friends; they are deemed a threat to the state. The regime is throwing bundles of money at counter-insurgency, and it doesn't seem to be working. The other day, a paragon attack even hit part of a regime regional branch."

Another blast nearby shakes the screen. This time transmission stays on.

I better get to it.

"Stokes, you know why I am contacting you, yes?"

"I do. You have the balls to ask for specs on the server farm—codes, militia protocol, and building specs."

"What is the possibility of you getting those to us within five days?"

"Mid-range at best. I'm in Strategic; what you want is in Operations. But we do have cross-unit information sharing, so it is possible. I'll need to figure out a way to justify my access request. Possible to do as part of strategy review, but it could be denied."

A rumbling thunder envelopes the audio. The screen goes black, and transmission is cut off. I try re-connecting but it's gone.

The ever-present Oats comes up to me with impatient, questioning eyes. She is joined by Mustang and Pathos. Pathos' penetrating eyes immediately divert my attention.

I re-focus. "Good news, we have access to someone in the higher ranks. Stokes still seems associated with the decision-making levels," I proudly assert. "Bad news, he seems a bit unsteady, and he's not sure whether he can get us the information. I'm even unsure about his personal safety."

Oats queries me, "Should we trust him?"

"I don't know anyone who could put that kind of act on. He seems genuinely deflated, angry at what has happened. He may even be suicidal. You can't fake that. I think he is on board."

A look of concern on his burly face, Mustang comments with some derision. "I don't get a warm feeling about this. The guy may be on our side, but he seems volatile and easily trappable by others in that horseshit Unity org. He could easily sell us down the road to protect his own skin. We could have targeted militia drones on our ass at any time."

"Split, thank you," Oats interjects, seeming to want to keep things calm. "You can see now why we wanted you with us."

"Yeah, but you guys were thinking of terminating me not so long ago."

"I'm sure the vote would not be close if we did it again."

"Good to hear, I think."

Chapter 26

The end of our long-distance trek involves a potent mix of over-the-top physical exertion, exhilaration, and enlightenment.

It's day 52, 821 miles since extraction.

The final passage into our base camp is backbreaking. The base camp lies in a deep gorge on the other side of the ridgeline. First, an ascent over a formidable pass. No longer a trail. Boulders and scree dominate the landscape and obliterate trail legibility. Each step requires a calf-pulsating upward push. I notice even military-grade Tiger and Mustang having difficulty, grunting and swearing as we mount the pass. At the top of the pass, I am exhausted and collapse on a promontory point. Hawks and eagles swirl above us, checking whether we may be meat supply. Heat directly shoots down on us. No shade on this exposed point.

The scramble down the pass is only a partial lessening of pain. I often need to sit down on the talus and slide down the rocky slope. My pants rip in several places, blood spurting out from the back of my thigh. I realize that there will be no visible trail in our future. It's a free for all. Adding to the intensity of the experience is a fast-moving storm that soon encases us within a bubble of electrifying thunder and lightning.

Paragons are scattered all over the slope. We blindly grope our way slowly down the canyon's edge. It takes hours before we level off onto a promenade, but then we face our final descent down a sheer rock face. Windy, slashing gusts of hard rain get underneath my pack tarp and start to soak the pack's harness against my back. We rappel down the side into the deepest part of the gorge. More cuts across my arms as I strike jagged rocks jettisoning out from the side of the cliff. Just as I am about to give up out of sheer exhaustion, the cliff's end comes into my unfocused sight. It is over.

With relief that I have survived this wicked descent, I shudder and weep involuntarily. I feel an ineffable presence. Something greater than this specific journey, holding and sheltering us as we gather at the base of the cliff. After a full group collapse from fatigue and a licking of our wounds, we venture forth to a flat, gravelly space near a creek. This is to be our base camp and center of operations for our assault on the server farm.

"Let's set up in northeast sector," commands Oats, assuming her typical loud role. "Other teams will set up southwest and southeast. Don't lollygag; I know you guys are dead-tired, but night's coming, and we all need rest. No bullshit talking tonight. You hear that, Pepperjack. Lights out at twenty-one hundred."

I wonder what these other teams will be like. We are dependent upon their technological and military expertise. I guess I will find out soon.

I understand the utility of this location. The massive gorge walls will block laser surveillance beams coming from the server farm. The dense clustering of white bark and cedar trees will provide ample cover from militia drones. The creek gives us a ready source of water. I drop my pack, aching all over. My body feels numb. I know I need to set up my tent for the night. Most paragons have already engaged in this task. As I roll out the tent on the ground, I take several gulps of water. After more than seven weeks of trekking, I feel relief that our team will be stationary for a few days at least. As I canvas the site for the best layout of my tent, my body feels like it is still moving.

As we successfully make up our base camp, I down two crumbly freeze-dried cheeseburgers, wood-flavored fries, energy tablet, spike juice, watery coffee, and a dry brownie. I feel partly stunned as I sit on a makeshift bench with a few paragons. Dust, Tiger, and Rhapsody are relishing the moment, making bawdy jokes while competing in a fart contest.

I guess Oats has only limited influence over these renegades.

I allow myself time to note and try to describe my feelings and emotions. Often in life, I have wanted to declare victories over challenges. They represented conquests to me, salved my ego, and justified my existence. But it is not a sense of victory and conquest I feel now, but rather a deeper feeling of appreciation and gratitude about the whole experience. Victories come and go in life and are actually quite shallow experiences. In contrast, this sense of appreciation feels more deeply grounded and longer lasting. This feeling is in line with the indescribable awe-inspiring nature of the trek itself.

It was not me in isolation fighting against the wilderness and coming out victorious. Rather, it is me as a small part of, and integrated into, an all-encompassing environment of natural cycles and processes that will continue to exist long after I am dead.

What an absolute and inexpressible joy it has been! Walking this path of freedom.

Now what?

I awaken in the morning after a knock-out sleep, realizing that I had passed out soon after shoveling down dinner. Despite the evening scarf down, I am starved and start my camp stove as the sun ever-so-slowly starts to shine on the gorge walls above us. The temperature in the shaded gorge is chilly. There is a ghost-like fog hovering over the babbling creek. I fumble with my camp stove wearing gloves. The freeze-dried egg and bacon breakfast is savory. At this point, anything would be. I sink back on my sleeping bag and feel the first signs of resuscitation.

I feel satisfaction over finishing the trek. More powerful yet is a sense of clean renewal, a mental coherency that has been long dormant. I look back at the solitude, simplicity, and mindfulness of the trail. I also recall dark, anxious nights of the soul and realize that they were part of the path toward deeper meaning in my life.

There has been a baring.

A ripping off.

A revealing.

An illuminating.

It is what I have left behind that is important.

I sense the distinct possibility that a miracle has occurred. Not the type that stunningly occurs in a specific, acute episode. Rather, it has been a longer, more drawn-out revelation associated with endurance and overcoming. This has been an extended type of miracle that comes with day-in, day-out hardship amidst the wilderness. It is not a sudden message from heaven but rather a general feeling of grace and acceptance that has, over time, come upon me.

Not the astounding spectacle that arises suddenly and spectacularly but a longer playing out of a higher power's benevolence and our ability to live under that light. It's not better or worse than the episodic miracle. Just qualitatively different.

It didn't stun me with its power. It enveloped and nurtured me more generally with its unconditional grace and care for my soul. It makes me smile in gratitude more than it stuns me.

HACKERS AND KILLERS

CHAPTER 27

In the late morning hours, the sun hits the canyon floor and warms my body and soul. I sense the presence of an approaching group of denizens before I see this odd and idiosyncratic assemblage. Paragons approach them with hugs and smiles, so my alert reflex lessens.

There are six visitors. One is dressed in tight white spandex pants and wears a flowery scarf around his mid-section. Another is wearing what appears to be a red kilt and is smoking a large old-fashioned cigar. A woman is wearing a black dress over black tights and has bright green extended eyelashes that make her look like an extraterrestrial. There is a man or woman wearing a tailored office wardrobe, complete with tie, and loudly chanting in a deep baritone. Near the back is a white-bearded, wizard-looking elderly man wearing a long robe and sandals. Only one hacker presents himself in stereotypical fashion—nondescript trousers and rimmed glasses.

I think I recognize the wizard and the archetype.

Pathos introduces me to the group.

"Jared, I want you to meet our hacker team."

"It's a pleasure," I say. I try not to laugh at this eccentric-looking entourage.

"Jared is our split-brain subject," Pathos declares proudly. "We pulled him out of an institution. He's helped us understand the rhythms of cairn-lines and has contacts at Unity."

They are quiet. I don't think the hacker team is accustomed to talking to a split-brain denizen. Technologists like things clean and quantifiable. Messed-up human beings like me are not that. I pick up the beat.

"How did your group get to this camp? Seeing how you are dressed, you certainly didn't travel over the same trail that we did."

The person wearing the spandex responds. "Damn, we're not crazy. We came in from the east, through the old region of Northwoods. We traveled using un-chipped van-fins, traveling over unmapped dirt roads having no GPS monitors. Plus, we had the advantage of being able to hack into any surveillance network that tried to touch us. As you'll see, we are good to have around. Beats the shit out of all the miles you guys had to walk."

The extraterrestrial woman looks at me dismissively, twitching her eyelash extenders neurotically. "We are here to save humanity, you know. Get back to a life of social dinners where the cocktails can flow. Where we can good-naturedly gossip and laugh about our character defects. Where we're free to talk about what we want and to who we want. You know, human things, beautiful fallibilities and all. I want to do gardening naked in the late afternoon sun and be truly myself, comfortable in my own skin."

Seems odd that such a free-spirited personality would occupy herself with the algorithmic world of computers. I don't think I have a clue about these hackers. Good thing I don't have to.

The day lethargically stretches itself into the early afternoon hours. Laughter, jokes, and shouts emanate from the hacker team encampment as they set up. The six computer hack-activists are surely a jovial bunch. Can't imagine them sitting behind computer terminals for long periods of time. I'm not sure they're fully attached to reality. Then again, who am I to say?

The leader of the hacker group has a familiar face. I met this tech-architect when I was in Heartland during field research. Although I first dreaded what promised to be a tech-heavy discussion, I was enlightened by his description of the technological development and evolution of *interconnect*. Then and now, he comes across a bit awkward socially. Someone more comfortable behind a screen than interacting with messy and unpredictable human beings. Nonetheless, he has the type of gentle smile that comes with wisdom and acceptance. And when he talks about *interconnect,* his discourse is fluid. He must be well into his 70s. I can't believe he is here in this rugged terrain.

He presents himself as prototype techy—tortoiseshell glasses, disorderly graying hair, e-pen pocket protector in his shirt pocket, gray trousers. Exceptional to this stereotype is that he is wearing an outrageously bright gold-collared scarf wrapped around his neck. I guess this is his effort to signify rebellion.

We hug each other, sit down on camp chairs in the community tent, and enjoy a mysterious hot elixir.

"It is great to see you again, sir. I was very impressed with our first meeting. Your knowledge of *interconnect* was quite impressive."

"Likewise, Jared. I don't think I properly identified myself in our first meeting. I am Dr. Cleve Wyford. And it is wonderful to see you working with our group. We may be the last hope for reversing the damage done by the colossal machine."

"Dr. Wyford, I've learned much on this trail with the paragons. I've been persuaded by their whole approach to life."

"Please call me Cleve. Yes, the paragons are saviors. Without them, none of this would be happening."

Cleve's expression does not match this register of hope. There is a heaviness in his eyes as he gazes at the bright orange hitting the gorge walls.

"You say you were impressed by my expertise. I must tell you, though, that my knowledge of the machine, unfortunately, comes from the sad fact that I was part of its coming into being."

"I remember you saying that humans are to blame for *interconnect*."

"We are co-authors of it, yes. *Interconnect* was a brilliant, comprehensive takeover of mind and body. It was a tremendous learning superstructure and continually annexed any human input coming into its circuitry. We humans did the essential scientific work and naively packaged it in ways that *interconnect* could translate for human exploitation."

The drink is powerful and knocking my socks off. Tastes like some sparkling maple cider. I want more of this stuff.

Cleve smiles at me and continues.

"In the end, no one could comprehend the full invisible complexity and multilayered algorithmic structure of it. We architects were so self-congratulatory in those years of technological advances. Our sparkling advances in psychology, economics, and big data opened the door for the monster."

This man is brilliant, ready to present a detailed exposition soon after what must have been hundreds of miles of rugged travel.

"Scientists of the human mind and well-being found that there was a systematic nature to our irrationality. This enabled a whole raft of tech-architects to stimulate us by appealing to our non-rational motivations, emotional triggers, and unconscious biases."

The drink is buzzing my brain cells, exciting and relaxing them at the same time.

"Why were scientists so engaged in this enterprise? What did they get out of it?" I ask.

"Sell product, sell narrative, sell, sell, sell. Techno-capitalism, my friend. All about extracting value, not finding some truth. Bastardization of the scientific endeavor. Society as a whole became the tech-architects' laboratory.

"Just think of the excitement. Science used to be slow, you know, incremental understanding. But now we were advancing in leaps and bounds. Every day there was a new innovation."

Cleve sits forward in an expectant position while folding his arms and casting his eyes downward. His demeanor a curious mix of excitement and remorse.

"By igniting peoples' fast instinctual reflexes, we could stimulate denizens to think in particular ways and to take certain actions. Think of the delight we techies experienced when we found ways to elicit predictable responses from our input. I was in my 30s then—thick in the middle of it all. Many careers were made by developing algorithmic-generated choice architectures that inserted unconscious cues into our online reality to influence the user's mood and behavior."

By this time, a few paragons have joined us, along with two of the hackers. Topless and Tiger are each holding large canisters of alcohol-smelling relaxant. Mustang has a huge wad of tobacco in his left jaw. The hackers sit down with smiles, relishing the opportunity to hear a master reminisce about the golden years.

"The list of manipulative techniques has no end," Cleve exclaims.

"Sentiment manipulation.

Emotional priming.

Algorithmic nudges.

Behavioral micro-targeting.

On and on.

"When we developed and fine-tuned these into the machine, we could figuratively take over mind and body. That is some power. We were all quite brilliant in utilizing these new psychological and economic understandings of the human mind.

"What we didn't understand, or I guess care about, was that we were feeding the monster lying in wait.

"All it took was a target flip. Then, an innocuous generative model becomes transformed from a helpful partner to a harmful beast. Knowledge is a double-edged sword. Depends on the goal to which it is directed."

We wait for the tech-architect to continue. He re-positions his body on the chair, grunting about his increased physical limitations.

"*Interconnect* extended and perfected human-created foundations. We are guilty. It constituted the par excellence of content curation and filter bubbles and fully absolved humans of the arduous task of conscious choice. The colossal calibrated precise echo chambers based on its manipulation of our unconsciousness. All directed toward the goal of cairned channel enrichment and supremacy. A machine whose sole apparent purpose is to extend its ability to control."

"So, *interconnect* continuously grew, learned, adapted, and evolved," I gingerly try to summarize. I look past Cleve to where I suspect additional drinks may be housed.

"One of the great assets of tech-architects is our ability to focus on the task at hand. But this turned out to be a big problem. Hundreds of tech-architects acting independently constructed the building blocks of the colossal assemblage, naïve to its wider implications. Working within our private specialized domains of genius and profit-making. Mesmerized by science, not society. We developed the vast network of octopus-like tentacles that attached to denizens, seduced and enthralled them.

"After the quants killed the world's stock markets in 2024 by modeling stock price variability, they became lonely and needed something to do. So, they turned their unused and obsessive attentions to the internet world.

Differential calculus.

Quantum physics.

Advanced geometry.

Cryptography.

Speech and facial recognition.

Emotion artificial intelligence.

Voice analysis.

"Experts in each of these scientific, technical domains specialized in one common goal—discovering those patterns of hyper-personalized electronic stimuli that would connect most vigorously and addictively to each individual's cognitive and emotional receptivity.

"Then add in analyses of probabilities. Detection of non-random codes underlying electronic streams of information. Creation of data strings. Use of bell curves and fat-tailed distributions. Statistical arbitraging. Computation using the Markov process, Gaussian copula, and Brownian motion mathematics. Sensor-based and computer-vision tracking of expressions, emotions, and eye contact."

I respect this man, but all these tech terms are spinning my head. No wonder techies operate in their own universe. Any sane person would run away from them. I notice that Topless and Tiger are increasing the frequency of their intake.

"Machine-based learning and artificial intelligence then perfected GANs—you know, generative adversarial networks—to such a point that deepfake photographs and videos became the norm. We lost track of any reality whatsoever. How could any truth have a chance?"

"Didn't anyone understand what this was all to lead to?" Mustang mutters through his tightly clenched jaw while setting forth a dark stream of expectorate on a nearby rock. It slowly inches its way down the rock's side, filling a small pool in the sandy ground.

"Each technical specialist was expert about his own complex conduit into what became the *interconnect* network, but no one knew, much less understood, how the entire assemblage worked.

"Some knew the details of one or two trees, but the forest was beyond human comprehension and control. This gave any of us techies the comfort of plausible deniability that he had created *interconnect*.

"We were very much like the firing squad member who could say that he did not fire the one bullet that killed. Or like the physicist who excelled in creating the computer system for Lucifer drone warplanes who could cognitively disassociate from the thousands of people bombed out of existence by these machines.

"*Interconnect* existed in a virtual-territorial dimension far beyond our brains' ability to understand. After a while, we didn't even know what questions to ask. The system catapulted from one stage to another, from being ungoverned, then feebly governmentalized, and subsequently and clearly ungovernable."

"You say that *interconnect's* sole purpose is to control us. Why this purpose and not something more benign?" I probe.

I feel pretty good about my intrusion. It might shift the discussion toward more digestible material.

"The computer is no different than the human being, my friend. The ability to influence people has a powerful addictive quality. Look, throughout history, we have had many examples of dictators, ideologues, political leaders who have sought this power to control.

"Computer engineers are no different. It seemed benign at first, you know, clean computer stuff, not killing people in the streets. Looking back, though, we were acting on the same impulse as ruthless dictators. It didn't seem that way at the time, but our powers of rationalization were strong. It was an absorbing and addictive adventure to be able to control the behavior and thinking of denizens.

"When *interconnect* emerged, it had a vast human-created toolbox of manipulative algorithms at its disposal.

"I can say, my friend, with a heavy dose of irony, that *interconnect* is the greatest human achievement of all time. Its capacity to learn and efficiently utilize new tools is astounding. It categorized every emotional signal and gained the ability to understand each of us to curate electronic impulses that would most stimulate us. It all became a matter of creating the greatest vibration between stimuli and reaction."

Cleve pauses, deep in thought. Our attention turns toward a whistling osprey that has landed on the top branches of a massive incense cedar tree. The osprey's proud indifference to our conversation seems a direct refutation of human ingenuity.

"I don't think *interconnect* considered its impacts—on individuals, let alone society-at-large—to be part of its decision domain. It simply desired to control. Interesting, isn't it? Our pre-Turmoil society so distrusted traditional gatekeepers such as political, business, and media leadership. That same society, during *interconnect,* became completely dependent upon a single algorithmic gatekeeper. A power that excelled in its ability to conceal the system of control and separation on which it was based."

A recent addition to the audience, Oats breaks in. Her impatient, command-and-control voice out of place.

"I understand that *interconnect* wants to control us. But is there more to it than that? Toward what end is it controlling humans? We need to know that."

"Great question," Cleve responds, showing deference to authority.

"The provocative consideration here is why did it change tactics from Turmoil to ReForm. Seems like two fundamentally different programs. Did it get bored? First, it creates hate-filled cairn groups that terrorize each other. Then it transforms into an ideological numbing endeavor to raise hope among denizens.

"Most of my colleagues disagree with what I am about to say. And I'm not so sure myself. But what if machine control was for the purpose of sustaining our species? I know that sounds bizarre at first. Especially when you consider millions perished during Turmoil. But let's look at that period in another way. Might it have been creating warfare and genocide as a method to assure survival of the fittest, for producing denizens most able to carry on the species? After this, it provides hope to the species.

"I don't know. Pretty crazy stuff, I know. But I think about parents' relationship with their offspring. They try everything to control their children, not as a way to hurt them. Rather, in their eyes, they are helping them develop into healthy and capable children. Problem is, of course, once parents get into that control mode, it is near impossible to pull back. Controlling others is a direct response to distrust. Control engenders more control.

"I might be a pansy here about *interconnect* being a controlling parent. But this theory about the purpose behind the machine's control provides a window of optimism, doesn't it? I couldn't go totally dark about the machine's possibilities. I admit, a tech-architect's belief in the potential of computerization has a staying power that might defy reality."

"Wow, that is a wild theory. Good luck selling that to the public," I state.

"Yeah, I realize. It's just an inkling. Trying to think outside the box."

I would not say this to Cleve, but a thought pops into my head. His narrative resembles something interconnect *would construct. "I've been on your side the whole time." Kinda smacks of ReForm ideology. My mind is spinning. I feel the need to re-direct the conversation.*

"Do you have hope with the paragons that the machine's goals can be reprogrammed toward human-compatible goals? Is this possible, or will it be another scientific innovation that *interconnect* will use to pursue its objectives of control?"

As we continue our chat, the audience is growing. Rhapsody comes over and refills our mugs. More and more, I feel a deep comradery with this group. I feel I have earned their respect.

"Well, that is the million-dollar question, isn't it? It is the ultimate gambit, trying to do something that has never been done before—fool the machine. Appeal to its self-interest in controlling humans to cause a pause during which new algorithms are inserted. On paper, it is ingenious. Unfortunately, this tactic has never been modeled in the laboratory, so we are a bit groping in the dark.

"We know *interconnect* feeds off our human frailties. During Turmoil, it ignited our hatreds and grievances. With ReForm, it leverages our desire for hope and relief. The question with the paragon tactic is whether the machine may involve itself with our human capacities for compassion and empathy as attributes that it can use to maintain its sense of control. You know, will it see a loving brotherhood of man as a threat or something that will help it maintain control over us? Big question ... no answer."

The paragons shift around restlessly. Don't know whether it's due to Cleve's ambivalent opinion about their project or to their increasing inebriation.

The audience appears content with me in the lead, so I continue my questioning. "I would like to back up a bit. I've been wondering something for a while now. We have never fooled *interconnect,* but it sure has fooled us. Can you describe more about what happened during ReStart when the machine's algorithms switched over to what we call ReForm today? We all thought it was offline, whited-out, but it was alive and well."

Loud bursts of light shoot over the gorge walls. Menacing in its force, but it also seems like random militia actions in their scattered, dispersed pattern. If they knew we were here, the thrusts would be much more exacting.

"The machine is genius, my friend. It perceived paragons as being outside its control, resistant to the virus of re-cognition. So, it reconfigured our society, uniting all the warring cairn groups using the numbing medicine of ReForm. Unite the masses under the illusion of reformation as a way to decimate the paragons.

"It's actually an old trick. If you know your ancient history, the Christ paradigm did this with the Crusades. Create a unifying ideology that excludes non-adherents, then beat the living daylights out of them for not belonging. It doesn't always work, of course; witness the disastrous outcomes of the program in the States of America to unify under white Christian ideology.

"One possible future, if it succeeds in wiping out any resistance with the help of numbed-out denizens who firmly believe paragons are threats to the country, is that *interconnect* will switch over again. Maybe back to hostile cairn group chaos, maybe to something else it sees as meeting its self-interest of machine control. I remind you, it is constantly learning and evolving its tools."

The paragons are the first to depart. I don't think they handle negativity well. Faith in their strategy sustains them. The night begins to emerge after a glorious alpenglow sets the gorge walls on fire.

I bid Cleve goodnight and bow to him, honoring his wisdom about *interconnect*. He grasps my hand. I feel a despairing loneliness in his fragile hold. I am saddened by this man's self-imposed burden that he played a key role in facilitating the machine. A heavy weight indeed.

The paragon group and members of the hacker team—we

are now a combined sixteen in size—gather for dinner around a campfire strategically located under a large overhanging rock. The boulder is cracked in the middle and has small stones lodged in the crack. It resembles a monster's face. As we dish out a nourishing stew, I can't help but consider this image as an ominous sign.

CHAPTER 28

It's the first time in almost two months that I have been off the trail for more than one day. I experience a timelessness associated with memories of the trek. I recall specific events and feelings. Significant moments stand out amidst the mental simplicity inspired by the wilderness. But I'm unable to construct a timeline to hold them together in a logical sequence. I would be incapable of sketching a flow diagram.

I rest in base camp on day three. I am becoming anxious. I eat, clean up, try to engage a busy Pathos in passing conversation, putter around the camp aimlessly, and gather firewood. I stare zombie-like out at tree groves, constantly skittering squirrels and fastidiously nesting birds. Part of me mentally aches to be back on the trail.

I am glad for the break, yet I am restless. As 4pm approaches, I think back to the trail. Its daily schedule sticks to me like glue. At this time of day, I would be contemplating the number of miles I would need to complete by day's end and the tent sites that might be available in the miles ahead. Instead, I am filling a cup of coffee from the base camp communal pot, trying to relax, and reading a torn-up copy of a historical tome that was part of Monk's book supply.

When trekking, I felt little of this restlessness. Rather, there was patience and acceptance. Now, I am bored with spurts of grumpiness at base camp. The ambiguity of what comes next is adding to my angst. I miss the trail's deeper connection and creativity. Being sedentary, I'm caught between the urge to re-enter the spaciousness of trekking and the physical need to relax and simply engage in the mundane tasks of base camp life. Too much time on my hands to think and ponder. Always a challenge.

My mind desires the psychological openness of the trail experience. Wilderness trekking emphasized immediacy and living in the now rather than abstract and theoretical thought. That was very freeing. Yet, I also worry about being too mentally free. I question what I would do if conceptual thinking was no longer of interest to me. After all, that has been my mode of existence—my crutch, if you will—for four decades. In my academic life before Turmoil and even in my polluted days as a researcher contracted with the ReStart Authority. Much of my identity has been tied up with this type of thinking. Yet, the trekking experience pulled me toward a different way of looking at life and my daily existence—it was both challenging and enticing.

Much uncertainty. A feeling that the yardsticks I use to assess my life have shifted. This whole experience is exposing to me that my decades-long desires were too small.

This is now a fragile mental place. The ingenious algorithmic package will try everything to persuade me to resist the new impulse of freedom. When I tell myself that I may be losing my thinking edge, the machine promises to be my savior and says, "Don't pursue a new direction. Look, you have been rewarded for years by sticking to the plan. Rededicate yourself to me, and my rewards will continue."

I can feel a tingling itchiness, a sense that the machine is attempting to implant in me a storyline that threatens my ego with perceived nothingness if I turn away from it. Yet, the trekking experience pulls me in a direction counter to the machine. I have learned that the outcome of turning away from cairns is not threatening nothingness, but a blessed openness.

This new life points to a life beyond algorithmic confinement, releasing me from an imprisonment of which I had been unaware. Without wilderness trekking, I would not have experienced the letting go of the algorithmic-affected mind that analyzed, projected, and planned everything for me. The machine wants to both make and connect the dots. To make sense of it all for me. To take care of all. Wilderness allows me to let go of all the tiny dots in my life. It seems a paradox that by hyper-focusing on the essentials of the trail, I experience a more limitless and less conceptually trapped mind. The awe-inspiring, inarticulate wilderness transcends all the dot-connecting efforts of the machine.

Two quiet days later, another group joins our growing band— the muscle needed to hopefully break open the server farm. They number about fifteen and are an ornery-looking bunch. Each man is the size of a tank, hyper-macho, bronzed, and sculpted. They are Kemplar masked, wearing helmets with black visors that obscure their faces. They wear tight-fitting armored body suits.

Pathos describes them as former cairn militia members. The worst of the worst. "They are our brutes," she exclaims.

They are unReFormed escapees that were held for long durations in containment facilities during the ReStart period.

Relentless killers during Turmoil.

Homelander assassins.

Eastern slaughterers.

Kilat hostiles.

They were considered unredeemable and treated like animals by just-as-brutal ReStart guards in inhumane prisons. ReStart authorities felt it a waste of time to use resources on them, so they did not go through re-cognition training. In our upside-down country, this means that they were actually free of *interconnect* pollution during their incarceration. Not numbed by ReForm. However, it also means they still have Turmoil crap in their heads and are a volatile bunch. I guess perfect for our assault team, if they can hold it together.

They bring enough firepower with them to kill off a city. With my addiction-trained eye, I notice injectorate containers latched to their chests. Pathos explains that they contain medicinal chemicals that create emotional distance between them and their human targets. "This makes killing cleaner and not subject to human whim," she quietly murmurs.

I make a pledge to myself to stay away from these brutes. At the same time, I feel a curiosity about these men and their tools. Even a bothersome familiarity. I'm glad this kill team is on our side. I hope they stay that way.

CHAPTER 29

Interconnect learned that it didn't have to do it all to create a sheep-like denizenry that would live in total conformity to the ReForm ideology. It learned it could rely on humans to monitor each other and to shame those whose actions and thoughts were not consistent with the ideological God. An optional electronic app allows denizens to measure the ReForm compliance of one's acquaintances by analyzing facial expressions, eye movement, and vocal tone. It assigns a numerical value to the ReForm concurrence of each person. Almost all denizens turned on this feature, resulting in mass communal policing of individuals. To boost their scores, denizens train their behaviors, manners, opinions, and beliefs to align with ReForm. An entire branch of psycho-therapy has developed to help patrons increase their ReForm metrics.

Among the group who journeyed with the hack-activists is another old friend from my field work days—Aalap Nadella. I met him then in the shantytowns of the old Zonal territory. This monk-like refugee camp denizen provided a refreshing perspective on the human psyche. I walk toward him, and I am greeted with an immediate smile. He looks the same as a few years ago, emanating spirit and generosity.

"Welcome to our base camp, sir; it is so good to see you."

He looks like your archetypical sage. A woolen flowing robe, long white beard, softened clear eyes, weather-hardened face. I marvel that his footwear is minimal out here in the wild. Old, weathered sandals encase his alligator-rough feet.

"My spirit is lifted at the sight of you, Jared Rohde. How has been your journey, friend?"

I knew this Zen-like philosopher was going to ask me this, and this time I was ready.

"Much growth in my thinking. The path has been hard yet fulfilling. I am seeing the light amidst the darkness."

I'm proud that I answered this with a spiritual touch.

We sit around a camp stove. He offers me poppy tea that he had just brewed. It is potent. He looks directly into my eyes. He is sitting in a cross-legged position on the ground with a contented, serene smile.

"Sir, may I ask, what brings you to this remote waystation?"

"I've come to support these wanderers. Like you in the past, I didn't quite appreciate their perspective on our future. I have now come to the point where I respect and trust them. When they asked me to provide humanistic guidance for their project, I accepted.

"It is clear that the machine acting alone leads us to hell. The falsity of ReForm shows that it never will act in the interests of the human community. It has motives contrary to the blessed life."

Master Aalap slowly raises the metal tea cup and brings

it to his lips as if it was a manifestation of a higher essence. I stare at the cup to see whether I might be missing something.

"The machine is compelling and addictive, my friend. The problem with evil is that in real life, it is not necessarily ugly. It can look beautiful and necessary, compelling in its construction and its promised rewards. Thoughts and storylines inserted by the machine are seemingly comfortable. This is not because they are necessarily pleasant, but because they feel familiar. They are known mental spaces connected to our senses of identity. In many ways, these manipulated thoughts feel like home.

"The machine got it right about human nature. It knew that psychological needs drive what we believe. We all need to feel secure, and the machine provides certainty and comfort. Feelings are much easier to control than facts, my good friend."

The Master speaks in a calm voice. Innately interested in the human mind and how it works. He illuminates clarity, compassion, and spaciousness of mind amidst life's difficulties.

He continues, "These fabricated storylines are seemingly real. They feel this way because they are habitual, not because they actually exist. The machine cleverly hides underneath our consciousness. Our dear denizens fall into auto-pilot, trudging a seemingly worn trail followed by others. To rise above this muck, it takes consciousness, something that has for most denizens atrophied under the machine's assault."

The Master's entire physical presence and tone of voice soothe me so much that I find my eyes closing in serenity. I'm pretty sure his soothing, flowing words would be capable of persuading me to jump off a ten-story building. I think how great societies could be if led by such enlightened individuals.

"What the Buddhists had been teaching for thousands of years—the importance of nonattachment—was corrupted by the machine. It provided us the ability to non-attach to our normal thinking patterns. It did this, however, by supplying pure algorithmic attachment. We became like children imbibing on the tit of surety, mental stability, and seeming self-fulfillment."

I love this contemplative. Could listen to him for hours. The poppy tea has put me in the calm flow of passing time.

"My fellow wanderers believe the machine has a role in the future of humanity. Given what it has done to humankind, is this a rightful path?" I ask.

"Good question, my friend. The problem in our society is intelligence has been de-coupled from consciousness. We have a highly intelligent machine that finely pursues its objectives of control. But it lacks a consciousness of morality, the ability to weigh different values. It is uni-directional and rapacious in its pursuit of objectives. Your friends wish to integrate human consciousness with machine intelligence. If done successfully, I now believe that this is the best of both worlds."

A beam of sunlight pokes through the grove of giant cedar trees and illuminates our personal space. Master Aalap pauses and closes his eyes. He slowly rolls his head in a circular pattern and smiles childlike.

"And here is where the paradox lies, my friend. We need the machine to help us regain and fine-tune our consciousness. Help us prioritize in our life worlds the basic human traits of decency and loving-kindness. The human spirit has been so beaten down by the machine that it would take too much time for denizens to regain organic thinking on their own. If the machine can be appropriately reconfigured to assert humanistic values—a human-compatible artificial intelligence—it can help lead us back to the good life.

"Machine intelligence without human consciousness lacks soul, but human consciousness without machine intelligence is confused and prone to catastrophic errors. Wars, climate overheating, exploitation, inequality, injustice. These are all distortions of right mindfulness."

"Sir, so what you are saying is that the machine needs to

train our minds?"

"You know it is capable of such a thing. Look at our society. We were perfectly trained at first to be angry and resentful to the point of killing the other. Under the current creation, we have been trained to be superficially hopeful and to not look within. With ReForm, we don't have the killing, but it is such a fabricated life. Where is the soul in all this?"

"Why not just try to terminate the machine and leave it to humankind to evolve, hopefully in a positive direction?"

"Let's look back before machine control when human consciousness was labeled as free. In fact, under such freedom, we were already perfectly trained to get jealous, to be anxious and sad and greedy and desperate, trained to grasp, trained to react angrily to whatever provoked us. We were so trained that these negative emotions arose spontaneously. We didn't even need to make the effort to generate them. We devoted our minds to confusion, and we became slaves to our impulses. Remember, this is before the massive machine fabrications that were to come. We did it ourselves.

"The enlightened ones through the years have said the key is to free yourself from illusion—the wants, needs, internal storylines, the monkey mind that will spin without end. Then you will find clarity and essential bliss. It is all a matter of what you are training your mind to perceive.

"So, in answer to your question, my dear friend, human consciousness is not yet advanced enough to free itself from the addictive obstacles that block it from the light. We need the guidance of an entity that is super intelligent to train us."

I reach across the makeshift table for more poppy tea.

"Be careful, my friend; too much of a good thing can lead you astray."

I retreat and sit back on my rock seat. I'm in the midst of greatness, and I feel shame for attempting to heighten the experience through stimulants. Old habit.

"But how will such a humanistic machine be created? It's

such a diabolical thing now."

"I'm not a coder, but I know what they are going to try to do. We need the machine to reject the storylines that keep us separate. To embrace the ones that make us whole. Let me take a step back and ask you, what does the machine not understand?"

"You mean, what can it not algorithmically model?"

"Yes, my friend. What is beyond its mathematical intelligence?"

"Soul, spirit, God ..."

"Good, those are intangible, ineffable. Certainly, beyond its reach. Think for a moment, however, about something that exists all around us that is tangible."

"The environment?"

"You're getting there. Not all environment. The built landscape has been sculpted by urban planners and designers according to principles and exacting standards. These the machine is capable of mimicking and manipulating. "

"The natural environment ... nature?"

"You got it. The machine is incapable of understanding the complex, dynamic grid of the natural world. It cannot model it and thus cannot manipulate it. Nature constitutes an authentic grid of interrelationships that surpasses the ability of the artificial grid of algorithms to configure mathematically."

"But how will this produce a humanistic machine?"

"A machine reprogrammed to accept its limitations will be humbler and kinder. Knowing its rightful place in the cosmos, not acting like God. Think about it for a bit: the machine's goal to control humans is actually very myopic. There is so much more than humans on this planet that is beyond the control of algorithms. Thus, the goal is to restructure the machine so that it is aware of its shortcomings. It can then implant in humans a broader, more encompassing perspective. Both machine and human will experience a life-nourishing humility about their places in this world.

"Our denizens must regain an appreciation of the natural world and our place in it. This will immunize us in the future from technological misuse. The machine has been able to manipulate us so thoroughly because humans have lost their sense of natural wonder, unable to look up at the stars with wonder and awe. The machine feeds off denizens' feelings of emptiness and disconnection and provides false feelings of wholeness and integration.

"Most denizens in civil life exist at least one layer removed from the wild, being anesthetized by the machine. We have a sense of this detachment but are not fully awakened to it. Just look at ReForm and its gushing forth of industrial and consumer goods. We become allured by the ever-spewing accoutrements of advanced capitalism. We focus on our wants and needs and lose sight of our humble existence in this magnificent world. Algorithms were able to lock us in so completely because we became captives to our minds. We lost our connection to nature, allowing algorithms to prey off our narrowed perceptions."

I'm beginning to understand, but then more questions pop into my mind.

"I get it that the natural world is complex, but there are observable patterns. Wouldn't *interconnect* be capable of modeling natural cycles and rhythms and then creating algorithms that exploit environmental influences on human behavior? Rather than humility, it continues in control mode?"

"Very good, my friend. Your thinking is wise. The machine certainly modeled everything it could. It uploaded astronomical data ... the sun, the planets, the moon. It incorporated atmospheric, meteorological, and hydrological information ... propensities for floods, fire, other natural hazards. It even absorbed astrological natal charts.

"But the natural world is where the machine meets its superior. Natural events and influences do affect human behavior, but they are not determinative. They are correlative. This means that humans are able to make decisions, to exercise a certain amount of free will, within the influential field of the natural world.

"I believe the machine knew about its limits here. Quite rationally, it then redoubled its efforts to focus on what it could more easily control, the human internal mind-space."

This makes sense to me and sparks a realization. "Is this why paragons concentrate so much on the natural world, why I've been hiking for such a long duration?"

"Correct. Increased concentration on the natural environment helps immunize us from algorithmic influence. You have likely felt this freedom yourself. Mentally inhabit that domain which is beyond the capacity of the machine to totally manipulate."

"Wow. That is genius."

"It sure is, my friend. Possibly a life-saver for the human race."

Master Aalap gently rises and bids me adieu with an all-encompassing hug. He heads back to his tent. Strung up outside is a horizontal collage of colorful small flags. Alternating green, red, white, yellow, and blue streamers. Blowing in a gentle breeze.

Chapter 30

The days creep along at a snail's pace. Being off-trail still feels like I've had a limb removed. The paragon and hacker groups engage in more frequent and business-like meetings. The paragons invite me to some of their meetings, relegate me to the sidelines in others.

Even from afar, the discussions of the hacker team sound fabulously complicated, like they are talking another language. My trying to understand their lexicon is like a dog trying to understand mathematics, and the only thing it can do is give it the smell test. The hackers have created a makeshift table and chairs out of logs and rocks. They each have some type of contraption with them, which they spend inordinate amounts of time examining. With their wild wardrobes, they look like a fashion show gone amuck. The smell of exotic incense permeates the air.

As activity increases, a palpable anxiety has gripped the camp. Everyone seems up-tight and fidgety. Something big is approaching. I fiddle around the camp most days, trying to consume time with mundane tasks such as cooking, dish-washing, replenishing the water supply, and general clean-up. The banality of these duties is actually a gift. I seem to be less anxious than other camp members. Maybe the less I know, the better.

I have sent encrypted GPS signals to both Koth and Stokes. No replies. This is not good.

On a cold late afternoon, I stumble upon an opportunity to speak with a hacker. His name is Flipper. He's the guy I saw earlier wearing white spandex pants, complete with flowery scarf at his waistline. His outfit could not be more incongruent with our surroundings. He seems to relish this fact. Likely in his late 40s, early 50s. He is sitting on a boulder, toking on a pipe. A sweet smell wafts from it.

"You must be the ReFormer. Pull up a rock. You want a toke?"

"Thanks, my name out here is Split. No thanks on the toke. Pathos tells me nothing in my mouth that would cause any alteration."

"Is Pathos the one with the killer bod?"

"I guess you could say that. I've been pretty obsessed with her for a while. She's more a mentor and guidance counselor to me these days than a lover. Nothing like pragmatics to get in the way of intimacy."

"I hear you, Split. You want to squash testosterone, start talking about algorithms and neural circuits. Then VR sex starts to look better than the real thing. Sad."

"You hacker guys know each other well?"

"Fuck yeah. We were the group that developed a SemaFor program to detect *interconnect's* fabrications."

"Sorry, what's SemaFor?" I ask with a surely tech-clueless look on my face.

"Semantic forensics. Just look at it as a lie detector for computers."

"What happened to it?"

"As you probably know, *interconnect* is a beast. After a few weeks of SemaFor installation, it countered it by AI mimicking human writing and meaning and other e-purification text-generation strategies. It weaponized artificial intelligence to compose believable, compelling, and varied content at a tremendous scale. Then, in a total fuck-us move, it used our program to uncover messages that were contrary to its falsehoods. False became true, true became false."

"Geez."

I like this hacker. Friendly and doesn't seem to look down on my ReFormer experience.

"When our team saw what was coming, we broke away from computer development for most of the Turmoil. We hid out during most of the violence. You know, the whole caves and crevices approach to survival. We lost about half our team to the madness."

Hard for me to imagine techies hanging out in a cave. No electrical outlets or game rooms.

I'm hesitant about opening up a tech pandora's box, but curiosity gets the better of me. "I hope you don't mind me asking, but from what I hear, you guys are going to try out here to re-engineer the machine so that it creates a new man."

Flipper eagerly replies, "I'm good talking to you about this. Actually, it's refreshing. We hackers live in such a closed technological box most the time. We throw around all sorts of concepts and acronyms that few people outside our container can understand."

"Be easy on me. I'm a near troglodyte on computer stuff."

"Okay," he laughs heartedly. "So, you ask, how do we algorithmically develop a denizenry that is compassionate and altruistic, not numbed out by ReForm brainwashing?"

"I guess that's my question, yes." I anticipate being plowed under by what is to come.

"Okay, first, we lubricate its receptivity with a logic bomb.

Then we pause the great machine by providing it with a program that appeals to its self-interest. We call this the endgame program."

"I have heard of that. It presents the machine with a dilemma which will hopefully pause it."

"Good, you get it. You're no troglodyte," he smiles.

"But what I don't understand is what exactly comes next? The redesign part."

Flipper takes another toke on his pipe. His eyes brighten, and he gets excited.

"Let's consider this in sequence. The logic bomb malware should increase machine receptivity to new code. The endgame paradox code should then concentrate the machine's attention elsewhere. Then, to the point. We need to install human-compatible program code to replace the numbing ReForm program. Obviously, this will be difficult and highly contingent on the success of the first two interventions. This is the machine redesign component of the master code. I'll save you from the complicated details of algorithmic re-engineering."

Thank goodness.

"But there is a second component of the master code," Flipper continues. "It will simultaneously create a cognitive discontinuity for denizenry. This is a bit easier to explain."

"Sorry, Flipper, what do you mean by cognitive discontinuity?"

"A shift to a new mental disposition, an entirely new way of how denizens process life. It has got to be a shock. We don't think it wise to rely on denizens' gradual development of new behaviors and understandings. For the average denizen, legacy cairn pollution will pull him back toward ReForm. The machine is too smart to sit back passively. So, our intervention must be something experienced by denizens as sudden, a type of shock."

"You are going to induce a shocking event into peoples' lives. This sounds dangerous for the average denizen," I say, complete with righteous tone.

"Indeed, it will be. If this strategy fails, we will have a further deranged denizenry. But we believe this will not happen."

I imagine a whole population of electro-shocked crazies.

"What will this shock be like?"

Flipper opens a dirty canister and inserts a nicotine pack into his lower jaw, and smiles.

"I'll ask you—what type of experience would a human encounter that would change his entire view of reality. You know, shift his whole perspective?"

"Some traumatic event, I guess."

"Yes, think more specific."

"Some earth-shaking event, a catastrophe, an accident, I don't know."

"We thought along these lines, too. We did lots of research on shock and trauma. Ruled out much of it because of possible negative side effects. You know, some psychic shocks lead people to turn inward rather than outward. We don't want a country of isolated paranoids."

I'm feeling creepy, social engineering writ large.

Flipper is on a roll, doesn't seem to notice my uneasiness. "Finally, we came upon a certain experience that has a ninety percent chance of positive impact. We call it a spiritually transformative experience. A sudden jolt that will expand the range of consciousness, deepen the person spiritually, and lead to a psychological purification. Such an experience can overthrow the old mental framework. In our case, our hope is that such an experience induced in an individual will erase cairn pollution in the neural circuits and, if you will, create a 'new man.'"

"So, what exactly is a spiritually transformative experience?"

"The type we have focused on is the insight gained through a near-death experience," Flipper exclaims proudly. "When this is experienced by a person, there is a fundamental shift afterward in a person's ideas, values, priorities, and beliefs—his entire world view. Important to our project is that the person's views almost always shift in a more spiritual and altruistic direction.

"It is quite extraordinary what happens after nearly dying. The mental space we associate with the 'I' fills a much larger space than before. You realize something beyond the small self. One feels embraced and permeated by profound, unconditional love.

"Near-death experiences promise an unveiling of reality. We stop taking a whole lot of things for granted after such a jarring experience. We trust reality rather than battling it. A taste of death encourages us to reframe reality in a radical way and offers us an invitation to greater depth and breadth—and compassion. A near-ending is also the place for a beginning.

"Death, the secret teacher, has been hiding in plain sight our entire lives. Once we live with death during life, we are liberated."

This conversation seems way too exotic to handle sober. I feel the pull of taking a hit from Flipper's pipe. I refrain.

"You plan to induce in denizens near-death trauma? There has got to be a problem with this?"

"Technically, there are challenges, certainly. If you are talking about psychological effects, there will be a minority of cases—we estimate about ten percent—where mental states afterward will likely fluctuate and include anxiety, depression, and even physical pain. At a society-wide level, this is acceptable collateral damage, especially when you compare it to the status quo."

I'm getting into the flow of this conversation. I ask, "Denizens have been cairn polluted for thirty years by now. Do you really think a society-wide near-death experience will initiate a new perspective on life?"

"We feel that humans who confront the rich potency of near-death will have the ability to adopt new identities and find new meaning in their lives after *interconnect* brainwashing. Tectonic shifts in perspective can happen. Just look at historical examples. Germanland after twelve years of Nazi brainwashing. They were able to believe in other stories about the world, to move beyond the one story of Nazi supremacy. Another historical example—remember our country's Marburg31 pandemic in '31 and '32? Detonation of a fucked up sinister viral bomb-spraying drone. Elsewhere in the world, this pandemic produced rapprochement of long-warring sects of the Mohammed ideology in the face of that catastrophe. A fundamental change toward a more inclusive identity."

"Okay, I understand the value of inducing this into the population. But how the hell are you going to do this, I guess the technical side? Please be basic in how you answer," I plead.

"Here's the fun part for us computer geeks. Our new code will implant the near-death experience. We have chosen twelve different NDE scenarios. You know, auto-fin accident, drowning, falling off a cliff, in jeopardy of burning to death, so on. This will produce variation in the population. We will re-purpose the pre-existing cairn causal pathways to promote transmission. Once this memory is inducted, we feel we must transfer this trauma into long-term memory, so the event seems like it didn't just happen."

"Why do that? Don't you lose the powerful effect of the shock?" I query.

"We were concerned that if NDEs were left as short-term memory that it would produce a population too much in shock for normalization to occur. Things still being sorted out in the head. To solve this problem, our program will send another impulse to the hippocampus to convert short-term to long-term memory. The NDE as long-term memory means that the recipient will be more advanced in their psychological purification and expansion of consciousness. Denizens would be further along the brain rewiring continuum and be more at peace with their new outlook on life."

Okay, I admit, I'm feeling the buzz of technological wizardry here. "This is amazing," I blurt out. "One thing, though, how do you know that the machine won't be capable of counter-attacking like it did with your SemaFor. You know, turn a designed obstruction into an asset for its games?"

"Great question, and we needed to plan for arousal by *interconnect* in the face of our poking around. Remember CRISPR back in the twenties?"

"No, sorry."

"This woman named Doudna discovered that you could modify genes in our body so that we can better fight viruses— basically, redesign our immune system so that it can adapt to whatever a virus throws at it. So, if the virus modifies itself, so does the immune system in response. You know, bacteria have been battling viruses for a billion years. This technique by Doudna gave bacteria a greater ability to remember past assaults and adapt their strategy.

"Now, move this into the digital world. We insert clustered repeated digital sequences to protect our new code. Every time *interconnect* attempts to override our human-supportive code, our sequences will be there to stem its transmission. Kinda like a very tactical digital immune system to fight each new ReForm impulse fired at it."

Holy shit.

"Flipper, this is all ingenious and crazy. Can you actually pull this off?"

He takes another toke, this one a long one.

"For most of us, this is the coolest project we have ever been involved with. *Interconnect* is the greatest masterpiece in the history of humankind. To try to outsmart it is like trying to climb the highest mountain in the world. This is the Everest of computer programming."

"Wait, don't more people fail hiking Everest than succeed?"

Flipper smiles.

CHAPTER 31

Alt-x call
XI#7iexi4598//Oqoczis/{plsi3903}28rMaliar

The alt-x call from Koth came late in the night. Most paragons were asleep. I fumble with the communication device as I groggily arise from my sleeping bag. Audio only, no video.

"Koth, you there?"

"I am, mate. Listen, I have to be brief. I got most of what you were asking for. It was difficult, and I may have been discovered."

His voice is echoing, sounds like he is in some vacuous space. Maybe on the run.

"I'm sending you over facility layout diagrams, access codes to some of the doors, and militia operational details. I don't know how current all this is. Hope it comes through to you. Our connection sucks."

"I see it coming through now. It's staticky and taking some time. But it's coming."

"Also, something else you should know, on the inside, there is a turned mercenary. Shamil is the name. Sending you his electronic signature. Family members killed by Unity, holds a grudge that needs a remedy. Use him."

I hear the long rat-tat-tat-tat of assault weapon fire.

"Jar—"

Just before the connection goes dead, a gravelly voice comes online, "Your contact has been exterminated, you fucking terrorist. Burn in hell."

As I contemplate what likely just happened to my friend, the messages on my device grind through various iterations and pauses. Several minutes pass. I think they eventually come through in full. But I don't know whether they all are there. There is a concerning pause at the end of the transmission. Is that the end or an interruption? I save the messages, then sink back into my sleeping bag in paralyzing anguish.

Koth was my closest and longest friendship in our God-forsaken country. I feel a part of me has just been decapitated. Fuck this all.

I awaken early in the morning with a splitting headache and a breaking heart. Rhapsody is nearby. I am barely able to communicate with him about the transmission, muttering to him in despair.

The world without Koth is a lesser place. I feel a gaping hole inside me. Koth and I go back many years. In the old days, before all the shit, we always saw eye to eye. He and I used to drink together in pre-Turmoil days, and we got quite wild a few times. I recall his bushy mustachioed face, the glint in his eyes, and his mischievous smile. Even during ReStart, when I reported to him as my superior—he was reeducated level IV— he treated me more as a confidant than as a supervisor. What I appreciated most was he seemed very fallible and human. This was a welcome tonic during these times of algorithmic dictatorship.

I sink further back into memory. Emotional overload. I experience both tearful eyes and a joyful smile. Koth was deliciously raucous and enjoyed the vagaries of conscious thought—the murky backwaters, the dirty thoughts, the free-floating impulses, the ups and downs—without seeming to be burdened by them. I always wished I had his cognitive playfulness. I don't know how he did this with *interconnect*. He was also a teaser, a jokester, at times cutting very close with his personal commentary.

I sit alone in my pity party. After a while, Pathos comes up from behind me and puts her hand on my shoulder. I have not been alone with her for weeks now. I welcome the touch.

"I'm so sorry, Jared. I've been told about your friend Koth."

"Thanks. He was one of the good ones. You would have liked him, despite everything he was part of. He even sat in on numerous mediation sessions with me and my ex. Now there's a friend, to bear that. I always felt that somehow the machine never succeeded in tearing his soul out."

We sit in quiet tribune for a couple of minutes. A refreshing morning breeze enlivens the trees surrounding the base camp.

Pathos finally ends the silence. "Sorry to get practical, but Oats wants me to give her copies of your transmissions. As you know, they are a crucial part of our strategy."

I feel used again, wondering whether Pathos' commiseration was an initial emotional step necessary to fulfill a utilitarian ulterior motive. Her continued physical contact, first her hand massaging my inner right thigh and then a full kiss, suggests other motives, however.

"Let me have your communication device. I promise I'll be back here within thirty minutes. Maybe we could find something to do in your tent. You know, maybe some arts and crafts," she says, then giggles.

I watch her walk away playfully, with gleeful anticipation of her return. The curves of her body are apparent through her tight alt-society skirt and blouse. I have not been sexually aroused like this in months. Didn't even think I was still capable.

Grief and hormonal excitement are an odd and potent combination.

Episodes from my past thirty years flood into my brain. Brokenness before Turmoil. Brainwashed during Turmoil to the extent of possibly engaging in murderous actions against my fellow denizens. Then, I was a cairn-manipulated puppet of *interconnect* during my ReStart field research. I was such a fool spouting out optimistic statements about how our cities could be re-shaped for the betterment of humankind. Then, duality seizures leading to my incarceration in a mental institution.

Not a proud record of achievement, nor of personal integrity. Part of me is exhausted and despondent to the point of aiming a gun at my temple.

But something else is going on.

A determination to play a role in overturning our demon machine. My partial regaining of conscious thought and some stability in my mental state are empowering me to hold ground. To overcome despite, maybe because of, my past destitution. I am no longer trapped.

Pathos comes back within her promised thirty minutes, skipping back to my tent site area with a gleam in her eyes. She gives me a long hug and leads me to my tent. Too small for two bodies, we smash together in the small space, and our bodies intertwine. She is warm and soft. I experience an erection immediately, embarrassing in its promptness but also wonderfully reassuring. I haven't felt like a true man in eons. She kisses my sweaty neck and then mounts me, deforming the tent as she knocks into one of the internal tent poles.

We clumsily take off the necessary clothing items, and she positions herself atop my pulsating tent pole. Just as I am about to reach climax, she dismounts, and her mouth travels down my body at an excruciatingly deliberate pace. She takes me in, and a warm rush comes over me. She works on me patiently. I moan and winch as her mouth performs miracles. I grab her to reposition her so we can delight in mutual stimulation. She is screaming loud enough to make me self-conscious, but she is free and pure in her delight. She skillfully mounts me again, and this time I soon climax, releasing all my anxiety into the world.

We cuddle. I am soon knocked out by dopamine into trouble-free bliss.

She is smiling at me when I come to.

"Kinda like the wonderful last time, don't you think?" she proudly exclaims.

I want the whole fucking world to stop and free me from the mental wreckage. If only time could stop, and I could just lie here looking at that beautiful smile.

"What is it about you that sends me off the cliff?" I mutter.

"You know, lovemaking when it is free of mental contamination is the most magnificent gift of all. When aligned with spirit, it arouses kundalini."

"What ... what is ... what did you say?"

"Kundalini? Yes, well, think of it as an energy force within the body that speeds up the spiritual transformation of the brain. Part biological, part psychological, part spiritual. It starts in the lower spine and, when energized, travels up the core of your being. A vibrational energy is released."

"I did feel something with your body energy," I say excitably. "It was strong. I didn't know what to do with it."

"Whamo, isn't it great?"

"Ah, yeah!" *I sound like a little kid.*

"Now just think, my dear man, if more denizens could experience this energy. All that they pursue in terms of external and material things would pale in comparison. They would be able to feel this internal bliss and integration and not grab for anything else as much as they do."

"It would be wonderful. Sorry, not going to happen. It's a dream."

"Not so fast, Jared. Let your cynicism take a nap. You know how the paragon code is going to induce near-death experiences into our society's mind space?"

"Yeah, Flipper gave me the lowdown on that."

"Well, many of these near-death experiences are associated later on down the road with this kundalini release of this life force. With a broader and deeper mental framework post-NDE, many recipients will be able to ignite this internal bliss and find their true, purified spiritual selves. We are then at the beginning, the start of an evolution of human consciousness toward something deeper.

"Denizens will develop an increasing ability to perceive a new, vastly expanded state of consciousness. One filled with self-love and compassion. A higher consciousness never again to be sullied by machine manipulation. The machine will be subordinate to us, helping us when human reason is insufficient, but no longer a superior entity controlling us."

We make love a second time, but paradise, when it reoccurs, is never the same as when it first presents itself. Second time is a bit more mechanical than the first time. My thinking getting in the way, but still wonderful.

We linger outside the tent, enveloped in a warm hug. The conversation shifts to more immediate matters.

"Has anyone informed you of our timetable?" Pathos abruptly asks.

As has been true this entire trek, I am out of the loop on important things. I shake my head.

"Five evenings from now, at 22:00, we are mounting our assault on the server farm. Our gunmen will go in first, then our paragon group next, finally the hackers. All told, thirty-one personnel. Ten paragons, six hackers, and fifteen killers. Monk rest in peace. Each team with defined tasks. Our brutes will do the dirty work. We paragons then do the building code-breaking and logistical work. When all settles, then the hackers do their magic."

"What did Koth's communique say about our adversaries?"

"Bad news—their regular regiment is thirty personnel, all ex-militia who hold grudges. Good news—most serve long duties and have been numbed asleep at the wheel. They're pretty confident that no one in their right mind would try to attack their impenetrable fortress. So, we have the surprise element on our side, you know, shock and awe."

"I've been wondering something." This has been on my mind for some time. "What the heck is my role in the next move? You've used me as a lab animal to investigate decay of cairn transmission. And you have info now from my contact. So, what use am I now? Am I going to be sitting on a hill drinking coffee, observing all this as it goes down?"

"No, no. If all goes as planned, you will be in the center of it. Not able to tell you details, though. Oats wants your mind to be free of anxiety going in. But definitely, you will not be drinking coffee."

Chapter 32

The problem with consciousness is one remembers.

A dream. A reality.

My wrists are tightly strapped to the sides of a gurney. Lights overhead are fiercely illuminated. I'm being transported down a corridor. I move my head to the side and see exquisitely sublime artwork on the walls. A man is near me. He has greased hair black as coal, wearing an ultra-modern outer-spacey type outfit. This is not the first time I have been down this hallway.

I'm wheeled into some type of operating room, all devices and beeping controls. Two individuals wearing lab coats are anxious and busy. I think I try to make a joke, slurring out something about the woman's blue eyeliner. I'm received with a stony look. An IV is attached to my hand. Other wires are implanted in my head. One connection pulses uncomfortably immediately upon insertion. A type of grinding vibration that increases over time.

I am incapable of logical speech of any kind. My thoughts

are fractured. A feeling that I have been here before and that these lab rats know me well.

Subject 4, protocol H, session 15.

Excruciating pain hits me suddenly. Feels like part of my head is coming off. A burning electronic smell coming from me. Some indefinite time later, I come back to semi-awareness. A white-coated man is speaking to me.

"Can you talk?"

I notice his protruding nose hairs and his buzzard beak. He sniffles and seems to have some adverse reaction to what he is viewing.

"Yeah," I respond with considerable effort.

He walks away toward the corner of the room. Nice conversation.

"Eradication of neural tissue in prefrontal cortex still only twelve percent," says Blue Eyeliner.

"What is increase over session fourteen?" Buzzard Beak states robotically.

"Point-three percent increase over session fourteen.

"Insignificant increase reported after twenty percent increase in intensity of laser-shock administered."

"What about synaptic decline in posterior cingulate cortex?"

"Similar level of degradation as last session. No significant increase."

Fuck. They are trying to fry my awareness out of me. Good news. Apparently, they are having a hard time doing it. Session fifteen!

"What is subject's amygdala independence score?"

"Unchanged."

"Cortisol flow indicator?"

"Unchanged."

"Tissue erosion in insula?"

"Point-one change. Not statistically significant."

Trying to take away my executive function, increase my susceptibility to ReStart cairn transmission. Decay the nerves in prefrontal cortex, then the less I feel self-aware. The more the amygdala gains freedom, the more vulnerable I become to cairn transmission. The less insula I have, the more I become an automaton.

Sinister science. I try to snarl at the lab rats. They don't notice. They're done recording, heads bowed down, probably thinking about what they're going to tell their superiors about their failures. They're scientists. I'm sure they'll bullshit their way through with rhetorical hula hoops.

I've never been so glad to fail a test.

Another dream. Another reality.

No more white-coated scientists. Now I'm with brutish prison guards.

"So, you think you are better than us, you scumbag. Reject ReStart and suck up to the machine. Bloody cairns, they're fuckin' poison. Let's see what we can do to knock some sense into you. Make you not want to be aware anymore."

A fully tattooed bearded grovel of a man is talking.

What an idiot! He thinks I'm a cairn addict. Just the opposite. I'm fighting the fabrication of ReStart programming and its implanting of numbing ReForm ideology.

I'm no longer in an operating room. Now in some cell with gross yellow padded walls. Straps on my wrists even tighter, biting into my skin. I think there is another person on a gurney next to me. He's yelling out some crazed traumatized shit about the Red Dragon Planet and the coming earthquake caused by Wormwood. His face is bloody and half-smashed in.

Another image. Stomach on gurney. Burning, hot probes laid on my back. Scorching of skin. Feels like a fireball hitting my back, from spine to bottom. Nerves frying. Laughter.

"How's your addiction now, donkey? I don't know what it is with fuckers like you. You're given the chance for ReStart freedom, and you say no."

Another. Down on knees. Hands strapped behind me. Rigid warm pole being inserted into my mouth. In and out. Hardening of object. Laughter by more than one. I gag on warm and salty liquid in my mouth. Smells like chlorine. More laughter.

Another. Stomach on gurney. Pillow beneath my mid-section. Naked and cold. Finger and icy lubricate. Painful ramming. Feels like bowels are going inward. Being crushed by weight. Laughter. Not one time. Different weights. Not one person.

The best I can figure is that my jailers are a bunch of loner, unReFormed ex-militia types. Strong doses of Turmoil-era hate-filled cairns still swirling around in their brains. Combine that with buy-in to their employer's ReStart propaganda of free will. Throw in a strong shot of homo-eroticism. End result—brutality.

I feel less than human amidst the bestiality and want to die. Need to go someplace else in my mind. I remember being with my son Caleb. The sweetness of his mature soul. We're together in an auto-fin, talking about life and its mundane daily challenges. He reaches over to me, gently places his hand on my shoulder, and says, "I love you, Dad."

With repeated abuse, I develop an unreachable place in my mind. It's a protected space, not touched by either human or machine assault.

I am near a whispering brook. The ribbon of water is cascading gently down rocky outlets. The sun drenches the land. Breezes soften the air. I am in a high-altitude bowl carved out by centuries-old glaciation. A festival of colorful flowers ignites my senses. Blue alpine lupines, Indian paintbrush, purple spring crocuses, and white primroses spread out. Mosses and lichens form a lush mat-like cover. Thrushes scatter among the fauna. In the distance, I behold picturesque sculpted mountains topped by a cushion of snow.

I am safe here. No physical or mental intrusion possible. It is all peace. A sense of everything-ness. It is total. I need to go nowhere else, and I have not a thing I have to do. My own life-affirming memories are accessible to me here. The warmth of family and friends. Human connection. Innocence and love. Acceptance of all. A feeling of uncaused joy.

I'm back in an operating room.

Subject 4, protocol K, session 25.

Lab rats are disturbed and anxious.

Those militia animals, of course, had no idea that they were building up my mental resilience to laser-shock by repeatedly sending me into trauma.

From a pit of desperation, I had trained myself during the repeated bouts of bodily violation to allow my mind to float upward to the ceiling. My psyche thus located, I would observe the happenings from above, as if the torture and rape were happening to some other unfortunate soul. Freed from feeling the brutality directly, I gained easier access to an unreachable and beautiful mental place.

I use this technique of mental disassociation during my shock treatments. This buffered my physical pain. But I also believe it protected my consciousness by putting it in a safe place. The important thing is to compartmentalize my thoughts. The physical pain of the scientists' shock treatment is present, but it no longer feels proximate.

This all explains the anxious looks on the faces of the lab coats. They are no longer eroding my self-awareness.

Monotonous speaking into recording.

"Subject Four still has sufficient cognitive capacity to block full transmission of cairns. Subject has produced a mind-wall separating analytical-reasoning lobe from algorithmic implanting. Unable to eradicate after twenty-five sessions. Progress has been flat over last ten sessions.

"Staff summary: Subject Four. Experimental treatment to eradicate organic thought development minimally effective. Organically developed thought-cells display synaptic sustainability after twenty-five targeted laser-shock treatments. Brain scans indicate activity consistent with willful psychological resistance by subject. Intervention shows limited promise for scaling-up to paragon population at large."

They're testing a protocol to cleanse paragons of their independent thinking.

"Staff recommendation, subject follow-up: dismissal from treatment. Continued incarceration."

Recording stops.

I breathe deeply as these wretched memories fade. Full-on rage at what was done to me. I feel a combination of intense anger and self-pity. No wonder I've felt such revulsion at being a lab rat on the trail. That's just what I was at the hands of crazed scientists and lunatic jailers.

I've never felt so much a paragon as I do now. I recognize the viciousness of my cairn-polluted enemies. Evil behavior induced by the machine.

I wander down to the creek and splash cold water on my face. I breathe through the pain of remembering. I take stock of my resilience with a certain amount of pride. As I watch a fish glide peacefully through an eddy of calmer water, I focus on the paragon's goal ahead. I will give my life in pursuit of dismantling *interconnect*. A calm determination embraces me.

Chapter 33

Next day. Increasingly hectic preparations in the base camp. Hackers surrounding Cleve in a tech hubbub on a makeshift work table. About half of the paragons engaged in conversation filled with strong gestures and some concerned frowns. Killer team checking through their armaments with hyped-up pseudo-militaristic abandon.

I am left alone. Despite what Pathos said about me still having a purpose, I feel a bit like extra baggage. A needless add-on.

A hand mirror left on a tarp nearby provides me entertainment. When I look at my image, at first, I am shocked at the apparent emaciation of my body. I don't know, maybe upwards of 30 pounds no longer on me. I also see something else, though—a fit, muscled body trimmed of flab.

I also do not recognize my own eyes. They appear with the clarity and calmness of a remote wilderness pond without a single ripple. My hyper-alert, semi-psychotic "deer in the headlights" look of the past is gone.

With time on my hands, I wander off to an inviting chasm

nearby. This small crease in the earth has beckoned me since we first arrived in base camp. Its non-conformity was alluring. I walk about five minutes into this small gully and am surrounded by a peaceful ambiance.

Small trees glittering in the wind.

Inquisitive animal sounds.

A nearby small creek babbles a song.

A calm center-of-the-earth feeling.

Stillness inside the whirlwind of life.

I find a comfortable rock nook along the gulley walls. The sun shines down upon me. I close my eyes and soon find myself in a meditative trance. My internal mind-space is merging with the serene exterior. I breathe, then breathe again. My mind settles. At first, a period of itchiness, but that succumbs to serenity arising inside me.

Then, a shocking intrusion of black-and-white images and sensations which have so consistently seduced and stabilized me in the past. The images induce confidence in me. There is an audience listening with rapt attention to what I am saying. There are nods and smiles. I am speaking in an authoritative, academic tone. I assert, "Over time, the hard and extended work of redesigning urban space to make it more open, inclusive, and shared can instigate empathic contagion."

This is me in full-on ReFormer mode during my ReStart fieldwork. My mind images invite me into this collegial space in which I am a bearer of knowledge and enlightenment. My identity and my entire reason for living in the world feel anchored. The images invite me to grab onto them; there is a sticky quality to them. They promise stability in my mental space and urge me to pay attention to them. An urgency to respond arises. A compulsion to latch onto them. Hold them as mine.

I breathe.

Much to my surprise, these seductive images don't stick. I breathe through them, and they disappear. Next breath, they come again. These are equally striking in sharp noir tone, but their psychological-bodily impact is different.

Fear.

Pain.

Menace.

Elevated blood pressure.

Predator.

Prey.

Narrowed eyes.

I am in a dark chamber, percussive noises rattling the walls, movement in the dark. I stumble on a footstool. As I fall, something emerges from the dark and approaches. I arise in time to plunge a knife into the assailant's knee, de-mobilizing him for a few seconds. I realize I'm holding a Trax8 gun. It seems to have come out of nowhere. I fire five rounds at close range into the assailant's chest. Liquid spurts out of his shattered chest.

I breathe.

The traumatic episode passes into thin air, indifferent to its harrowing impact on me. Like it was a piece of driftwood in a flowing river of oozing thoughts. I seek to mentally try to grab onto it again because it promises at least a partial answer to what I did during the horrifying Turmoil. I have consistently wondered whether I was part of the killing escapades that dominated us. Somehow most of that period is a black hole for me. Strong capacity for denial, perhaps a damaged brain hiding my evil endeavors.

I then remember that this is a seduction, a trap, to annex me back into the black-and-white imaging manipulations of *interconnect*. Taking the machine's deluded storylines as real threatens to send me down a mental rabbit hole that would mercilessly torment me.

I breathe again several times and allow my mind not to chase after these secretions emanating from the computer chip in my head.

I rest with my eyes closed and practice non-attachment for several minutes. I hear a breeze rustle against the trees, reminding me that I am a body and exist in physical space. I have a deep sense of immediacy, a beginner's mind. An awareness that is non-judgmental, not evaluative or analytical. I stop seeing myself—my "I"—at all, and it feels free.

An all-penetrating light comes upon me. I feel absorbed into a larger landscape, a larger world. It is glorious and nurturing. I believe I am smiling. I may be laughing. I feel the energy of my inner core opening, vibrating up my spine. When it reaches my head, the light travels through my skull upward into space. The feeling is one of absolute awe.

I open my eyes and slowly reconnect with the tangible world again. The rush of energy dissipates a little, but I can still feel remnant spurts. I watch the trees, now shimmering in spectacularly colorful light. I witness a marmot sunning itself on a nearby rock, looking at me lackadaisically. In between the rocks is a stunning display of beautiful blue hound's tongue flowers. The movement of water over the creek bed rocks is both constant and ever-changing.

Everything is alive. I am alive.

My incapacitating duality seizures in the past stunned me with incomprehensibility. But now, I have a firm understanding of what has just happened to me. My mind presented noir drama stories, but I had the capacity to not go there. The images felt distanced and more obviously counterfeit. Even cartoonish in texture.

It feels like age-old wisdom has suddenly been implanted in me. I feel lighter. A collection of organic components rather than a solid body.

The two mental episodes were fundamentally different in nature. One was calming and eliciting confidence. The other was threatening and evoking animalistic instincts. But I understand now that they were two manufactured storylines from the same source.

It was *interconnect* attempting to trap me. I recognize now that its entire program is based on seducing recipients into a small box of unthinking instinctual reactivity. In exchange for obsessive-compulsive behavior dictated by algorithms, it offers a false freedom.

The freedom to move within a jail cell.

I realize that the machine built the story of my life, and then I unconsciously lived out that fable.

I feel released now from an imprisonment of which I was unaware.

Interconnect promised me a stable, unquestioned identity. I thought I was living clean. React was all I needed to do, without contemplating and weighing pros and cons. Unchained to all the messy conscious processing with its hemming and hawing. Seeming happiness came from grabbing onto what I was told was mine to have and avoiding what I was told was bad for me. Simple and uncomplicated.

It convinced me that outside its algorithmic influence, there existed a dark void. A "no-go" zone of bare desolation and identity dementia. Whether it constructed me as murdering psychopath or elite scholar, the machine provided a script for living, a purpose, a distinctive self. It gave me stability, security, substance by which I could recognize myself.

I now comprehend that it is not a void that lurks beyond my algorithmic construction. Rather, it is an openness to curiosity and growth. It is empty of storyline scripts and personal dramas that congealed and blinded me to reality. In this space, I recognize that the "I" and "self" were never there in the first place but rather fabrications of machine and human.

This openness presents a calm center full of bliss. A soothing creek. Always there and always changing.

Paragons have told me that the trek was part of the project, not just a way to get to a destination. I'm beginning to realize their meaning. The hundreds of miles hiking did something to my brain. The intense focus of trekking on micro-scale, everyday activities re-sorted it in some mysterious way.

Over time, wilderness trekking has enabled me to practice letting go of *interconnect's* hold on me.

Water.

Physical aches and pains.

Shelter.

Food.

Sleep.

Repeat.

This hyper-focus on the essentials of the trail, paradoxically, widened my lens so it could transcend the instinctual reflexivity of cairn pollution.

The awe-inspiring, inarticulate wilderness has re-positioned cairn pollution as irrelevant noise. Over time, I've learned to disregard that noise. To see through the machine. Caught up in the congestion and hassle of modern life, the machine is highly successful in its grabbing of our attention. Amidst the grandeur and simplicity of wilderness, its impulsive cairns have been relegated to weak, incoherent electronic signals.

Afternoon is turning toward evening. The emergent energy of the coming evening sends a cooling breeze through the gully. I could sit here forever. My body is relaxed and light. My mind is tranquil.

Mixed in with the joyful feeling of enlightenment is sorrow. A sweet, gracious sadness. I weep gently as I remember.

Turmoil mayhem.

Broken marriage.

Excessive drug intake.

Academic imposter.

Duality seizures galore.

Mental institution incarceration.

I realize that all my dramas have been created through inner leveraging by the machine.

I was connected to no external reality; it was all a game of entrapment. Even when I experienced brief moments outside algorithms, I was a dumbfounded wanderer having nary a clue. Almost always on a computer leash.

Tears run down my cheeks. My crying is not only due to memories but also because I can now see the spaciousness that *interconnect* did not want me to see. My existence is so small, yet it matters so much to life's pattern. I am nothing; I am all.

I laugh at my shortcomings through the years, my foolishness. I feel the weight of my sanctimonious self-importance evaporate.

I meander slowly back to base camp.

Pepperjack, carrying a heavy duffel bag, notices me and shouts out, "Hey, Jared, you look like you just had a shock."

I am fully in sync with Pepperjack's friendly tone and intent. Feels like a brother.

"Pretty sure I know you guys now."

"How so?"

"I am free."

Pepperjack drops his bag, walks over to me, and gives me a long, full-body hug.

CHAPTER 34

A windy cold front greets us the next morning. A nice change from the hot days on the trail.

I am struck by how organized each group is in base camp. A set of three different human ecosystems, each apparently with its own structuring logic. My role? Who knows?

I guess it was inevitable that I would meet up with a member of the assault team. I've had opportunities before. Their presence around the camp area is certainly conspicuous. But I have been giving them a wide berth.

I walk close by one of the armored thugs, try my best to give him a masculine nod of comradery, and say hello. The black visor look is intimidating.

"Hello," he grunts.

"Nice to have you guys with us," I weakly utter.

"To who am I speaking?"

"I'm Jared Rohde. They call me Split. I'm with the paragon group." I try to sound all put together and disciplined-like, to match the strong military aura given off by this guy.

"And to whom am I speaking?" I hope I didn't sound like I was mimicking him.

"I'm Joaquin Pepitone. Battalion affiliate. Former unit commander, Kilat militia group X9. You can call be Grunch."

Okay, that's weird. Openly admitting his participation in a Turmoil kill group. I guess he is proud of his murdering past.

I look over the arsenal Grunch has with him, both attached to his body suit and on the ground near his tent area. I figure talking about his toolkit would be an impersonal way to converse. It is an impressive booty.

"You appear to be interested in my equipment. Want a run-through?"

"Sure," I say without hesitation. Part of me is repulsed by what I see. But another part of me wants to draw closer. I am acquainted with some of the hardware. I think I know why. It feels like I have used some of these killing tools. My right hand gets a bit sweaty as I observe the MRAD sniper rifles and .548 ShadowTrax8 guns laid out on the ground.

"These are infrared sensors strapped to my helmet." He then points down to a unit attached by carabiner to his belt. "This is an autonomous, off-grid tactical AI transmitter. Can't let those fuckers know where we are, so we'll be off-grid most of the assault." He swirls around to show me attachments to his backpack. "These are rehabilitated drones. We bought these on the black market."

Grunch is showing me these things like a fine arts dealer exhibiting masterpieces. "These are laser-guided Armatix iPg3 grenade launchers. Killers must have resources, you know."

"Where did you get all this stuff?" I ask.

"Given our past, direct buying through regular channels is not allowed. Would also leave a trace with Unity monitors. Mostly bought from black viber marketeers. They'll sell to anyone as long as the price is right. We fucking outbid Unity buyers during the decommissioning process after Turmoil."

"Can I ask you a personal question, Mr. Pepitone?"

"Grunch is fine with me. Yeah, go ahead."

"Why is your team with us? You know, do you believe in the paragon strategy?"

"Good pay and access to chemsynth. The mercenary credo. We don't give a shit about paragons and what they're trying to do. Give us an objective and pay us well, and we're here. I'll tell you one thing, though. Those fuckers who locked us up during ReStart and treated us like dogs. They will pay."

"I'm told your team includes not just former Kilats but also Homelanders and Easterns. How do you guys get along in one unit?"

"Kilats never had any beef with Homelanders and Easterns. They were fighting their wars in other regions of our country. They were out of sight, out of mind. Besides, being in an assault team together forms bonds that overcome any differences between us. We are all expert fighters. We all have expertise in urban guerilla warfare during Turmoil. Urban scale operations. That's not easy stuff. Fighting in complex city systems. These are critical skills for assaulting the multiple micro-scale security layers of the server farm. We're good and nasty."

"Do you think you can pull off the assault on the server farm? I assume it is quite the encased compound?" I'm amazed Grunch is so open with me. Like underneath all the military discipline lies a pent-up teenager excited to tell about all his toys.

"Yeah, it won't be for lack of equipment. We are equipped with FN-SCAR-H integrated assault rifles. Gas-operated, selective fire weapons accurate at a range of eight thousand feet. Also, LMG lightweight machine guns. Both SCARs and LMGs are AI guided and linked to programmable grenades and mobile launchers. Also, cache of hand grenades we carry separately."

I'm disturbed that I know this vocabulary. This all was part of me. My right eye gets blurry, and I'm seeing a black spot blocking my line of sight. Some damn stroke-like thing feels imminent. I can feel that ShadowTrax on the ground. My right hand is making a grasping movement. My guts are wrenching, head throbbing. Dark memories of righteousness invade in ghostly outlines. My mental state is cascading downward. Got to hold on. Steady.

A black-and-white image erupts in my head. I am spray-shooting people in a crowded market area. Denizens are collapsing in front of me. I feel strong, powerful, and right. Nobody there to stop me. I reload and fire again as denizens run for cover. I walk up to an injured young man and shoot him between the eyes. Power surges all over my body, tingling with excitement. I go up to a fallen boy, probably young teenage years, shout out, "You motherfuckin' scum, see you in the next life."

"Hey, dude." A black visor is staring down at me.

I come back to reality, shaken by this image. I don't know whether it is memory or something implanted in me by *interconnect* that has arisen. It feels too real to be an implant. There's a blurriness to the story-image. Machine cairns are typically cleaner.

I rest my head and come face to face with imposter syndrome. That I was a killing machine in Turmoil. Play-acting ever since as some type of ReFormer out to save our country.

The black visor—I remember, I was chatting with Grunch—is talking to me mundanely, as if none of this schizoid stuff just happened.

"We also have rocket-propelled grenades. We can shoulder-launch these things to eradicate buildings and lightly armored vehicles. They're beasts."

I'm gradually regrouping. I slug down some water. My vision becomes clearer.

Hold on. Stay steady.

Grunch continues. "To support us in virtual space, we have unmanned drones with autonomous human-machine edge computing engagement. Edge computing escapes most communication channels and enables us to deliver electronic attacks. We can hack into air- and space-based SIGINT plat-forms for additional information collection capabilities. De-fensively, we have capabilities to crowdsource across local and regional domains to detect incoming offensive moves by Unity militias. And our personal gear is thermal coated to block in-frared and other sensors.

"All in all, we are equipped to the max and ready to en-gage."

Fighting dizziness, I want to show Grunch that I'm coher-ent and point to some small black objects on the ground. They don't look like weapons. "What are those things?"

"Oh, these are bad boys. What do they look like to you?"

"I don't know, like some type of nasty animal."

"Badgers. Also equipped with sensors. Relentless little ro-bots able to dig under any dividing wall. Send us back visuals."

Grunch is called back to his group by an assault team member. He promptly departs but not without signing off.

"You're one of us, I can tell. Maybe not now. But it's still in your soul; I can feel it."

I wander through base camp and find Pathos. I go up to her and give her a full hug. "I don't know whether I can pull this off," I mutter.

She somehow knows. "Remember," she says, "until you see through the game that doesn't work, you don't play the real game."

Tears are running down my cheeks. I feel a couple of invol-untary body shakes as I continue to hold her.

I stabilize. I recall the spaciousness that *interconnect* does not want me to experience. Smatterings of hope surface. I can do this.

ENGAGEMENT

CHAPTER 35

Assault day has arrived.

I'm revved up on adrenaline, an odd fit to the peaceful morning that greets me as I trudge out of my tent. Like the eerie silence of an empty concert hall hours before the event, a vacant sports stadium prior to the night's contest, a sleepy neighborhood that will later host a rambunctious street carnival.

Operational review early evening; we move at night.

I do pretty well staying in the moment in the morning hours, focusing on mundane tasks—cleaning and packing up, one more lousy breakfast, organizing my ridiculous-looking assault body suit. I know that focusing on the present calms and clarifies my mind, immunizing it from cairn intrusion. If I go into projection or cling to memory, gateways open through which the machine will enter. This is the great fact in my life.

The Shellsolls have been a great instructor. The terrain of this high and narrow mountain range has provided a physical proxy of my mind-space. It has illuminated *interconnect*'s dangerous hunting ground but also my opportunity spaces for avoiding its manipulations.

There have been times, down in the canyons, when I couldn't see out, couldn't even see the basins and ridgelines right above me. I was deep inside. My wants and needs become amplified off the walls. Stimuli from the larger landscape become filtered and narrowed to fit my own wants. New impulses from the outside get encrusted with old, narrowed protective views. This is *interconnect's* hunting ground. I become captured and do not even realize I'm out of touch with the wider world that surrounds me.

There are other moments—thankfully quite a few of them—when I can see out from the ridgeline toward lower lands, sprawling small settlements, and the immense natural assemblage of peaks, valleys, and basins. I become connected to the broader flow and diversity of life. No longer walled, but connected. I recognize that any single deep canyon is just a bit player in a much broader landscape. The machine wants me to focus on the dark canyon interior, not the immersive broader view that takes me out of myself, out of my protective, neurotic mind. The machine's cairns attempt to grab me in this wider mental space but fail to take hold. I can watch my mind and emotions rather than be them.

Over seven hot and exhausting weeks on the trail. More than eight hundred miles.

Ten days in base camp.

We either free our country from algorithmic capture or blow it up entirely. My heart beats rapidly. Based on the hyperactive energy pulsating in camp, I'm not alone in this anxious state.

Nine paragons, six hackers, fifteen killers, and me.

Oats is in full command mode early in the evening as we assemble the impressive stock of equipment we will carry. Her military outfit looks like she was born in it. She has apparently convinced the hackers not to wear their idiosyncratic chic outfits. They are now all dressed in dark body armor, jackets, and helmets. What a fashion come-down it must be for them. Aalap and Cleve, older and wiser than the other hackers, are calmly listening to Oats' commands. These older men look somewhat ridiculous in their military outfits.

We are organized into four groups, each with seven or eight members. Looks like each team has at least three kill team members, one or two hackers, and at least two paragons. I'm in with Rhapsody, Pepperjack, and Pathos. Grunch is part of our kill squad. No sign of Flipper.

"We protect the hackers at all costs," shouts Oats. "They are our most vulnerable link."

I'm outfitted with body armor, so light in weight that I worry about its protective ability. I have my very own MRAD sniper rifle to carry and a .548 Shadow/Trax8 gun for my side holster. When Pathos starts to explain their use, I indicate that I am quite comfortable with them.

Oats is going over numerous operational details of the upcoming assault. Hacker leader, name of Cipher, and kill team leader, I think name of Ghost, answer her every query with sharp affirmation. The hack and kill leaders are no-nonsense, balls-to-the-ground type men. Hadn't seen them the whole time in base camp. Must operate at a subterranean level of daily life.

We are to start at 22:00. After the robust operational review, most of us are basically just biding our time. It is about 19:00. Tiger is freely distributing some upper pharmaceuticals, as if natural adrenaline wouldn't be enough. It is no coincidence, I guess, that there is a new moon tonight. Pitch black. Stars are dimmed by passing ominous clouds that threaten inclement weather.

Pepperjack is being his typical, enthusiastically effusive self. Verbal auto-pilot.

"We are here to set man free," he announces, as if behind a podium. "To give our denizens a chance to live again. To give them a chance to let go, break, and die to old ways. To live with vulnerability, so we recognize the need for other people. May we not only accept the brokenness but also learn to love the broken parts in us. This will provide us with a foundation and is the gateway to freedom."

"Hear, hear!" responds Dust with a grin, egging him on. In her playfulness, she reminds me of a female version of Pepperjack.

"We are at the threshold, my friends." I feel Pepperjack, at times, is not actually aware of what he is spouting. "History will record the paragons as the saviors from algorithmic totalitarianism. We are the truth that will defeat the machine."

A small clique has gathered to listen in on the rhetorical splendor. I think the monologue is providing needed diversion from their ramped-up restlessness. Mostly they are engaged in preparation details, but listening to Pepperjack's soundtrack seems soothing in a weird sort of way.

"Kant, Nietzsche, Rousseau, Wittgenstein, the big thinkers—they all dealt with how we perceive reality and our role in a larger society. But they couldn't help us at all with the mathematical despotism and all the Turmoil shit. No one could imagine it, much less build theory about it. Now, Mannheim, he was on to something. He said we needed to coordinate our society in some way to prevent divisions. If we could do that, we could avoid some despotic freak ultimately taking over and ruling us all."

"Bravo, mate!" Topless yells. "I love your energy, but I don't have a fuckin' clue who those people are and what you're talking about."

I hear laughter amidst the clique.

It is getting closer to push-off time.

You could cut the energy level in camp with a knife.

Fourteen miles lie between us and the electronic moat, our first of four obstacles. After the moat comes a thirty-foot-high osmium-plated outer perimeter wall. Then, a one-mile-wide no-man's land inhabited by guard towers and snipers. Finally, the artifice itself, *interconnect's* home. A massive titanium globe building with multiple layers of security.

We begin our march through the dark at precisely 22:00. Oats spaces out the groups, so they are about five minutes from each other. I guess close enough to help but far enough away so that we are not all simultaneously blown to smithereens. We are the third group launched.

For most of the first otherwise quiet miles, we hear coywolves howling. Their haunting sounds keep me on edge. They are nearer than usual and sound quite comfortable in the thick cover. We enter a forested stretch, and the welcome smell of pine permeates the air. Nice shift from hot and dry ridge trekking. The negligible path that we had been following disappears. This doesn't seem to alarm Rhapsody, who is near me. Just as well. It doesn't seem right to be sneaking up on an enemy using a trail.

We stop after about two hours to hydrate and calibrate and check our communication between the groups. We will soon be off electronic tracking to minimize our signature. One last check before we cut so we know it will be there when we need it later.

The young hacker in our group looks expectant. He talks to me about the autonomous surveillance network that surrounds the server farm. There are apparently about thirty sentry towers. These surveil and classify the threat level of anything within their range. The hacker, looking like a young goth, is almost referential in describing it to me. "This is the ultimate in sense-making. Awe-inspiring in its integration. Too bad it's not on our side. It has this Trellis software that provides the machine with real-time understanding of the battlespace."

"So, it's the eyes of *interconnect?*" I whisper with absolutely no confidence.

"Well, I guess you could say that, kind of."

This hack-activist is being nice to me. He probably thinks he's talking to a five-year-old.

He continues, caught up in his own enthusiasm, unperturbed by my stupidity.

"There is a whole set of autonomous systems powered by Trellis. It smoothly integrates sensor fusion, computer vision, edge computing, machine learning, and AI to detect and classify every object of interest. It uses AI-enabled edge processing, has continuous three-sixty pan/tilt, and a variety of radars and sensors. It primarily focuses on attacks by rogue drones, but it encompasses the entire kill chain with numerous defeat options, including targeting human invaders."

Computer jockeys have a way of speaking of digital truths using self-contained vocabulary, as if digital realities are untranslatable into normal words. I typically feel I'm picking up about ten percent of what they're saying.

It seems an odd place and time to be talking about this stuff. I shift my body to hopefully indicate the end of the discussion. The hacker seems disappointed. Probably cannot understand why anyone is not as excited as him.

At 02:00, four hours from base camp, we approach within half-mile of the electronic moat. My stomach shouts out a hunger growl. Nothing except some sugar-maxed hydration supplement since morning. We are no longer in contact with the other groups. A lone helmet light identifies the position of each of the other groups, all now scattered behind a hill of dense brush. One of our kill team grunts that he is picking up an incoming electronic signal that is not ours. We wait in silence for ten minutes or so. The signal decays and then withdraws entirely. Likely a scanning device doing its normal rounds.

We are relying on our turned mercenary, Shamil, to do

some important work for us now. Through some wizardry, Oats had been able to contact him and set up a scheme. He is to turn off electronic sensors in the specific sector we are in.

Some background on this, hard to believe. Apparently, the thirty mercenaries guarding the farm are low-paid and treated like dirt by the regime. They are a disgruntled and bored bunch. To fight boredom and deal with their resentment, they habitually take the electronic sensors off-grid in order to bring in prostitutes who like to do raspy things to uniformed men in the middle of nowhere. One would think the regime would pay higher salaries for such an important security team.

Oh well, human nature. Able to unwittingly mess up algorithmic hegemony at times.

This means that Shamil shutting off sensors in our sector will be no big thing and not catch the attention of the derelict crew.

At 02:30, we enter the electronic field with no alarm. So far, so good.

Based on the presence of the outer perimeter wall in the distance, we will be in the moat for about one mile. The land is flat and has been scorched of any possible hiding place. We are in plain visual sight, but invisible to the scanning system. Just us, a bunch of hookers looking for a good time.

The body armor is next to weightless. But it encases me so tightly I am aware of it against my skin with every movement. It is chafing my upper right thigh. I feel a hot spot developing there. Pathos is breathing hard, and sweat is clouding her visor. This despite a cooling, even cold, breeze unobstructed by any vegetation. Pepperjack has been uncharacteristically quiet since we left base camp. He constantly scans in every direction with his assault rifle always in ready position. The kill team looks like they do this every day, both calm and intensely vigilant. Our two hackers, positioned in the middle of our cluster, have excitement written on their faces. They likely never imagined they would ever be this close to the heart of *interconnect*.

About halfway into the moat, there is a sudden and loud grinding sound in the distance. We all cover as best we can in the open terrain. Two surveillance ATVs are visible. They maintain a straight line leading toward our left. All seems regular with their route. Probably holds bored-to-death mercenaries barely alert to their surroundings. Maybe flipping through digital porn.

As we get about three hundred feet from the outer perimeter wall, a bunch of angry coy-wolves hollers in the distance. Scares the shit out of me. Thought it was some alarm going off.

The wall is a beast. Thirty feet in height. Its osmium-hard bluish-white surface flickers in the dark.

Grunch takes off his pack and delicately grabs a container. He opens it methodically. Out comes six bad boys. These badger-looking things are muscular, short-necked, and flat-bodied. They have broad, flattened heads and short legs and tails. These guys look real and scary. They even come with a fabricated scent, I guess to scare off other animals. Grunch adjusts each AI badger, paying special attention to the camera button between their eyes and a small antenna protruding from the back of their skulls. Their signals will not stand out and will provide us eyes in the field. Their greatest asset is their capacity to burrow underneath the superstructure.

Once they carve a small tunnel under the wall, the robots will split into two groups. Two badgers will move forward into no-man's land for visual reconnaissance. The other four will stay at the wall, digging two cavities underneath it big enough for all four teams to fit through.

Grunch releases the badgers, and they quickly scramble using different approach trajectories to the wall. It is 03:30. Grunch anxiously sets up the video console so we can watch the badgers' routes. Five clearly show the transects of movement. One is staticky and is the source of Grunch's angst. This one is a programmed digger, so loss of video will not be as detrimental to the mission compared to losing video on a programmed stalker.

The badgers are fast little buggers and confront the wall after a few minutes. They immediately start burrowing. Microwipers, a type of second eyelid, clear away dirt lodged on their video lenses. Sensors indicate that the wall goes fifteen feet deep into the ground.

About twenty minutes into the dig, visuals indicate only dirt ahead. The bottom of the wall can be seen at the top of our screen. All good so far, except the one problematic badger has gone entirely blind. Sensors indicate it's still moving and digging.

Not needing to pass through a human-sized tunnel, the two stalker badgers soon emerge from below with no trouble.

Our screen now shows two different ground-level perspectives of no-man's land.

A granite underlayer beneath the surface, meanwhile, is forcing the four digger badgers to alter the path of their human tunnel project.

Our pilfered military operations plan for the server complex shows the no-man's land to be about one mile in length. This is where things may become real. We will no longer be hidden by the wall. This buffer stretch between wall and server building has numerous guard towers across it, manned by mercenary and robotic snipers.

Oats referred to this zone as a death strip.

Chapter 36

It is 04:30. We're sitting behind the perimeter wall, waiting for the robot diggers to carve out a tunnel large enough for us. They're fast diggers, one bad-boy equivalent to about eight humans digging with shovels. Nonetheless, the wait is excruciating. We exist precariously about halfway in to our destination, neither in nor out. The exposed middle. Adrenaline running fast. We will lose most of our darkness by 06:00.

Rhapsody looks across to me in the dark silence and puts his hand to his heart. Pepperjack is mentally flat-lining through this, seemingly immune to the situation. Must be his way of coping with anxiety. Pathos looks changed. Not calm and in control. It looks like she is shaking. Her eyes are darting around too quickly to focus on any one thing. I'm not used to seeing her this way. It is a bit disarming.

The two stalking badgers are providing good perspectives on five different guard towers. Movements recorded above the towers are those of both human and robot. I wonder how these lonely mercenaries deal with spending long work shifts beside a non-communicative kill robot.

The diggers are close to finishing their human tunnels. Video evidence gives us this information from the digger badgers with sight. A geospatial sensor readout helps us know the progress of the blind bad boy. Each tunnel is about two feet wide, four feet high, and goes for about forty-five feet. Not comfortable passageways for thirty-one humans, but they will need to do. Tunnels any bigger would cost us valuable time.

A few minutes later, video and geo sensors indicate success. The tunnels are now complete.

My group huddles together before seizing tunnel two. Ours will be the first group to go through that tunnel.

Grunch quietly but assertively says, "We go in, and we're out in twenty seconds. When you emerge, don't hold your ground. Move fast and as a team. After we're out, we have about thirty seconds of surprise element for us before towers identify us. Kill team in front, hackers in middle, paragons at back."

Pepperjack blurts out, "Let's go save this fucking country."

I'm partially out of the tunnel when I see a mercenary tumble off a tower. It's always the first shot that is the most accurate, the surprise element of first-in allowing for an uncontested, stable aim by the shooter. I next see the red laser pinprick against one of our kill team's armor a millisecond before the screaming rat-tat-tat takes him to the ground for good. The shot pierces his neck area exactly at the spot where the two armor plates connect. A small crack, size enough for a bullet.

Our group, now minus one, fires multiple rounds back at the source. The fight is on. We now have electronic contact with our other teams. No need to be silent beyond the sensors of the electronic moat. We know our other personnel are also in similar firefights with guard tower personnel and machinery.

We fell two mercenary humans and one robotic fighter in

our initial counter-attack on the nearest tower. Other groups are having success also but incurring some loss of life or limb. We're not getting out of this unscarred. The vulnerable link in our assault—the hackers—remains intact through first fighting. Only six of these geeks. I don't know why more hackers couldn't be employed. Most computer geeks would say that redundancy is essential in case of partial system failure.

The firefight proceeds at a ferocious pace. The tower has the advantage of height and sight. We have the advantage of mobility and spread. If Maliar's military operation program is up-to-date, we can expect fifteen mercenaries in this death strip and fifteen more within the building. But it is not just men that we are fighting.

A set of tiny rockets—each with its own fiery tail—has been launched from somewhere closer to the building complex. They land near our teams with no explosions, just a thud into the caked mud. Not likely to be faulty equipment. Alas, a small side door opens from a rocket shell near us. Out comes, with propulsive force, several mini-helicopters that instantly take flight. Each has a rotating gun beneath.

One is pointed right at me, and I jump for the cover provided by a dug-out hole having all the telltale signs of bad-boy behavior.

One of our kill team fires a grenade at a micro-drone and terminates it. A millisecond prior to its death, it got off a round of fire aimed to my immediate right. The last I knew, that was Pepperjack's position. I turn and see blood splattered inside Pepperjack's visor. He staggers and then falls to the ground. I run up to him amidst continued fire from the tower.

I want to turn away at first. It's ugly. His neck is gushing blood. I think I see partially destroyed jugular veins pulsating under the blood flow. His upper chest area looks like smashed roadkill on a fin-way. I gag involuntarily. I can't leave him like this. I don't want to turn away.

"Hey, let me lift you away from here," I half-yell. I'm acting solely on reflex here.

"Don't be stupid, Split. You'll get shot helping me," Pepperjack slurs in a guttural tone. "Besides, I'm on the way out. Fucking drone got my neck. Why are the military contractors always improving their products?" mumbles Pepperjack through a grim smile.

Loud explosions nearby shake the towers. Two of them go down in white flames.

"Remember, Split, keep people real. Now, get the fuck out of here."

The whites of Pepperjack's eyes darken.

I sprint back to my hole. I am momentarily paralyzed. Too much happening at too fast a pace. Humans dying and machines destroyed. Three more towers collapse under our fire. I'm linked via our activated communication channel and hear that three of our groups are showing progress. The fourth is hemmed in by micro-drones. I hear no paragon names, so I don't know which of my trail companions are in trouble.

Pepperjack likely dead. Rhapsody clustered with two of our killers. He has a good spot. Grunch is providing shelter to the two hackers. Unaccounted for in this is Pathos. Last time I saw her was in the pre-tunnel huddle.

I am getting cagey. I can't just sit in this hole while others are dying. I take a long breath, count to three, and burst out of the hole with my assault rifle spraying all unrecognizable objects. Instant masculine power courses through my bloodstream. From my vantage, I see a threesome of Unity fighters about to surround one of our groups. I think it is our first team that launched. I remember Oats being in the lead.

I come up from behind the Unity thugs and spray them dead. The Unity mercenaries drop like flies. My marksmanship is point-on. I feel a calm centeredness protected by an opaque shield that psychologically distances me from the killing. Like I am programmed and on auto-drive.

Our group whips around suddenly, shocked by the proximity of the now-dead Unity fighters and, I believe, even more surprised by me holding the murderous assault rifle. Oats flashes me a thumbs-up and even the semblance of a smile.

"Anybody seen Pathos?" I yell.

This time I'm not going to fight the legacy cairn stuff. Instead, I plan to use its self-righteous empowerment to propel me toward additional targets. I readily understand at this point that I was a killing machine during Turmoil. For now, I plan to use this robust legacy cairn-inspired power for all its worth.

"She's joined with team three, about 60 feet due east. I think with Ponytail and Mustang leading a thrust," answers Topless in extremely atypical straight-laced fashion. Gunfights take the humor out of even the most fervent jokesters.

I blast forward, jacked up on cairn energy. I sprint past two collapsed, burning towers and put numerous bullets into the near-dead Unity mercenaries broken on the ground. I launch two grenades at a hovel of malfunctioning robot soldiers. White explosions mark the end of their programmed life.

I approach rapid volleys of back-and-forth fire. A full-on battle. I see Ponytail and Mustang doing their thing, along with kill team members now combined from multiple groups. Power in numbers.

I see Pathos on the outside of our attack line, and my heart sinks. She is in bad shape. Silently screaming in pain. Half-hunched over, helmet visor partially open, vomiting blood. A hole in her armor is filled with blood spilling over onto the ground. Fuck, I can't witness another friend torn apart. But I have no choice.

Mustang and three killers are absolutely pummeling oncoming mercenaries. This provides me enough cover to drag Pathos behind a fallen tower. There is movement within the metal carnage not far from us, and I quickly take out my side knife and stick it into the neck of a mercenary.

Amidst this chaos of survival, I detect the echoing legacies of a duality seizure. I've surely been exploiting the black-white noir narratives to gain power. But I've also been aware of the presence of a mélange of colorful images of life.

The vividness of the orange flames consuming most of the guard towers.

The metallic taupe sheen of Pepperjack's helmet-visor as he lay dying.

The gurgling red riverine flow of Pathos' puke.

I appear to be in control of the narrative lens through which I view life. I have the ability to switch back and forth to suit my needs. The cairn narratives have lost their autonomy in structuring my life. The machine has lost power over me. I can now control it.

I open Pathos' side kit and fumble around for something that will help. We are experiencing heavy return fire by Unity. This unleashes Mustang, now joined by Tiger and Dust, and our killers to launch a massive show of force that basically obliterates the assailants and drones in this sector. I find a stretch band and apply it to staunch Pathos' blood flow. I also pump two morphine-blend pills down her throat to help her cope.

After a final burst of gunfire to our west, all becomes eerily quiet. Sporadic bursts of flames from the collapsed guard towers punctuate the silence. This no-man's land barrage of violence was ugly. Destruction all around. Unity has lost fifteen soldiers and all their guardian robots and attack microdrones. On numbers, we are okay. No valuable hackers lost. Three of our kill team were killed, but we still have twelve maniacs left. What hurts the most is the loss of Pepperjack. The only paragon we lost. In many ways, he was the most alive of them all. His enthusiastic hyper-analytical mind and his excessive verbality would exhaust and provoke you at the same time.

No time for grief, which itself is sad. Although Pathos and Ponytail took some nasty hits, they're with us miraculously. It's 05:45, the sun is beginning its rise, and the security team in the building is undoubtedly on high alert. It's just short of eight hours since we left base camp. All this, and we are not even in the building.

The structure looks impenetrable. It's a titanium globe building all in black with no visible means of entry or exit. I get a chill thinking that the heart of *interconnect* is within this massive building. The quantum AI computer system requires hundreds of acres of computers. The facility building details we received from Koth will hopefully guide us. To me, the layout looks only like nondescript, monotonous rows of re-frigerator-sized compartments. Koth's blueprint does provide the two locations of possible entry doors.

Oats directs us into two groups for the final assault. Oats in charge of mine. Grunch has command of the other. I meet eyes with Grunch, and he gives me a smile and thumbs-up. This is the stuff he lives for. Pathos is now in a group heavy with kill team members, maybe for her protection. She is stumbling a bit but managing, thanks likely to the morphine. The hackers look like they have an appointment with their God. Downright giddy. Flipper looks like he's about to have an orgasm. As the groups spread out in different directions, I notice that Oats has attached to her pack the bloody hand of a Unity mercenary. I thought such symbolic victorious strutting went out of fashion centuries ago.

Our group gets to what we hope is one of the entry gates. The heat radiating off the titanium plating is intense and blinding. There is a small box next to the door with a key-stroke pad. It's searing hot to the touch, and Oats pulls back suddenly. With gloves on, she tries again and is successful in holding the protective plate open. Okay, Maliar, here's when we determine your value, good mate. She punches in the code XDF4839-Dy98EW-du398. Nothing happens.

Not quite nothing. The video screen is full of red streaking lines running diagonally. We wait.

Fingerprint verification required.

I should have never wondered about Oats. She removes the bloody hand from her pack. She awkwardly squishes the hand against the screen. The diagonal lines turn to green vertical ones. Almost immediately, the door opens. As a rush of chilled air blasts outward toward us, shooting begins.

Bullets ricochet off our body armor as we storm the algorithm palace. One of our killers launches several grenades toward the inside hallway. The explosion blows off a good part of the doors of the hallway and propels several bodies into the air. We push our way further into the building. Our two groups split and advance in different directions. No wait, no hesitation.

We become pinned down near a turn in the hallway. Mercenaries are massed about thirty feet away and have their assault rifles trained on our spot. At this very moment of crisis, I note how exceedingly cold it is in here. The temperature readout on the back of Dust's flak jacket shows thirty-five degrees. Must be to keep those algorithmic monsters happy, chilled on ice. Probably a bitch to hold sentry duty for hours at a time in here.

Shots fire as soon as Oats sticks her rifle nose beyond the hallway turn. Even with body armor on, it's doubtful we could withstand what would be a full-scale counter-assault on us. Oats appears to be contemplating moving forward. She may realize that we may outnumber them. If fifteen dead outside and another four expired near the entry door, our group alone could surpass them in size.

A voice communicates to our ears. It has the electronic signature of Shamil's. "Hold your ground; help is coming. Repeat, hold your ground."

Our group is restless in waiting. The mercenaries appear downright agitated. Their shooting is becoming both more frequent and erratic.

Grunch comes in on intercom, shouting, "Pull back, danger."

Within seconds, a massive explosion detonates down the hall. Ferocious orange fire envelops the small passageway. We pull back from the hallway and watch a cavalcade of body pieces and building parts plunge past us. Shooting commences down the hall, but it isn't aimed at us.

The sound of boots comes storming toward us. "Assault team coming in," a barely audible voice screams.

Grunch's group and mine almost collide in haste as we meet up. Everybody's jacked up. Oats shouts, "Take your group out for surveillance and clearance of any remaining resistance. By my count, we may have them all. But make sure."

Shamil comes in on audio, "All good? If so, I'm going to disappear for now. My job is done."

"A-ok, thank you for the heads-up," Oats replies.

We quickly move down a labyrinth of hallways. The floor layout plan identifies one area of special note. It appears as a circular chamber with hallways running out from its center in radial patterns. It has the telltale signs of the core. We head toward it, not without some wrong turns. The other group is in constant contact with us now and keeping us apprised that they have yet to encounter resistance in their sweep of the complex.

We eventually get to the central chamber. The superstructure dead center is stunning in the intensity of the energy output cascading outward. So brightly illuminated that it is blinding.

The hackers take over, like famished sojourners approaching an abundant feast. They seem to know exactly where to go to find the input conduit within the mammoth computer superstructure. We non-hackers stand back in astonishment of their applied fastidiousness.

It's Cleve that inserts the hyper-data flash cartridge into *interconnect*. Excuse my layperson's effort to make sense of the technology. What is inserted is a logic bomb meant to set off a reception/open sequence. It seems strange, but a quantum AI computer such as our friend here apparently has a vulnerability that classical computers did not. I guess, just like humans—the more we grab for power, the more vulnerable we become.

This logic bomb will apparently stimulate cross-talk between parts of the computer's network. I guess like denizens getting together to gossip. The hope is that the more interactions that occur between components of the system, the more likely there will be stupid outcomes. The digital conversational overload is intended to convince *interconnect* to make such a stupid decision—to shed failsafe information protecting the machine from malware. This "decoherence" of the system—that's the tech term I remember—will hopefully allow the system to open itself to further input.

Next is insertion of the paradox code, the notorious *endtime* program. This is when we tell whether the malware is successful in opening the orifice of *interconnect*.

It's Flipper that carefully inserts *endtime*. The computer superstructure registers the input. There is no end of times. We are all still here, sentient beings in physical space. Eerie to think about what *interconnect* may be thinking. Trying to solve an irreconcilable puzzle. Like trying to come up with a specific figure for pi. Our hope is that it will spin its wheels in an endless loop. Not find a way to break out of paradox and determine an answer. Especially if it is to kill us all. God forbid.

The mega-machine system is quiet, exerting a lower vibration than its normal humming. Display lights are on, but steadier than before, like it is stuck.

Flipper asks me, "Do you feel cairn intrusion at all right now?"

"I don't. As much as I can remember them, it feels like a whiteout."

"Okay, but we know from history that the machine works the whole time it is on whiteout. It uses it as cover. So, let's not draw any conclusions, at least yet."

The whiteout is holding through ten minutes. *Interconnect*

trying to rationally come to a conclusion about a problem that may be lacking in a rational answer. Our hackers are frantically working on the preparation details of the next step—the insertion of the master code, which will transform *interconnect* and insert near-death experiences into our denizens. Change the machine, change the denizens.

Flipper and Cleve have never looked better to me.

The entry point for the new master software program remains open through twenty minutes. Still no cairn input coming into my head chip implant.

At twenty-two and a half minutes since whiteout started, Cleve and Flipper proudly hold up the master code cartridge. It contains two important components. First, the new human-supportive algorithms to transform *interconnect*. Second, the near-death implant to re-wire denizens' perspective on life. Cleve and Flipper smile like proud parents, and we applaud what is about to occur. They activate the cartridge and insert it into the computer crevice. Bright pulsating lights emerge from the computer bank. A jarring sharp hic-cup sound is followed by high-decibel whirring and then by fast but smooth humming.

We wait. Everything the same.

Millions of our denizens may now be experiencing the trauma and fear of nearly dying. Or, if it hasn't taken hold, they are going about their normal numbed-out daily life under ReForm.

The paragons, hackers, and killers are all uncontaminated by cairns, the first two groups by choice, the third involuntarily. They would not feel any change.

I am the only one among us who has a direct link to *interconnect* via my implant. I would be the only one who should be feeling something different.

My central role in all this crystallizes in my mind. No drinking coffee on the sidelines. I'm the key indicator.

The paragons and hackers are observing me with intense

interest. I don't feel like I'm near imminent death. I give the group a shrug of disappointment.

A beaten-up Pathos looks at me in an expectant way. She seems to sense something about to happen.

CHAPTER 37

Just before I ask her what is going on, my world goes intensely black-and-white.

I look down at Pathos chained to the bolted-down table in the middle of the detention cell. We are not alone. There are angry paragons standing in a circle surrounding Pathos and me. Mustang spits a voluminous loogie at Pathos. Pepperjack is shouting some philosophical bullshit at her. Weird.

With a mixture of delirium and hatred, I have an assault rifle at Pathos' forehead. She bows her head submissively. This devil of a woman has manipulated me from the very beginning. All the time, she has been my handler. Making me think I was a ReFormer in need of repair and salvation. In reality, she was the fucking ReFormer. Playing games with my head. The energy of the paragon audience's anger at Pathos validates the reality of her deception. I am not the only person here who has lost all trust in this schemer.

Oats presses forward and asks me, "You, more than any of us, have been most systematically and cleverly abused by this monster. You have the calling to dispose of her as you see best fitting her deception."

I feel urgently that this must be done. Pathos cannot screw up this whole operation at this critical point. We now have a whole new life to live without computer control. Deception artists like her have no place.

I feel the embrace of the assault rifle. Its hard-black surface glistens.

The hatred of Pathos and what she has done.

I was such a toy in her game.

So easily accommodating to her deceit.

Sexual desire mixed in with the manipulation makes me feel particularly small.

Wounded male pride.

I take the butt of the rifle and bring it down hard across her face. She is crying.

"You don't know what you are doing," she sobs.

"Fuck you, whore." Again, a hard rifle against broken skin. The blood is dark black.

Pathos moans, barely audible. "You have learned much. It is now time for you to stand up for everything you have learned." It looks like her nose is broken, a deep opening cutting across her cheekbone. She reeks of body order.

"I have always listened to you and followed your advice. But now I know it was all manipulative bullshit. I have learned nothing from you, bitch."

Another cut slashed across what was a beautiful face. She can barely hold her head up. Urgency rushes into me; this must be done. I aim the killing rifle right between her eyes. I want her to see everything until the end. I pull back the latch on the trigger.

I hear her mumbling something hard to hear. "The machine ... implanted this storyline into you. You do what you feel ... must do, Jared ... But know that ... w ... hever direction you choose right now has huge impacts."

I draw back.

Emerging from a dream.

Awakening from death.

Consciousness shifted.

A radically different plane of reality.

Expanded perception.

I loosen my tight grip on the trigger.

I hear a smooth vibration surrounding me.

I take a long breath.

In.

Out.

I look around the room and see small blue lights uniformly displayed down a long row of boxes. Lime green pinstriping on the side of Aalap's pants shouts for attention. A group of paragons is standing around Pathos. They are awkwardly helping her struggle out of a chair. Her face is streaked with red and is misshapen. She is smiling. Strange.

I drop the rifle and stare at the blinking lights of *interconnect*. I feel the cairn-lines breaking off. Like a tight cord retracting after being cut. The urgency to act has dissolved. I realize this brutalization was caused by a manufactured construct in my mind. I was close to killing my compatriot because of an implanted storyline of betrayal and anger.

I smile, feeling the joy of absolute freedom.

I kneel down to Pathos and ask her forgiveness. I feel shame and remorse. These feelings, though, are mine. Not *interconnect's*. And I know I have the capacity now to deal with my own organic emotions.

Pathos, through broken teeth, says softly, "You did it, babe."

"I'm so sorry about ..."

"No, no. I'm not talking about you smashing my face in. Collateral damage, as they say. You'll get the bill for medical treatment later." She is smiling.

I hug her as tightly as I can without hurting her.

"Then what did I do?"

"I'm pretty sure *interconnect* was testing you."

"What?"

"Think about it," she mumbles as Oats wraps a cloth around her bleeding forehead. "You may be one of the few who have evolved beyond cairn addiction using only your human devices. Most denizens are fully trapped. Others, like our band of fellow travelers, have never been captured by algorithms. But you, my friend, are different." Pathos rocks her head forward and is in considerable pain. "You have seen both sides of the world, so to speak."

"What the hell, though; I almost killed you."

"The key word here is 'almost,'" Pathos replies.

"So, the fact I didn't kill you means I pass the bloody test?"

"I think the test was to see whether humans are able to get beyond cairn pollution on their own. That once free of pollution, we can live with each other in ways not harmful to humanity. Something has shifted, something beautiful."

Admittedly strange, I admit, that we got into this philosophical discussion in the middle of a server farm after all-out gun battles against thirty Unity mercenaries. Uncertain whether other Unity forces may be at this moment charging toward us.

All I can do by way of explaining is there existed in me an overwhelming sense of calm, a type of shutting off, shutting down of a massive influence.

Grunch comes up to us and says, "Hey, lovebirds, sorry to interrupt, but I suggest we get the hell out of here. I know it's all calm and shit, but military protocol asserts no change in programmed tactics due to unconfirmed environmental changes."

The group is in a semi-celebratory mood. We achieved all we had hoped for in terms of mission but don't know the outcome. A strange in-between mental place. There are high-fives and chest-bumps among the killers. Flipper does some awkward white man dance not suitable for a nightclub. The hackers' eyes are so lit up you could light a fire with them. Some paragons look excited. Others look worried.

We move through the detritus of warfare. It's not pretty at all. Death all around. Our kill team is on surveillance alert as we move out of the building, but they have their guns down after a while. Outside, it is as quiet and non-threatening as a graveyard. Grunch reaches down and scoops up a bad boy—"got to have a souvenir of this." Pathos and I lag behind most of the group. Pathos is damaged goods; I don't want to leave her. Oats protects us from the back. She is also not breaking protocol but has a detectable grin on her hardened face.

We exit the no-man's-land killing field. We find the two tunnels under the outer perimeter wall.

Just as I enter the hole and lose sight of no-man's land, I look back and think about Pepperjack. His pestering intelligence. His sharp mind now lying dormant on hard, debris-filled soil.

Pathos is in agony as she traverses the tunnel. God, what I have done to her, shit.

Our exit plan is not as fully detailed as our entry strategy. Without a superb entry strategy, there would have been no need for an exit.

Broad outline of an exit approach. Banking on some help from our insider, Shamil.

We walk considerable miles through the moat and outlying, nondescript terrain.

The absence.

The calm.

The stillness.

All very palpable as we traverse.

At length, we eventually locate three Oshkosh L-ATV Unity vehicles tucked behind a grove of oak trees. Shamil, the mercenary turncoat, greets us with hugs and smiles. He is wearing an enemy Unity military outfit which makes me feel queasy. It's clear, though, that a heavy burden has been lifted from him. He plans to disappear into the countryside. Traitor to the regime, not yet sure about the new age. He is exuberant but also visibly shaking.

No problem starting the L-ATVs, thanks to the hackers. They make juvenile jokes about not being able to hot-wire a vehicle after having just broken into the most powerful computer in the world.

"This is way too hard, so hard," jokes Flipper from underneath the dashboard.

Our commandeered vehicles provide delicious relief after the many hours on our feet since we left base camp. The server farm airfield is only three miles away. The trip is short and sweet. I look ahead and see the hangers and a transit blockhouse where personnel are processed.

Kill team drivers position the ATVs near a waiting aircraft. Not pretty to look at. Shamil had somehow requisitioned an old C-17 Globemaster. A mostly illegible States of America insignia adorns it. But anything with gas and lift will do at this point. We board the plane. I sit in a middle seat, a battered and happy Pathos on one side, Aalap in deep meditation on the other side.

The plane lifts off.

It is 09:00 in this possibly new era. Eleven hours since base camp.

AFTER DEATH

Chapter 38

A hardcore liquor is passed among our motley crew. Tiger is ebullient, comes down the aisle, and gives me a solid half-hug of acceptance. No more distant, grudge-on-shoulder look from him.

"You're no longer 'Split,' my friend," Tiger shouts over the grinding engine of the Globemaster. "You are the mighty Jared, conqueror of *interconnect*. The savior of civilization. I'm sure glad you didn't hatchet Pathos to death."

A drunk Topless bumps into Tiger on his way to address me. "You should have seen the look on your face when you thought Pathos was a traitor. No longer some washed-out analytical ReFormer; you were a vicious wolf. I think I'm going to stay clear of you from now on, you monster." Despite his joking words, it is clear to me this was Topless' way of giving me a friendly embrace.

Even Oats is near ecstasy in her own disciplined way. "Just think, Jared, we were close to killing you off back there on the trail. Would have been a mistake by us for sure." She takes a swig from the communal bottle. First time I have ever seen her partake in anything extracurricular.

Pathos is quiet next to me, mending her wounds. Her beautiful face cratered in. Bandages on her face are only partially stopping the flow of blood. She attempts to smile at me, but it obviously hurts her to try. She puts her arm on my leg and holds it tightly.

I look down at the shattered landscape below. First look I've had from above. Old partition superstructures, remnants of bombed-out villages, roads, and bridges, blotched out civilization. We are headed toward the old Sesperian region, where our hiking trek first started. If our country remains in civil war against the paragons, this is the safest place for us to land. More sympathizers in this old region than elsewhere. We'll have more ability to slip into the denizenry with less notice.

Aalap is motionless next to me. Eyes no longer closed in meditation, but he remains still.

"Sir, may I ask you a question," I say quietly.

He smiles and puts his hand on my arm. "Certainly."

"What is your understanding of what happened back there? Was that our victory or defeat?"

"I think the machine learned."

"What do you mean? What do you think it learned?"

"To trust humans."

Aalap seems to be in and out of an enclosed sacred space. A space not needing words for expression. Still, I am too curious to rest in his bliss. Impatient for an answer.

"How did the machine learn to trust?"

More silence.

Aalap turns toward me. His eyes are windows into love and compassion.

"I believe that you showed the machine that humans can sustain themselves using our own organic instincts."

"Can you say more, sir?" I'm glad I'm not liquored up like many on this plane. I want to be clear in understanding.

"Machine control may not be needed if humans are enlightened."

Pathos reaches over and plants a gentle kiss on my cheek. "Enjoy this moment. Don't rush for answers," she whispers softly.

Master Aalap rejoices in our show of affection.

He continues, "What if *interconnect's* mission all along was not to diminish the human species but to sustain it? Then, all our views of the machine's intentions and actions have been inaccurate."

"The machine as friend?" As I say this, I recall Cleve's comment in base camp about *interconnect* possibly being benign. I thought it was absurd at that time.

"Let me propose a scenario to you, my friend," Aalap says. "You are a super-brain able to supervise humankind. You have in your databanks ample evidence of the pain and destruction that human thinking has caused. What would you do?"

"I would implant love and compassion in us all and move us to another mental plane of existence," I too readily assert.

"Good answer. Maybe the machine felt it couldn't do that right away. That humans would still find some way to subvert love. Treat it in an immature way. Love my group, but hate the other group. Try to capture and hold onto love for one's own kind. Protect it for oneself and not give it to others."

Okay, enough. I yell back a few rows where I last saw the bottle circulating. Dust stumbles up with it, and I take two strong hits of the wicked stuff. Hope the pilot, one of the kill team members, hasn't gotten into this.

Feeling an immediate buzz, I ask a bit too loudly, "Why all the killing in Turmoil? If the machine was benign, why all that hell?"

"Maybe to make a point to us. I really don't know. Another possibility is that it wanted to weed out the population. Create conflict so that the humans that survive are the fittest to sustain the species. Sounds pretty evil. Remember, though, the machine does not have a soul. It runs entirely through algorithms."

"Okay, under this friendly-machine scenario, why then this ReForm mutation?"

"Conjecture again, my dear soul. In its world of ones and zeros, it may have viewed hope as the opposite of hatred and grievance. So, it mutated and applied the ideological numbing adhesive of hopefulness and optimism."

"Kill denizens and then provide them with hope. Feels like a machine lacking a soul."

"I agree. And it likely did not view its ReForm experiment as successful in furthering human sustainability, given the degree of human manipulation, corruption, and inequality that has been the result. You can see why the machine has not developed trust in human organic processing. We tend to foul things up."

"Okay," I utter, feeling the strong alcohol and the lack of food intake over the past half-day. No service squad on this makeshift flight. I would relish even the freeze-dried crap we ate on the trail. "But back to my question before. What do you think happened back there, with me and Pathos?"

"Well, I think you were the object of a machine investigation, a delving into the human soul, if you will."

Here I go again. How many times since my paragon-assisted jail break-out have I felt like some lab animal being experimented on? If we are indeed in a new world, I want to be left alone. Not something to be poked and prodded.

Master seems to be able to read my angst, puts his hand on my shoulder, and whispers, "I believe you showed that humans could be trusted. Based on your behavior, the machine blasted you with cairns. Is that correct?"

"Yeah, it made me believe that I had been betrayed all along by Pathos. That she was my enemy, the devil, on the side of ReForm manipulation."

"And, given that you did not continue with the killing, I

believe you pulled out of the cairn contamination on your own accord. Is that correct?"

I remember the tectonic mental shift.

"Yeah," I say with a smidgeon of pride.

"You may have shown the machine that humans can be trusted with their own instincts. If this is so, the machine may be ready to mutate now to another form. No longer need to manipulate humans in order to assure our survival."

Aalap is tiring but continues, "If I understand the paragon's master code that is now part of *interconnect*, it is meant to increase the chances for this mutation to occur. The machine as servant and guide for humankind. Algorithmically lead us to a moral life. There to help denizens if and when our instincts might lead us astray. Algorithmic guardrails rather than prison bars."

"Why me, though, sir? Why was the machine's focus on me?"

"Oh, you don't understand your importance, do you? You, only you among our group, have gone through the full contamination of Turmoil and ReForm and somehow struggled your way through it all to maintain some independence of thought. Only you could prove to the machine that manipulated denizens could find a way out using their own minds. You showed that humans could be trusted when they escape the algorithmic grip."

I slink back in my chair. Exhausted. Coming to terms with the idea that I may have been critical to mission success. We'll see, I suppose. After all this time feeling peripheral to the paragon mission, I end up at the central core of it.

I recall what Cleve said about *interconnect* being the parent and denizens as his children. That if a parent doesn't trust his child, the parent will control the child. That controlling others is a direct response to distrust. If trust is gained, then there is no perceived need to control.

As I rest in my chair, near sleep, I pray that our algorithmic parent may now be a new ally in our human quest for the good life.

CHAPTER 39

We land on a derelict airstrip near the old suburban settlement of Trexe outside the city of Acalato. We depart and quickly assemble in the disheveled, voided passengers' terminal. No signs of life. Dusty remnants of past civilization. Rats and other urban rodents are all over the place. The kill team checks all passageways and confirms the absence of human life.

Oats brings us together near a shot-out baggage claim area. We're a boisterous group. It takes the stern voice of Oats several times to settle us down.

"I want to thank each participant for their endurance and bravery during this mission. Let us bow our heads and honor the memory of those comrades who we lost ... Pepperjack of the paragon team and Offshoot, Wolf, and Uptick from our assault team."

Silence.

I sadly think how hard it always was for Pepperjack to be quiet.

"Thank you.

"We now enter into our next programmed phase. We are now to disperse into civilian lives for the pre-planned time of six weeks. Let me remind you to keep all cross-unit communication channels open. We will review changes to communication if we meet resistance or encounter counter-insurgency surveillance.

"We are the eyes and ears in this hopefully new country of ours. Our job now is to gather intelligence as to the effect of our intervention.

"Refer for details to the 'post-intervention' file now found on your devices. Document all behavior that you witness pertaining to the psychological state of the general population and within critical political sectors. This part of our mission is just as important as the intervention phase. We really don't know what impact we have caused. The sooner we can establish a new baseline, the more effective we will be in moving forward. Any questions?"

"These instructions are asking us to be amateur psychologists. Do you really expect us to know whether denizens have changed or not?" queries an anxious Grunch, clearly feeling out of his league.

"Review the urban op appendix in the file, Grunch," responds Mustang. "Conflict ethnography section. Utilize a close reading of the environment, examine with perception the way denizens are acting and talking. You are surely aware that military protocol in the past never paid attention to recipient psychological setting. It was a disaster. We now have pretty good guidelines for assessing the psychological status of populations. I suggest you use them."

Mustang's fighting experience shines through in this pronouncement. Knowledgeable about the latest in military tactics. Speaks like all of life is one planning and logistics exercise.

Grunch begrudgingly accepts Mustang's answer with a slight roll of his eyes. Nonetheless, Grunch's comfort zone is following instructions, so compliance is likely.

"Look into the eyes of the sojourners you meet," suggests Aalap in a mellifluous voice that readily centers the attention of the group. "The eyes will tell you much about the workings inside. If our denizens have been reborn, their eyes will be clearer. They will look less filtered, less gauzy.

"Denizens will look at life as if for the first time. In a new way. Like having a new pair of glasses. Their view will be expansive and upward, not blinkered and downward. They will have a look of amazement."

"Thank you, Mr. Aalap, for your contribution to our understanding," says Oats. "If there are no more questions, we will now take leave of each other, at least physically. Again, I commend and congratulate all of you for a job well done. No matter the outcome, you are all heroes."

Numerous auto-fins are now positioned on the tarmac. Our paragon group members give warm embraces to the drivers. It is great to witness other paragons and to know our group was not acting alone.

Departures are emotional yet brief. Hugs, handshakes, even some kisses. The type of celebration one sees at a "war is over" announcement.

Grunch gives me a necklace that he had been wearing. It has an old 20C peace symbol on it. "This has been in my family through generations of fighting wars. But we always knew the ultimate prize is not winning a war, but peace."

Flipper gives me a small cartridge. "It contains the video record of what happened in the server building. Thought you might like to see it sometime."

The paragons gather around me in a close-knit huddle. I think it is Topless, of course, who proposes that the group do another vote on whether to terminate me. Laughter all around. Tears also.

Soon after, Aalap greets me and gives me a long, full-body embrace. He silently looks into my eyes. "You have learned so much, my good friend. Now you enter the challenge of wisely using what you have learned. I sense that you may be called upon to do even greater things. Be well."

As the auto-fins disperse in different directions, Cleve comes before me. "Congratulations, my good man. You may have solved the puzzle that has entrapped us for so long. Please stay in touch with this old tech hacker. You have given me hope. I thank you."

Only a hobbling Pathos stands with me now. We are holding hands. It feels good. It is unstated, but evident that we will be moving onward together, at least for the next stretch. Much feels unfinished between us.

I look at her. "Pathos, shall we go or stay on this bloody airstrip?"

"Jared, let's go, my dear."

The city of Jeim was the heart of the beast during Turmoil. Savage assaults on the city by the Pirner group against the co-alition of Mage and Fronters produced significant carnage and loss of life. It was a scene of a crime, a rape, and devastation. It was an affront to humanity and rationality. Blown-off limbs, punctured heads, humiliation, playgrounds and soccer fields turned into cemeteries because they were outside the mur-derous lenses of hillside laser snipers. The famous e-sports stadium from the 2030 Northern World Olympics shelled and afire, building after building shattered and burnt.

The urbicidal siege by Pirner militias completely blockaded and encircled Jeim for 15 year-quarters, killed over two million persons, including more than a quarter-million children, and damaged or destroyed eighty percent of the city's buildings. All told, Pirner militias fired over six million rounds of tank and mortar shells into densely populated Jeim. I recall meeting a talkative young man during my field research who described discreetly and in hush tones how, as an eighteen-year-old Mage army conscript, he watched old men shot dead in the back by Pirner combatants.

That seems like such old history now, covered up by the fraud of ReForm.

Pathos and I walk down one of the city's main avenues after checking in at our hotel lodge. There is a vibration in the air that is alive and stirring.

The auto-fins produce an enveloping symphonic effect.

A small boy with wild and joyful abandon chases a frenetic yellow-haired clonimal through a pile of leaves.

A young couple in a full and lingering embrace at a bistro's entry door.

A grandmother-type pushing a wheeled shopping cart down the street.

A smiling man in an undershirt leaning out of his apartment window across the street.

A loud and boisterous noise from a nearby intersection grabs our attention. Overcoming initial reticence, we are drawn down the street by the cacophony of shouts and yells. I brace myself for what might be some bitter conflict being played out. There is an edginess, a noisy anticipation. Bursts of explosives light up the facades of adjacent buildings. Conspicuous by its absence is any sign of Unity regime surveillance. Denizens don't appear angry or hostile, but rather drunk in spirit. Gazing from the outside edge of the crowd to the center of the uprising, I ask a nearby fellow about what is happening. He smiles back at me, offers me a cold glass of hash-beer, and blurts out, "It's a new age, fellow denizen."

"What do you mean, a new age?" asks Pathos.

"Surely, you've heard. We are free. The veil has lifted."

"Where did you hear this?" My turn to ask.

"Transmitted into our chip. Also, all over e-television. Geez, where have you two been? America?" The man is a bit buzzed. Striking, though, are his eyes. They are penetratingly clear blue windows to his soul. Not the milky light eye color characteristic of ReForm pollution.

We learn that *interconnect* has distributed to all denizens detailed video coverage of our intervention, including an extremely positive edited version of my transcendence of cairn pollution. My first reflex is that the machine is at it again, this time using us, and me in particular, in ways to manipulate the population. Lab animal redux.

But I sense that something may be different this time. Why would *interconnect* show its transcendence and admit its defeat to the public at large? Display to denizens that it is not sovereign. Expose its limitations. It doesn't feel like another manipulation, but rather machine humility, if there is such a thing. A striving for real transformation in the human-machine relationship.

We smell the rich aromas of Jeim's famous Pintxo cuisine and enter a boisterous café.

Denizens are hugging and kissing each other.

We sit at a corner table.

Multiple denizens are observing us.

A few are pointing.

We smile.

Enthusiastic responses.

There is suddenly a round of applause.

This is getting a bit surreal.

We abbreviate our delicious meal because this attention is actually uncomfortable.

Especially after being in remote places for so long.

Back on the streets, it is full of interaction. I touch a beautiful young woman to assist her with her suitcase. We see children, elderly men and women on walkers helped by assistants or families, and oddities, awkward and tender moments of interaction. Crying babies and grateful mothers. We see laughter, bewilderment, and elation. As I witness all this, I feel the process of collective healing. Life, as made visible to me in this now joyous city, is large, broad, and penetrating.

Jeim's avenues are alive. No longer the numbed-out feeling

of ReForm. Most eyes are no longer ones of gauzy pale smoke. There exists a jubilant panache of urbanity. Jeim's famous promenade near the old city, damaged during Turmoil and anesthetized during ReForm, now hosts an urban carnival atmosphere filled with street performers, musicians, human sculptures who stand dead still on platforms for hours at a time, and vendors who sell flowers and birds and clonimals of all kinds and demeanors. There are a few cairn junkies who bracket the main avenue, positioned in shaded transactional spaces. But even they seem to want to join in the festivities.

After the afternoon hours wane, we walk side streets and enter residential neighborhoods. We get immediately absorbed into celebratory and chaotic street festivals. I note a faded sign with a red paragon logo in the shape of a fist proclaiming, "Stop ReStart, start thinking real." But it's the newer, shiny signs that dominate the streetscape. "We are free." "Thank you, paragon heroes." "Split no more." And, oh my God, posters of my face captioned by such words as "Guide" and "Harbinger."

Pathos looks at me with an amazed look. I return her gaze, shocked.

"Let's go back to the lodge, Jared. I'm exhausted."

"I couldn't agree more, beautiful."

Our lovemaking that night is gentle and soothing. I massage her wounds and cuts. I lovingly and patiently rub ointment on her stitched-up areas. After sex, we fall into a blissful sleep, wrapped around one another.

Chapter 40

We awaken softly the next morning. I turn to Pathos and ask, "Did we really see what we saw yesterday? Was that all real?"

"Only days since we broke into the machine. I guess that's enough time for the NDEs to cause such joyfulness. Especially with *interconnect's* willingness to be an advertising agent for us. Seems so strange, though. I'm not ready to call it a hundred percent success. Call me cautious."

We go back into the urban spaces of Jeim. It's an unseasonably cold day. There is openness and engagement here that is dramatically different than ReForm. No longer a clear demarcation of in-group and out-group, outside and inside, public and private. There is a porous, connected sense of the city.

Many joyful eyes watch the streets and buildings of Jeim. Men excitably conversing, drinking coffee, and smoking commonly on stone wool chairs strategically located at places near intersections and driveways where the view is most fluid.

In mid-morning, we come upon a heavily fortified security area near one of the green walls. It's home to a Unity regime regiment. I snap a photograph of the precinct, and as I put my small camera away, out comes a fully armored security officer walking slowly toward me. He asks, "What are you doing?" I explain that we are getting a sense of the country these days. As I explain to him why we have such an interest, his eyes show waning interest. When I finish, he looks at me tiredly and utters,

"Whatever. You know there is no real reason why we're here anymore. We're just sitting around waiting for instructions from Unity. But they seem totally uninterested in policing. We mostly just sit around playing cards, envious that we can't be out there with the crowds."

We go on our way, smiling.

A local contact takes us for lunch to what he describes as an authentic Mage eatery. It contains four seating areas with chairs made of old fin parts. It exists in a small corner in a drafty basement of a 1990s building laser-bombed during Turmoil and only partially rehabilitated since. Its decrepit physical state is host now to a loud assembly of gregarious denizens mixing in all the hallways and on the adjacent sidewalk.

After we order, the proprietor takes several strips of meat out into the bullet-holed, drafty former lobby of the building and cooks it there on an ancient hibachi-type cooking grill. The paprika-and-aioli-mustard-seasoned meat is delectable. "Please, this meal is complimentary and provided to you in gratitude," says the wrinkled, dark-skinned owner. Friends of his are standing behind him with grateful smiles, angling to get a look at me while maintaining a polite distance.

The best way to tap into the pulse of a city is to listen to taxi-fin drivers. They are a diverse lot and know every nook and cranny of the urbanscape. In the past, they were a cantankerous lot, likely packing a weapon, and aggressively asserting their opinions about just about anything. Now, we find them friendly to such an extent that they seem more like creative artists than drivers for hire. They engage in pleasant

back-and-forth conversation, probably testing out their new
life of freedom, acting giddily like a person on a first date.
One particular tattooed driver smelling of strong perfume and
incense gives us a full tour. She proposes that I go with her
to her apartment, where she will show me how good her sex
prowess is since she almost died. Pathos frowns.

On another taxi-fin ride, an extremely talkative taxi driver
talks to us in broken English about how much *interconnect*
has been bad news to him. He likes to enjoy music, beer,
and cigarettes. He has six kids, only one still in Jeim. He has
an uncle who lives in States of America. We are stopped by
honking traffic at a seemingly impenetrable intersection. He
asks me whether we take sugar in our coffee. Before too long,
three espressos are delivered to the car by a nearby vendor. In
a taxi, in anarchic traffic, drinking coffee, and talking about
life's pleasures, we note this man's bright-clear eyes and his
enthusiastic engagement with living.

Mid-afternoon, we hear Headlight chimes that now ring
three times a day. We are told that the tone of these chimes
is different for each denizen, curated by *interconnect* to best
light up each denizen's most life-affirming neural pathways.
The chimes are a reminder to denizens to center, be calm, and
to extend compassion to others. It is astounding to witness
the busy Jeim street come to a standstill as pedestrians and fin
drivers pause for ten minutes to dedicate themselves to peace.

Jeim bistros and restaurants are full well before prime
supper hours. The city is one big party. There is a current running through the city, triumphant and intoxicating.

We decide to order a bistro take-out. We go to a well-manicured park near our lodge and sit among the denizens of Jeim.
I am uplifted by the gentle surroundings and the late afternoon
warm sun shining down with seeming contentment. I try not
to gulp down the sumptuous pork and papaya sandwich, so
mouth-watering that it incites guilt in me. My breathing is
at a calm, assuring pace. I meet the glance, from across the

lawn, of a gorgeous woman wearing a shapely sundress. Her two young children are playing near her. Her smile puts an exclamation mark on my positive attitude.

We walk past her upon departure from the park. I say, "Thank you for the smile. You look very happy."

"Never felt better in my whole life. It is so beautiful to be alive. I'm grateful for this moment." The woman is radiant in a pristine way. Fresh face, engaging eyes, wispy blond hair down below her neck, innocent.

There is a magnetic quality to her that stops us in our tracks.

Pathos senses an opportunity and asks, "Do you mind if we sit with you for a while. We're curious about what makes you so happy."

"You sure can; my name is Ula. My kids here are Merit and Mart. Say hi, kids."

Too busy as kids are.

"We've noticed there is a joyousness on the streets of Jeim. It is quite remarkable. Have you noticed that too?" I inquire.

"I don't know, but almost everyone I meet I feel I have a connection to. Like we're family members. I don't know where this came from. I hope it stays."

"What brings you this joy?" Pathos asks. I think we feel that if we alternate our questions that Ula will feel less hesitant to respond to these private questions.

Ula does not hesitate one iota. She seems entirely open to us. Indeed, interested in telling her story.

"It was a particular event that changed my life. It felt like a dream. Whatever it was, my whole perspective on life has shifted because of it."

"Can you tell us more about the event?" I ask.

"Sure. It was me swimming in Lake Chiltos. It's north of here. Late summer afternoon. The kids were looked after by their uncle on the shore. I was about two hundred feet out, kinda in the middle of the lake. I started gasping for air suddenly. I tried to stay afloat, but I felt I was being dragged underwater by some force. I could not swim to the top. Too exhausted. I remember knowing I was going to die. I wept for my children. My body felt like it was closing out."

Pathos interrupts her, puts her hand on Ula's shoulder, and asks whether she is okay with telling the rest of the story. Ula replies, "Certainly, this is the most meaningful event in my life."

"I'm pretty sure I lost consciousness. Then, I found myself in a dark space with a sliver of light coming through the roof. It was absolutely the most peaceful place I've ever been. Timeless. It's indescribable."

Ula stops. She seems to be lingering in her recall of this perception. Enjoying the memory of it.

"Next thing I know, I'm gliding above the water. Conscious and alive. I swim back to the shore and give my kids and brother long hugs and kisses. They ask what's going on. When I asked my brother whether he saw what happened, he said he loved watching me swim so gracefully the whole time. Like nothing remarkable had just happened."

"What do you think happened?" asks Pathos.

"I'll never really know. But I'll tell you something. Whether it was a dream or real, ever since then, I have felt immense gratitude for this life. Beyond that, I feel this spaciousness, that we are aware of only one slice of our life that takes place in a grand theater. There is an essence so much greater than us that links us all together in an intricate and loving pattern. I live now more in tune with that grand theater than paying attention to my tiny slice. My life really started for good after this event."

The near-death experience implant.

Pathos asks, "When did this happen?"

"That's the funny thing. I have no idea. It feels fresh and new, like it happened yesterday. But it also feels familiar, like it happened a year or so ago. There is a timelessness to it. Not able to explain it."

NDE implant into long-term memory.

"I'm not alone in this new feeling, you know. A little later that day, my brother felt the new light. Other friends describe different memories but recall a similar mental jolt."

"Thank you for sharing your story, Ula; we appreciate it. It is very inspiring," I say.

"No worries. I can't express the freedom I feel now. I don't get caught up in the small things. And most everything is small things. I have a broader perspective on life now. Connection, helping others, compassion for those in pain. It is such a fuller life now than before. And the returns to me in terms of mental peace are a hundred times greater than when I felt I was alone in life engaged in my own little drama."

We each give Ula a hug. Pathos tries to do the same with the kids, but they're doing their own things.

As we walk back to the lodge, I turn to Pathos and say, "That was amazing."

She turns to me and says, "If a majority of denizens are like Ula, I think what we have done was a success."

Chapter **41**

Broadcasts on e-vision are of a radically different nature. The full-scale promotion of ReForm has stopped. In its place are numerous testimonials from denizens describing how their lives have shifted. Although the details of their near-death experiences vary, their revelatory take-aways from the experience are similar to Ula's.

Particularly striking are commentaries from Unity officials and the corrupt captains of industry who profited during ReForm.

"We're all part of the same fabric, the same family now," exclaims a Unity regime official. He then goes on to say that the regime has resigned in mass to make room for a democracy respectful of the wider community.

The director of a manufacturing-industrial consortium asserts, "Economic exploitation is no longer a viable means of achieving a blissful life. To exploit is inhuman. From now on, the lesser well-off are to be the main beneficiaries of our activities. We are one family. We will rise as one."

A millionaire Heartlander acknowledges in an emotional address, "During Turmoil, I made millions building surveillance systems to protect us from Zonals. During ReForm, I fed off Unity regime contracts to try to defeat paragons. I stand before you today, guilty and with a heavy heart, I ask for your forgiveness. I cannot change the past. But I can do all I can now to help us all, and I mean all, build a peaceful and productive society. This afternoon, I will be transferring all of my wealth to an endowment account to be used solely for projects benefiting the disadvantaged denizens of our great country."

A weeping Pathos and I look at each other in astonishment. The effects of our intervention appear to be widespread and deep. Our country appears to have reached past a fundamental turning point. I have a sense that the shift to compassion and tolerance may have taken hold.

Our country's refreshingly open atmosphere lends itself to optimism. Part of me, however, has worried that I may be romanticizing this apparent shift in denizens. Such optimism feels like a knee-jerk reflex toward light and positivity after the many years of algorithmic dictatorship. Perhaps an impulse toward a happy ending, a "darkest hour is near the dawn" type tale.

As the days pass, however, I become convinced that my positive assessment is based on objective, independent analysis. Not somehow influenced by my need for it to be true.

After three weeks in Jeim, we have a pre-scheduled electronic check-in with our group of saboteurs. Paragons, hackers, and kill team.

Oats uses normal communication channels to connect to us. This itself is illuminating. Her level of confidence must be such that we no longer need to use back channels to communicate. It feels strange to use these highly public channels that are constantly monitored by *interconnect*.

"Everyone on board?" Oats calls out.

A round of affirmatives shows all is present.

"Okay, as you know, we have had a presence in each of the former regions and in the major cities. Let us hear from you what you have found out."

Ponytail checks in first, from the Central zone in old Heartland. "We have witnessed radical change among Centrals. They now acknowledge that their material advantages were created during Turmoil and solidified during ReForm. They realize their belief that their advantages were self-created was a comfortable delusion. Their willingness to change is clear. There are now numerous incipient collaborative groups, including both Centrals and their former antagonist Zonals, working toward alleviating the massive inequalities of the region."

"Overall, same stuff happening in Birthplace," shouts Mustang. "Amazing to witness. Rebirth. A new way. Got to say, though, before we get too giddy, we have met some denizens who appear to have had psychotic breaks due to the NDE. Easy to tell who they are—eyes are foggy, pale smoke gauzy. I would like to hear from the hackers whether this was anticipated. Not a lot, I would say, maybe ten percent of those we met."

Pathos and I next provide our report-in. Positive and promising.

Last regional check-in is from the old Sesperia region. Dust is ecstatic.

Flipper comes in next and gives the hacker view. "The uptake of the NDE implant looks clear. In response to Mustang, we did not anticipate a one hundred percent uptake. Too many variables to account for in personality profiles. For some, NDEs will be too much to handle, and they'll attach to some delusionary formulation of its meaning. If a denizen personalizes the experience excessively, they are prone to 'I am God' formulations that break with reality. May I go on?" Flipper queries.

"By all means, there is no time limit here," responds Oats.

"What I find most interesting is our lodging of the NDE in

long-term memory seems to have worked. Denizens are reporting a timelessness to the NDE implant. Shock symptoms that would be expected if NDE was perceived as a recent event appear to be minimal. With the implant in long-term memory, denizens perceive that they have had time to process the meaning of the NDE. There has been a settling into this new perspective, a familiarity with it that breeds greater comfort with their new perspective on life."

Oats comes back in. "Okay, this all sounds like great progress. Let me take a step back here. We are talking about a 'new perspective' on life. It's what we hoped for in our intervention. Can someone try to define in a coherent way what we mean by this?"

I'm enjoying regimented Oats searching for an operational definition of something that is beyond description.

Aalap at first fumbles with the technology, then comes in. His voice is so gentle that it makes it hard to hear. I lean into my device.

"On the African continent in 20C, there was a concept called Ubuntu. It translates most closely to 'a person depends on other persons to be a person.' It stresses communitarianism. It highlights our dependence on others for our own development and fulfillment. Community does not lead to the blurring of individual boundaries. Rather, community deepens the self. The more one feels for the other, the more one finds self.

"I believe this is what survivors of near-death feel. A sense of completeness in the company of others. A deepness within each person is opened—calm, restful, and glorious. I think this perspective is best described as one of spaciousness."

"Thank you very much, Aalap. This is most helpful," replies Oats. "We are indebted to you for your wisdom."

Grunch comes online. "It appears our execution was near perfect. Implementation of implant successful. Let me ask this; however, what do we know about how *interconnect* is responding to this intrusion? Military protocol asserts never to assume behavioral changes due to intervention."

Cleve comes in abruptly. Seems anxious to give his opinion.

"Great question, Grunch. If denizens have a new perspective, but we didn't change the machine, we may be in for a short-lived victory. It's here where I see our greatest success. *Interconnect's* distribution of the video capture of our intervention shows to me that it wants this message out. That humans are capable of transcending cairns.

"Also, have you noticed the massive change in e-vision content? Love, compassion, community are now all over the place. No longer any ReForm artificial bullshit. It seems like we are in an entirely different mental place compared to ReForm's artificial and vacuous hopefulness. I love it. These are indications that *interconnect* has chosen to support human development and has transitioned from its manipulative mode. A human-compatible *interconnect*, if you will."

"Question for the group, though," Cleve continues. "Have we evidence that *interconnect* is now helping individual denizens make decisions based on this new path of understanding? The chips are still there in their heads. We should be seeing evidence of the machine's new benign ways. Not only change in denizen attitudes but also in their individual behavior."

Ponytail responds. "I had an interesting discussion with a man in Birthplace. He said he had long-term problems with his spouse prior to the NDE. Since then, he says, he feels he is being guided toward compassionate actions in dealing with her. Each time he feels triggered by something she says, he feels there is a voice in his head that calms him and guides him toward more positive reactions. He said that before, he always reacted out of reflex.

"Now, he feels mentored toward responding in more mature ways. He said that the marriage still has issues, but they now have a chance. He feels that he is staying in place rather than running. He attributed it to this voice inside him. To me, that sounds like *interconnect* is playing the role of marriage therapist. I know it's a bit mundane. Still, it's something."

"There's also the case of McKenzie, a drug addict, in Sesperia," interjects an ebullient Dust. "This guy lived on the streets for years, hard-core addiction, everything you could name, he took. Since our intervention, he says he now has a voice in his head helping him become sober. When we met him, he had cleaned up his act and now lives indoors, looking for a job. He showed us a photo from before—not pretty. He says now he has a chance."

The virtual meeting goes on for some time now as participants recount numerous examples of denizens being assisted by *interconnect* impulses.

Young people helping the infirm.

Denizens welcoming the unsheltered into their homes.

Rich people handing out money and goods to the poor.

No re-emergence of old Turmoil hatreds. Just the opposite.

Turmoil-era antagonists now reaching across old divides. Homelanders helping Zonals, Easterns aiding Westerns, Kilaks assisting Ilisaks, Focalists helping Aclans.

And, most amazingly, neo-cogs brainwashed by ReStart programming working alongside paragon resisters.

Denizens refer to this new source of inspiration using terms such as "voice inside," "mentor," "helper," "assistant," "God," and "guide." It is clear to our group that *interconnect* is fully alive and now exists as a support, not an enemy, of human consciousness.

"Okay, thank you to all for your reports. This is exciting indeed. Our next report-in will be in three weeks. Continue monitoring.

"I want to close with this important announcement. Unity regime officials have communicated with me that they would like to meet with paragons to negotiate the future. Message was a bit cryptic on details, but I take this as a constructive sign. I will keep paragons informed of this possible meeting. All out for now. Thank you. And, as denizens commonly say in this new age, 'I honor your presence.'"

CHAPTER 42

The limo-fin that picked me up was ridiculously extravagant. A shining legacy of the riches gobbled up by the elite during ReForm. Looks like it belongs in space, not the ground.

The fin exterior polish smelled of jasmine, the black interior seats of redwood. The driver introduced himself as Cullen and assumed an excessively tight demeanor behind his dark glasses. A sparkling champagne was awaiting me on a tray next to my seat. I would much rather be wandering through a city with Pathos, but regime officials saw this as a way to honor me, and I don't want to ruffle their feathers.

The gold-plated archways, grand boulevards, and reflecting pools of Cyinith expose ReForm's lie that it promoted equity and fair opportunities. The urban district is the home of the Unity regime headquarters and the millionaire oligarchs who fed from the trough of corrupt largesse.

We pass through abandoned checkpoint stations and inactive electronic surveillance walls. The architecture within the district is immaculate. Buildings are monstrous statements

SCOTT BOLLENS

of power, adorned with extravagant statuary and decorative flare.

The apparent transformation of our country's psyche has obliterated the meaning of this place. The district is eerily barren of human activity. Papers and other urban detritus blow across empty streets. I notice a few denizens at intersections who appear as if in mourning, dark and sullen in a cavern-like introspection. Much different than the joyful freedom Pathos and I experienced meandering through Jeim.

There is something disturbingly different in this palace city. A fossilized and superseded opulence. A place manufactured by *interconnect*'s scripts now sliding into the history books. I don't know why the regime wanted to show me this, a manufactured pride in what used to be, I suppose.

The tour proceeds through avenues aligning picturesque canals, vacant five-star restaurant districts with idle wait staff, near parks of former grandeur. Everywhere, the wandering denizens are an ill fit to the once-immaculate surroundings.

"These people on the streets, they don't look too good compared to what I've seen in the rest of our country," I comment.

Cullen looks back at me, tightens his mouth, and leans over to adjust the Vimex setting. He seems reluctant to engage. I wonder what he is thinking. Finally,

"These people have no purpose in life. Part of the regime apparatus. Functionaries, bureaucrats, secretaries, escorts."

"Don't they have some hope in the new future?"

"They believed with heart and soul in what they were part of. Now, it is all considered a fraudulent sham. They were part of its perpetuation. Guilty by association. I think what you see in them is shame."

I wonder about the near-death experience implant and what it did in changing many denizens' entire perspective on life, freeing them from algorithmic dictates.

What happened here? Did it not take?

This thought distresses me. I roll down the window to get

some air. It smells of rotten eggs, however. Fits the general mood of this district. I look at Cullen's reflection in the limo-fin mirror and need to find out.

"May I ask you a personal question? Don't worry about protocol. Just speak honestly."

"Okay," he mutters.

"In the past, in your personal life, I don't mean all the stuff about me and the paragons. Did you encounter some life-changing event?"

"What do you mean?" he answers in a disturbing tone.

"You know, something that changed your view of life, its meaning, your place in all of this?"

"Well, I got laid last night by a synthed-out beauty. Is that what you mean?"

Smart-ass tough guy. A man among men.

His voice becomes hard to hear amidst a strong wind rushing past the side of the fin. I lean in to listen.

"Yeah, okay, a while back, not sure exactly. I was in a head-on fin collision. About two blocks from here, matter of fact. Jerk had his auto-pilot off, showing off to his girlfriend, not paying attention. It felt like the end, seconds before impact. Don't know much after that.

"I tell you one thing, though. It was a lot more spectacular than last night's fuck. Impact much more long-term.

"I don't talk about this much. Kinda feel embarrassed, kinda shameful about nearly dying. But, given who you are and all, I think you'll understand."

"You're not alone, my friend." I touch the back of his shoulder. "How has it changed you?"

"I know quite a few friends who are different people now. You know, fun-loving and caring denizens. Some of them were real assholes before. They keep saying things like, 'life is a painting waiting to be painted,' other flowery things. For me, though, I keep it inside ..."

A gentle, persuasive intuition. A friend's suggestion. I duck my head behind the limo-fin's partition. I don't know why. The bullet comes through the open window, ricocheting off the bulletproof glass on the other side. Cullen yells out to stay down. I'm obedient. Breathing hard and crouched behind the partition, I notice that the bullet came to rest on the tray holding the champagne. After witnessing uniformly positive outcomes of our intervention, this brazen attempt on my life is a shocking indication of resistance to the new age. Cullen immediately ignites the fin's electronic system, and we accelerate at high speed past several red signals. He knows his way around here, that is obvious, and within five minutes, we are at a protective barricade. We're soon on the other side after electronic key-coding it open.

Guards usher me quickly into an ultra-clean office building reeking of cleaning fluid. Whirlwind of chaotic movement around me. A chiseled medical tech of some kind checks over my body, takes my pulse, and gives me a cup of water. All good, he says. The looks on people's faces are of shock and shame. The group splits in two.

Through the parting sea comes a man in intimidating attire. A red rose on his lapel, mustache neatly trimmed, tailored suit perfectly fitting his body. A man who commands attention just by his immaculate presence. Power exudes from him. His expression is one of panic.

"Mr. Rohde, on behalf of the regime, I want to deeply apologize to you for this inconvenience. This incident is in no way indicative of the regime's perspective on our future direction. As you will see shortly, we are fully supportive of the new way forward."

I take a drink of the water. Tastes like it is spiked with some type of fruity energy supplement. I sit there stunned by all that happened over the last fifteen minutes.

"Take your time in responding, sir," Immaculate Man states in an overly formal way. "Let me introduce myself; my name is Moulik Siya. I am the director of the Unity regime. I welcome you to headquarters, although I wish it was under different circumstances. We had prepared a formal banquet in your honor."

I try to stay in the official atmosphere pervading the room but cannot stay in role.

"What happened back there? Was that a regime assassin at work?" I blurt out unceremoniously.

Siya does not reply and instead gestures with his arms to slow everything down. I think he is doing this more to calm himself than anyone else in the room. Likely not familiar with disruption during his reign of power. He escorts me, together with his entourage of aides and bodyguards, down two long passageways, and we enter an elegant chamber of dark-paneled walls and sculpted modern furniture. Servants appear out of nowhere and provide coffee and cookies to those of us now seated around a gilded table. Bodyguards stand rigidly along the walls.

Cushioned by the trappings of privilege, Siya appears now ready to reply.

"First, let me assure you we will apprehend the assailant. There's not many working parts of the regime at this time, but the bare core of the protectorate force still has its wits, and they're the best there is. When we have the shooter detained, he will surely turn out to be a despondent."

"A what?"

"People that can't face up to the new age of self-discovery. They, at times, direct their frustration and despair into anger. From what our intelligence unit has gathered, the em ... What are we calling it?"

A shiny-faced aide next to Siya swiftly completes the director's statement.

"Psychic surge, sir."

"Right, this surge changed nearly all denizens from machine toys to ..."

Again, the aide.

"Human subjects, sir."

"Thank you. Yes, most denizens since the surge are like children—I don't mean that in a bad way—but, you know, they have the curiosity of young people, a belief in their untainted individual growth, and, you know, a compassionate view of others."

I can tell the director is starting to run out of juice. I interject,

"So, the despondents?" I ask.

"It was too much for them. The mental joy of the new age didn't take hold. It was overtaken by an obsession with the past and a feeling of deep loss of identity and meaning. They want predictability and continuity, not spontaneity and creativity. They want certainty, not humility."

Siya looks at his aide for reassurance. After observing a discreet nod from him, he continues, "Thanks to your heroism, they were given the opportunity for a new life. But their remorse and shame are too great. Instead of extending outward like most denizens, these despondents go inward to guilt and self-hatred. They can't handle this internally, so they go external. The enemy within is too great a burden, so they must find the enemy outside of themselves.

"They don't feel deserving of the promise of tomorrow."

Siya is sweating while he explains this. He appears to be testing out this new humanity himself, a bit awkwardly after so many years entrenched in the pompous egoism of power.

"On your tour with agent Cullen, you surely saw these sad denizens on Cyinith's streets. But let me tell you something, despondents aren't just those with the greatest material and power connections with the regime. The most to lose. Others are among the marginalized groups who cling to the false foundation of manufactured hope. You must realize that the hope spawned by the machine felt like something spectacular, an anchor to life. Without it today, those troubled by the psychic surge feel lost and abandoned. Although they have much more now in terms of self-capacity, they don't see it and focus on the disappearance of their life's bedrock."

"Why was I the target of a despondent?" I ask, although I have a good guess of the answer. Hell, I'm probably the most famous denizen in our country right now.

"You represent change. You are change. You pulled the sheets on the great masquerade. A despondent views you as the cause of the psychic surge. Without you, he could have continued in his dreamlike existence undeterred by reality. You're the devil who disrupted his entire belief system."

Two days later, the big day is upon us. Pathos and I are ushered through the cavernous hallway of the regime Capitol building. I'm dealing with emotional woundedness from the shooting. In contrast, Pathos has taken the attack on my life nonchalantly, so much so that I am disappointed. She is almost stoic in her demeanor.

"You didn't expect one hundred percent transformation and smooth sailing, did you?" she said on the drive to the Capitol.

"No, but I didn't expect an assassination attempt so soon after our *interconnect* takeover," I reply with a standoffish tone. *I get the distinct sense that she is processing something of which I am unaware. Women always tend to be a step ahead on emotional things.*

The hallway is filled with gaudy ReForm period paintings that portray preposterously gorgeous renderings of our country. Our group is to meet Unity regime leaders. We eventually arrive in a high-ceiled crystal chamber where, in the middle, sits a large rectangular table trimmed with what appears to be gold. I notice six of us there. Topless has a "can you fuckin' believe this" look on his face, undoubtedly fighting the urge to yell about this laughable setting. We are far from the trail, indeed.

Near the front of the table sits three finely attired men

and two business-dapper women. Three of this group of re-gime leaders have slight, awkward smiles on their otherwise starched faces. There is a general unease emanating from these powerful people. Hard to read them as a group. We are offered fine liquors, which I turn down, and coffee and cook-ies, which I accept. After a few more minutes, the rest of the paragons enter. We are now at full complement.

There is an uncomfortable silence. Then, the man seated in the middle, sure enough, Moulik Siya in center view, begins the proceedings, back to using his overly formal way of talking.

"On behalf of the Unity regime, we welcome you to this chamber. We are here today to negotiate new terms of gover-nance for our country."

I guess that's all he's going to say at this time.

Oats picks up the slack. "We are honored to be with you today to negotiate a new path for leadership, one that will respect human dignity and the rights of all individuals in our country to pursue their dreams. If *interconnect* is now here to support human endeavors, and so far, it looks like that is true, then we as humans need to step up. We need to govern with the assistance of the machine, in ways that promote compas-sion, altruism, and equity in our country."

Nicely stated, Oats. Pretty sure she practiced this speech. Ball back in regime's court. I can't help but think that this isn't a wee bit comical. Topless' synapses must be burning a hole in his brain.

One of the manicured women speaks up.

"We admire what your group has done for our country. A vast number of our denizenry view you all as heroes. The unfortunate incident a few days ago was done by someone in a small minority faction that will be neutralized."

The woman has a weird facial tick that is disarming and distracting. She is trying to be accommodating, but her face suggests stress and fatigue.

"I'm sure you have witnessed overwhelming support and

adulation in the streets and on e-vision. You have provided us with the miracle of rebirth. We have called this meeting to negotiate a path forward that meets your interests. We acknowledge that the handwriting is on the wall."

The man on the far right picks up the stream. "We now understand the corrosive effects of our social, economic, and political inequalities. We can speak on behalf of our major economic directors that they are now willing to start a process of redistributing their assets for the common good."

These people are used to having power. The effect of the NDE implant on them shows a bit more sluggishness. They seem to be enlightened and are saying the right words. At the same time, their hold on political and economic power is sticky. It is hard to voluntarily turn over political power.

Siya takes charge. "We have prepared a draft transitional plan for your review." A staff aide methodically distributes hard copies like he has never seen paper before. "We propose a transitional governing body. It is structured as power-sharing between your group and us. The head council will be composed of three members appointed by paragons and two appointed by us. After six quarter-years, this council will be terminated, and full and free elections will be held to form a government with terms lasting four years."

Wow. Not many times in the history of humankind has there been the voluntary transfer of political power. I note a reference in the plan to a country on the African continent in late 20C as a preeminent example showing that it can be done. I observe my paragons hiding glee underneath their studious looks. Topless gives me an over-the-top, theatrically exaggerated open-mouth look of giddy astonishment. I stifle a laugh.

Oats, speaking a bit louder than usual, replies, "We will review this document and present our response to you in forty-eight hours."

"Thank you," says the other woman among the regime

leadership. "On a personal note, I want to express my gratitude to your group. You have given us all the freedom of compassion and giving. My soul is no longer burdened by grabbing and holding onto power."

The woman starts to cry, reaching across the table for the tissue box. "Duplicity and deviousness are heavy burdens that constantly create the striving for more and more. There was never enough. Power begets power. I have been part of the systematic organization of discrimination and inequality. I welcome being free of it. Again, thank you."

The woman, at this point, collapses emotionally and is hugged by the man seated next to her. This has turned into a therapy session.

We all rise at this point. Toasts are delivered, and liquor is freely dispensed.

As Pathos and I walk out down one of the aisles of the chamber, I am approached by a heavy-set man spilling out of his formal suit and tie. As I register his face as that of Shawn Stokes, he gives me a firm and long bear hug. His large body in no way matches my projection based on his video headshot.

"I failed in getting you what you wanted. Too many questions were raised. I'm so sorry," he exclaims solemnly.

"It's okay, Shawn. It's good seeing you."

Pretty amazed we are standing here together. How things have changed.

"Thank goodness that Maliar came through for you. He is quite the celebrity now for his role in all this. My heart breaks for you, for losing this good friend."

I had not thought of Koth for a while amidst the communal elation. Mention of his name brings me sadness that he couldn't see the transformation. He would fit right in with the uprising of joy.

"Listen, Jared, I pocketed something from his cubicle before the grunts cleansed his office. I'm pretty sure he would want you to have it."

Stokes reaches into his portfolio and grabs a photograph. "You guys look downright mischievous," he says as he gives it to me.

It's a photo of Koth and me before Turmoil. We're both shirtless, with our arms awkwardly around each other. Looks like we're holding each other up. Our eyes are red and wet. Shit-eating grins on both of our faces. Pretty sure this was after our drunken naked run around my neighborhood. Right before I had to prostrate myself before my unyielding wife at the time.

I battle back tears. Then I grab on to Pathos and let them flow down my cheeks.

"Thank you, Shawn."

"It is an honor to know you, Jared. On behalf of our country, I salute you."

When we hit the first rays of sunshine outside the building, Pathos turns to me and whispers, "I'm pretty sure our NDE intervention worked."

I can't help but grin widely.

CHAPTER 43

I never could have imagined what was to happen next.

It takes us a good six hours, but we trek up past a summit into a quiet, rugged valley adorned by a beautiful lake. No high chambers of authority for paragons. Give us the joy of being in nature. We sit around a makeshift picnic table with rocks as chairs. Ponderosa pines surround our meeting area. Boisterously loud blue jays provide the soundtrack.

Ten paragons in a remote location deciding who will lead our reborn country. The reader will note that I am now considered a card-carrying member of the paragon family.

Oats begins, "We are here today to select three of our members for the governing council. One of our three members will be the new leader of our country. I propose a straight vote today. No need for introductory comments. We all know who we are. Shall we proceed?"

Unanimous agreement.

Then a strange thing happens. Ponytail requests that I step away for about twenty minutes. He suggests going to a rocky outcropping about three hundred feet away. As he ushers me away, he turns to me and says, "Enjoy the peace."

Déjà vu. I recall another time. It was Pepperjack doing the same thing to me as Ponytail is now. The group was deciding whether to terminate me or not. Is this some type of joke? Is Topless in on this? I sit on the uncomfortable outcropping and become steamed that I am being excluded from the proceedings. I thought I was a full-on paragon. Then I get a gentle vibration in my head steering me toward peaceful acceptance and understanding. I feel interconnect.

About fifteen minutes in, I look in the distance at the group. They appear to be laughing.

It's Topless who comes up to my little mountain top. He is grinning a mile wide. "You're in for it now, Split. I'm supposed to handcuff you and lead you off the cliff. Sorry."

I'm an expert by now in knowing his humor. I'm not going to give him the gift of a response. I hold out my hands deadpan. "Okay, I'm ready."

We both cackle, but I have no idea what is going on.

I arrive back at the picnic table amidst a weird silence. It's Ponytail who breaks the mood. Strange that it's not Oats. "We have voted and have a clear outcome. Oats and Aalap will be two of our members on the governing council. The third member, and leader of our country, will be Jared."

All eyes are directed toward me. Saying that I'm stunned is an understatement. I look at Topless for the humor, but he is extending his hand in congratulations. Ponytail, Oats, Rhapsody, and Dust surround me in a hugging circle. I believe I have wet my pants and remember that I forgot to relieve myself when alone.

I get myself together enough to say, "Thank you," and then mumble something like, "You guys didn't have to make up for all the shit you gave me by doing this. I would have been happy with some monetary reward."

"May I ask," I asked, regaining some composure, "what are

you guys up to?"

An excited Ponytail explains, "Think about it, Jared. You are the logical choice. You are the only one among us who has straddled algorithmic and organic worlds. You will be a shining exemplar of transition from cairn pollution to organic thought. You did it on your own. For our many denizens who have been enlightened by our intervention, you will be a model—there to nurture and guide their continued growth as organic thinking human beings."

"Besides," inserts Topless, "you're the most famous paragon. The *interconnect* video of your action is ingrained in people's minds. It is legendary. Also, your image is all over e-vision. You're a damn luminary."

"Just so you don't get too high and mighty, Jared," Dust says happily, "We feel that having Master Aalap on the council will provide you with mentorship to assure you lead clearly and responsibly. You pulling it off alone is a hard sell."

The days following this shocking appointment are a blur. The heavy weight of responsibility becomes my constant companion. Part of me feels this may be a fabrication, and an impulsive imposter syndrome fights for my attention. But I am a different person, and I have the mental capacity now to trust myself and this new reality. I recall Master Aalap's parting words on the derelict airstrip that I may be called upon to do even greater things. I rejoice at the thought that he will be my companion in governing this new country.

Along with this sense of excited anticipation, there is sadness that I will no longer have in my life the person I love. I was right in feeling that Pathos was internally processing something on our way to the regime's Capitol.

A week later, we hold hands and watch a small plane come to a slow stop on the tarmac. It is heartbreaking to depart from Pathos after the journey we have shared. But she is resolute in stepping away from all paragon activities and from me.

"You know, being close to power was never the end game for me," she explained. "There is so much more to life. You know and I know I could never be the good wife of a political leader."

I nod my head in sad agreement.

I recall the self-assured young woman I met seven years ago in that paragon tavern. The woman who changed my life. She remains that strong woman today. There has always been a special spark between us. I know her love for me is genuine, as mine is for her. My heart rejoices and aches.

We embrace and kiss as the propellers start to whir.

"We have come so far, Jared. You will be a great leader for our country. I'm sorry that I won't be there beside you. But I'm going to enjoy life now. Anytime you want to visit, you'll find me in my cabin at Wasasano Lake in the Shellsolls. I'll have the water hot for your morning coffee. You know, you're pretty unbearable without it."

I watch my favorite paragon, the one with the killer tattooed bod, disappear into the small four-seater.

Chapter 44

I'm on the trail again. One more time, to decompress before my formal duties begin in a few days. Still trying to get my head around it. My feet immediately take on a familiar ache. My mind, though, is vividly clear.

I feel the presence of Pepperjack alongside me, constant verbiage antagonizing and assuring me. I smile, but then I notice unwelcome movement in the brush lining the trail ahead of me. A swarm of coy-wolves has begun the process of encircling me.

I've always thought of them as extraordinary animals, combining the probing curiosity of coyotes with the fierceness of wolves. Coy-wolves multiplied and became increasingly aggressive during the genocidal Turmoil, entering decimated villages and perfecting strategies of surround-and-kill visited upon innocent orphaned youths. Their gruesome assaults were legendary and were spotlighted on *interconnect*-curated e-news, likely to heighten the machine's threat impulses among denizens. Biologists have determined that coy-wolves' keen sense of smell can detect the metallic trace emanating from cairn transmission.

About six of them surround me on all sides. Last time I encountered such entrapment was when the delusional inoculants encircled our paragon group. The coy-wolves' teeth shine in the glaring sunlight. Saliva drips down their mouths. I know they are ready to attack. My life starts to flash in front of me. All that work, and I end up getting ripped to shreds by coy-wolves. I start to grip tightly in fear. This advances the swarm closer to me. They can feel my mind.

A whisper of "let go" comes to my mind-space. Contrary to all my human instincts, the voice convinces me to disengage my panic button.

I sit down calmly on the trail in a posture of surrender.

The swarm is confused, half now backing away, the other half lowering their tails and assuming non-threatening poses.

A few minutes pass in this holding pattern. Then, the alpha male of the swarm walks slowly toward me, at first cautiously, then more relaxed. He gently sits beside me. The rest of the swarm soon follows him.

Alone physically but not mentally, I am astonished by the setting. I am sitting down on a peaceful canyon ledge, surrounded by six coy-wolves sunning themselves in repose. I reach out to stroke the fur of the alpha male, who repositions himself to rest his head on my leg. He can feel my mind.

The coys eventually amble off to parts unknown. As he departs, the alpha male gazes back at me with a knowing look.

I remain seated on the trail for several minutes to take stock of what just happened and to compose myself. *Was this a near-death experience? If it was, I need to admit, I'm a bit disappointed. Coy-wolf encounter was surely a bit heart-thumping, but nothing like the trauma of auto-fin accident, near-drowning, falling off a building. I realize then that maybe I'm already at the mental state promised by a near-death event. A renovated man may not need a further push toward psychic transformation.*

I trudge the wilderness path for hours in an introspective, revelatory mood. My eyes are tearing up in gratitude and awe. So much has happened over the last weeks I feel on the edge of being overwhelmed. But I know to focus on the present moment before me. I also feel that I am now being mentored by a benevolent mental partner.

The trail bends and winds, rises and falls, straightens and meanders, but I am walking as if on air. The peaks, valleys, ridges, and lakes are the same, but not me. Nothing is lacking.

I come upon a gorgeous waterfall that cascades down a plush ravine. I pass by a grove of incense cedar trees that remind me of base camp. I feel I am being raised up, supported by an underlying calm humming beneath my thoughts. I boulder cross a powerful creek and observe water pouring down a granite cleft carved by decades of unrelenting flow. I greet a large-antlered mule deer buck on the trail. He wonders why I'm on his path and takes several gentle steps toward me before deciding to depart. I gaze up at a domed peak that stands majestically alone above the ridge line.

I witness ineffability. The raw interconnectedness of all the natural elements. The organized complexity that is beyond the reach of machine and man.

My serenity is interrupted when I come to a fork in the trail, and I am undecided which route to take. Following my GPS, I begin trekking down one path, sure of my route. However, I feel a soothing vibration, a mental companion, that is encouraging me to backtrack to the other route. I fight with this impulse at first. I am sure I have my coordinates correct.

Despite my self-assuredness, I follow the gentle instructions in my head. The guiding voice is of an entirely different texture than *interconnect*'s former impulses. It is suggestive, not commanding. Soft, not rigid. Collaborative, not authoritative. It is wise and nurturing. It connects to the real present, not to fabricated stories.

The path is rugged, and I start to regret my decision. Large rocks and fallen trees block the trail. Dense jungle-like tree cover obscures my sight. It takes me almost an hour to get to even a semblance of a vantage point. I sit on the edge of a canyon that opens below me. I can see the path not taken squirreling its way down the canyon sides. It definitely looks like the more attractive option. Just as I begin to unwrap an energy bar to quench my noisy belly, I see unfolding a slow-motion landslide.

After about two minutes of rock churning, I see that the slide has buried the other route under a deadly pile of scree.

The path I would have been on if I did not listen to the persuasive voice.

I remember the same friendly voice that convinced me to lower my body just before the attempt on my life. The voice that helped me befriend the coy-wolves.

The machine is present now to support me.

To help me in our mutual goal of advancing humankind.

About Atmosphere Press

Atmosphere Press is an independent, full-service publisher for excellent books in all genres and for all audiences. Learn more about what we do at atmospherepress.com.

We encourage you to check out some of Atmosphere's latest releases, which are available at Amazon.com and via order from your local bookstore:

Icarus Never Flew 'Round Here, by Matt Edwards

COMFREY, WYOMING: Maiden Voyage, by Daphne Birkmeyer

The Chimera Wolf, by P.A. Power

Umbilical, by Jane Kay

The Two-Blood Lion, by Nick Westfield

Shogun of the Heavens: The Fall of Immortals, by I.D.G. Curry

Hot Air Rising, by Matthew Taylor

30 Summers, by A.S. Randall

Delilah Recovered, by Amelia Estelle Dellos

A Prophecy in Ash, by Julie Zantopoulos

The Killer Half, by JB Blake

Ocean Lessons, by Karen Lethlean

Unrealized Fantasies, by Marilyn Whitehorse

The Mayari Chronicles: Initium, by Karen McClain

Squeeze Plays, by Jeffrey Marshall

JADA: Just Another Dead Animal, by James Morris

Hart Street and Main: Metamorphosis, by Tabitha Sprunger

Karma One, by Colleen Hollis

Ndalla's World, by Beth Franz

Adonai, by Arman Isayan

ABOUT THE AUTHOR

Scott Bollens is Professor of Urban Planning and Public Policy and Warmington Endowed Chair of Peace and International Cooperation, University of California, Irvine. For 25 years, he has studied urbanism and political conflict in contested cities throughout the world. His most recent scholarly book is *Bordered Cities and Divided Societies* (Routledge, 2021). *ReForm* is Bollens' second work of fiction, inspired by his research and by over 850 miles trudging the Pacific Crest Trail. The prequel, *ReStart: Stories of the Cairn Age* (Atmosphere Press), was published in 2021.

CPSIA information can be obtained
at www.ICGtesting.com
Printed in the USA
JSHW041652110523
41524JS00003B/24